CUPCAKE
NATION

by

SUSAN
ADELE
WIGGINS

ISBN: 1453612599
ISBN-13: 9781453612590

Pink Lilli Press P.O. Box 4007
Culver City CA 900231-4007

CHAPTER ONE

Jake Wellington woke without a care in the world. Again. In fact, each and every morning, Jake Wellington seemed to wake without a care in the world. As he threw off his crumpled Pratesi sheets and staggered, yawning into his luxurious, polished natural marble bathroom, one had to wonder....why would Jake have a care in the world? One. He was gorgeous. Not "follow him out of the corner of your eye" gorgeous. Jake was "drop dead, on your knees, here's my number, I'll iron anything you want me to. In fact you can iron that shirt you've got, on my back" gorgeous. Two. He was officially, as of this year, respectably, stinking rich. Three. (which is somewhat of a variation on number one, so it shouldn't *really* count). He need never sleep alone, and better still, she need never be less than exquisite, nor ever more than paid for.

He'd recently purchased his first home, a mansion atop magnificent Beverly Hills with the profits from Cupcake, one of the hippest non-denim related businesses to hit Los Angeles in a very, very long time. Open every day, Cupcake made a gigantic, top heavy variant on the little frosted pastel elementary school treats for, let's face it, Los Angeles' most beautiful, skinny people. Although snorting lines of cocaine off of a tightly bench-pressed rump still had its devotees, the latest thrill came from a cream cheese based frosting with an almost mystical, mind-altering cacao percentage. It was better than licking a toad. The LAPD never saw it coming. The drug cartels couldn't figure out a way to move in, since this shit was legal. What's more, Cupcake would gladly deliver to any rehab facilities located in the Southern Californian Basin for a very reasonable fee.

With an almost imperceptible twinge of guilt, he'd sometimes think to himself, this has all been just a little too easy. This did not stop, however, the emergent smirk that would arise on his full and luscious lips, as he smoothed away a rogue strand of hair with the aid of the nearest mirror. Oh well, if *I* hadn't done this, it would have been somebody else. And there will be others right behind me. He'd just heard about a company that was about to launch in conjunction with the most popular coffee bar in town. In the tradition of the late, great Hamptons Hotel or even the restaurant Indonesia, you had to *be* a model to get hired. You had to *be* a model to drive one of their cars. That is, a portfolio-carrying, *working* model. Rumor had it, that they had leased a fleet of sexy pink Cadillac Escalades for deliveries; sexy pink Taco Trucks for the street trade, and as a result, might very well be his first serious professional threat.

So far without fail, in the very, very early morning, say around 11, the most stunning creatures that the city could manufacture, lined up to purchase anywhere from one single to three dozen cupcakes a head. Blondes with razored pixies, raven-haired lasses with low to the nape chignons and brunettes with silken, Calcutta weaves, gathered propped a-top impossibly long, pilates'd legs encased in $240 skinny jeans. Some came directly from their blow-outs with silicone gleaming off their highlights. Some threw their children at their nannies as they rushed to beat the line. Nannies didn't usually mind because now, thanks to the Mrs., they would get their's delivered. No longer did they have to walk two dogs with the baby stroller, *every…single…morning*. They could keep one eye on little Zachary or Lillian; catch the last of Judge Manny (the fastest Talmudist hanging judge in the lone star state); get one more call in before the fresh coffee finished brewing and the lady would be back with a sugar-bomb in hand, complete with napkin and spork. If they'd remembered to turn on the dryer prior to her re-entry, the lady of the house would remain nicely calmed by the white noise, allowing a good four more minutes of peace. Jake was a healer.

How anyone could have imagined, in a town where it is a veritable crime to be larger than a size 6, that hordes of women would snake a line out the door and defiantly stake their Jimmy Choo'd strappy sandal'd claim on the pavement for a good 1400 calories at that, is anybody's guess. It was a place to be seen, like Studio 54's bathroom. But to be honest, you only ever saw the heavy girls with bad hair or tourists actually eating. The skinny ones just let the dark chocolate bag with the purple voile ribbon swing back and forth and back and forth in their fingers as they sauntered to their sedans, monster SUVs and coupes. Jake hadn't put the store name on the bag, just a little golden cupcake silhouette. Genius.

Stepping out of the shower, a still dripping Jake happened to catch a glimpse of the number of messages on his answering machine. It could only hold 400. It flashed 400.

It was time to get a real assistant, he thought, and went to his wardrobe to select the day's underwear, jeans, t-shirt, hoodie, thongs and baseball cap. He tossed the $1500 pile of casual wear onto his bed. He tried to catch a glimpse of his scalp in the ceiling mirror, he thought he'd seen some thinning. But that's impossible, he reassured himself. Anyway, I'll need a second mirror to see anything properly and thus make a quick mental note of it.

Skipping breakfast and the gym, Jake made his way down the hill straight into the bakery. It only took twenty minutes and being up so early in the morning, there wasn't a soul on Sunset. He parked his Porsche S4 behind the store in the spot marked "Jake's" and quickly made his way through to the kitchen. The day began at 4am for most of these guys, so the morning's first batches had been frosted and placed and replaced in the gleaming and perfectly refrigerated French display cases. Today the selection would be a blood orange cake with milk chocolate frosting, a dulce de leche with spiced buttercream, a fudgey bundt swirl cake with a morello cherry in the center and cherry frosting on top and lastly, a yellow cake with a chocolate sprinkle covered vanilla frosting for those plebeians who wanted to play it safe. This was one of his best sellers and it just sickened him to think about it. He'd fantasized all too often about shaving psilocybin into the batter but for now that just wouldn't be right.

"Hey Jake."

Jake focused to meet the gaze of Jill, the kitchen manager. A tiny brunette in her mid-twenties, Jill Ingram had been with him since he started the place. Back when he didn't sleep and stumbled around the building site covered in cake crumbs and frosting lashes. They'd met at a party and she seemed so enthusiastic about his ideas and so oblivious to the kind of car he drove or whether or not he could score drugs that he offered her a job on the spot.

"Hey Jill. What's news?" He reached behind her to get to the coffee pot steaming on the counter.

"Well I thought you should know that Her Sweetness scored the Baxter wedding."

"Shit."

"I figured you'd feel that way."

Her Sweetness was the totally resistible Deborah Sanchez, proprietress of "The Sweetness" a dueling bakery that had been in the game long before Jake, but whom he despised. In fact, everyone did. For however divine her pastries were, and they were some of the best in L.A., she was foul, rude and frankly, ugly. And fat. Deborah Sanchez was a fatty. Jake was sure she'd cut some deal with the devil because if baking was love, surely all her customers would be dead. And they weren't, nor were they the walking dead, which would be hard to tell in a town like this if it weren't for the harsh daytime lighting. Her business thrived all the more with an insolent and sullen staff, whose mean-spiritedness she encouraged. And despite reams of blogger complaints and curses, she still was at the top of her game, catering nearly every celebrity shower, wedding or press event where cupcakes were *de rigueur*. He tried not to think about it so early in the morning with a mug full of scalding hot coffee in his hand.

"We have to do better" he exhaled.

"Get ourselves a better batter?" blinked Jill. She knew she was on thin ice but what else was she going to do with her Master's in English? "Sorry. At least I'm not rhyming. Hand me that coffee will you?" She couldn't reach over him, he was too tall, so she placed her mug in front of him and waited for him to figure it out. He did.

"Anyway, Sweetness has that wedding, but you know we still haven't heard from Celeste about her daughter's bat mitzvah or the John Perry breakfast so things are still okay."

"You'll let me know, right? I have that meeting with Kasbah Pictures tomorrow regarding some kiddie movie they're releasing in a couple of months."

"Great. What in the fucking hell?....." They'd been braced by the loud clatter from behind of non-stick aluminum. Jill slammed down her mug without splashing (practice) and stormed to the back to see what was going on with that batch of dulces. Currently that batch (make it one to five dozen) was rolling around on the kitchen floor much to the amusement of a couple of bakers, but not to Jill's.

"That's 60 on the floor that we can't use, so at $4 a pop who's gonna eat the 240 bucks guys?" The laughter stopped immediately. "Sorry Jill" was whispered like a quiet prayer in church and everyone who wasn't standing in front of the ovens turned immediately back to their tasks.

"Don't worry about it," said Jake. "These things happen...try to be more careful fellas. OK? Back to work." He caught Jill's eye and winked. The two had long ago worked out a system where she played the bad cop, or rather, a small Doberman pinscher to his good cop, i.e. mellow happy golden retriever, which appeared to keep the staff efficient and in-line. All in all it was great place to work, if you had to have a job. Sure he was a baker and they're all a bit perverse, but in all honesty, Jake was a good guy. His staff liked him. His customers liked him. His exes liked him. The cops liked him. You get the idea? Let's not forget the bums, because the Beverly Hills bums *really* liked him, especially when he gave them a warm napkin wrapped mint julep or mojito cupcake with a cup of coffee so that they would go away from the front of his store. There was no booze in the cake, since it had all been baked out, but they didn't care a bit. As far as they were concerned it was as good as a stiff cocktail.

He turned his left wrist over to check the time on his Philippe Patek and saw that it was still pretty early. He walked to the front of the store and could see that even though they wouldn't be opening for another hour or so, there was a line beginning to form. He didn't like the customers to see him in there so early in the morning because they would start giving him pitiful looks and sad faces until he opened the door. Or they would pretend that it was blistering cold in the 74 degree weather and pantomime through the window a bad Marcel Marceau brrrrr shake shake stamp stamp sad clown frown could you let me in pleeeeeease it's freezing out here routine? He was getting ready to turn back into the kitchen and leave the premises until the afternoon's final run when he looked back and saw; he squinted his eyes and leaned his head in.....could that be....Ellie?

CHAPTER TWO

Ellie who? Ellie Calder. He leaned a little forward and to his left, just to make sure, and he was right. It was her. What was she doing here? Jill came up beside him to see what had taken up his attention so completely.

"Who are you looking at?" she asked.

"Oh, just the woman who smashed my heart into a million tiny little pieces" he exaggerated.

"I don't know about this one. Which one is she?"

"The one to the far left. The one carrying that dark brown bag." She caught sight of a rather plain woman in her middle thirties with an unbelievably enormous purse hanging from her shoulder.

"You mean the one with the huge purse?"

"That's her."

"Uh-huh. She's pretty," she lied.

Ellie may have been the one to bust Jake into a bunch of little pieces, but her looks hadn't had any part in it. Her looks were definitely innocent of that crime. This happened, of course, a long time ago, but not long enough, for him to walk outside and grab her around the waist and plant one on her, let bygones be bygones, how in the hell are you, you look great, gosh it's been a long time hasn't it, bygones. He'd already thought of getting into his car and squealing out the parking lot but for some reason he was still standing there. There was one more metallic clang from way back in the kitchen, but while the bowl twirled round and round in ever smaller rings, his staff came up to the front to see why these two were still looking out the window.

"Boss....is someone fine out there? For me maybe?" snickered Tony.

"Nobody fine would be waiting out there for you fool" snapped Maria.

"An old girlfriend of Jake's is out there" replied Jill much to Jake's annoyance.

"Which one?" asked Johnny.

"The one off to the side over there with that dark brown purse" offered Jill again. Jake was starting to get pissed. If she raised her arm and pointed he would have to clock her.

"Yo, homes, she's not even *like* you, dog."

Others trailed to the front trying to cram into the already crowded room to check this bitch out. Jake could hear the whispers behind him, when José exclaimed.

"Puta madre, I cannot believe this shit. This is some kind of joke, right?"

With that Jake had had enough.

"OK. Everybody back to your stations. Show's over."

He turned to find his keys and once they were in his slightly trembling hands he looked over at Jill.

"Got it covered? I'll be back later."

"Sure thing. You're not going to go talk to her, Jake?"

"No."

As he drove back onto Sunset, he hoped that he could cool off quickly. He sure as hell hadn't expected his morning to start out like this. Not good. The morning air cooled his face and his heart started to slow down some. Jake had a lot of work to get through this week and had no time for the vapours. He would just focus on that and forget about what just happened. In his world, as he knew it, this meant nothing at all. She was just a coincidental customer. Yet maybe she knew that he owned the place. Then she must know that he wouldn't want to see her. He was damn sure that he was nobody's daddy and she wouldn't dare come in to ask him for money. He was asking no questions, he wanted no answers.

BACKSTORY ON:

Ellie and Jake had been lovers probably three years ago now. She had been an old girlfriend of some guy he knew from college. He ran into her at Tops, the biggest local foodie equipment supplier for the area. Although it's true, she was nothing to look at and he didn't really know her, he couldn't help but be intrigued by the fact that the ex of one of those fraternity boneheads was going to fight him over the last remaining roasting pan on sale.

"You can get this on-line" she said with exasperation as she tried to yank it more securely towards her.

"So why don't you?" Jake retorted noticing that she had a pretty nice rack.

"What in the hell are you looking at freak?" she snapped. She was fast.

"I'm looking at the frigging roaster that you are obviously trying to crush into your tits so I can't get a hold of what is ALREADY MINE AND GO PAY FOR IT!" he yelled back.

Someone from the check-out aisle came running over shushing them both and waving his finger.

"Would you two please try to behave yourselves in here. Oh, hi Jake." The clerk smiled sweetly. Ellie watched him go from irritated to flushed and dewy in just under two seconds.

"Hi James. Sorry. I'm trying to buy this roaster here and it's the last one." James slid his elegant fingers through his long brown bangs, slowly drawing the hair behind one ear. Then he rolled his eyes and shot a cold hard glare at Ellie. No breeder was going to keep a roaster from his Jakey. Ellie had seen this all before and hoisted her magnificent breasts up a little higher in his face and replied "Sir, if this roaster is his then why is it in my hands?" James had nothing to say to that, which was not all that unusual for the poor dear, so he looked over at his darling and gave him a pout.

"She does have a point Jake" he softly blinked.

"Alright, fine, take the damn thing. Traitor."

Ellie's eyes flashed. She'd won! The boy's club had ganged up on her again, she hadn't backed down and she'd won! Then a second and more profound idea nestled into her consciousness....she hadn't won anything. Hetero- didn't really care, and Homo- didn't either. They were busy talking to each other and she was standing there looking like an idiot.

She paid for the roaster she'd fought over in aisle 3F and was making her way to the car when Jake approached.

"Listen, I'm sorry about that back there. I was out of line." She hadn't thought that this pretty boy actually possessed any manners and was a bit thrown while trying to put her package in the back seat.

"That's okay, really. It was a great deal, you have good taste and I respect a challenge. But seriously, go on-line."

Jake couldn't believe he was actually doing this but he listened closely as the words fell out of his mouth.

"I know this is weird but would you have a drink with me tonight? So that I may apologize properly?"

"Yeah it is weird and yeah I will. Meet me at Frankie's at 8? You know where that is right?" Jake tried not to show his indignity when asked if he knew where the hippest boutique hotel bar was located.

"Sure, I know the owner. I'll see you then. Oh and what's your name?"

"Ellie. Ellie Calder."

"I'm Jake."

"I remember from inside" she smirked. They both laughed.

"Well nice to meet you Ellie, despite the crappy circumstances and I'll see you tonight."

"Bye."

Anyway, that's how those two met up. Their relationship was by all accounts a rocky one. Neither one of them had really wanted to be in a serious relationship, and yet they had settled into what seemed to pass for one. Jake was definitely not one to stay with any woman for too long and he was too preoccupied with his business for any woman to put up with backburner status for very long. Ellie wasn't even in love with him, she was busy with her fledgling law practice and what did she need with an MIA semi-boyfriend? Sadly for Jake, just when he was starting to recognize that he may have feelings for her, although he still wasn't exactly sure, she pulled the rug out and left. In the past he had never been one to wonder if he was loved or not, since he always was. It was never even a question. This time round, he never got the chance to know if he really cared about her, or maybe even "loved" her, because she took the initiative and made the decision herself, something that women never did with him. She tried to explain…"It was never really serious, right?"

And he was loathe to agree. "Besides you're working all the time and you need to focus on that." Couldn't argue with her about that either. At least she had the intelligence not to suggest that they date other people, or cool things down, or the let's step back from the situation and see where we stand bullshit. She didn't wait until his birthday or some other special holiday to drop the bomb on him.

He played it cool, like he was supposed to, didn't embarrass himself by calling her or showing up unannounced at her door. He didn't send her flowers or cute e-cards saying "I miss you" with a bashful little bear. He just let it go and nursed this sick feeling in his stomach for what seemed like months. Ironically, everybody commented on how good he looked because he lost just enough weight for his cheekbones to pop out even more. Women started flirting with him everywhere; well they did that already, but now it was embarrassing. So he figured in the end, this was a good thing. Ellie had done him a favor, she was right and she just figured it out faster than he did. He wasn't focusing on what had to be done and he was lucky enough to be "dating" an intelligent person, not a cling-on. Now, he was in a great place. Except for that incessant stabbing on the left side under his ribs.

BACKSTORY OFF:

CHAPTER THREE

Anyway, as the cliché goes, time was the great healer it purports itself to be and Jake moved out of feeling disoriented by emotional confusion, to feeling like his old self again in pretty much no time. He did what every red blooded American male did in situations like these, he didn't think about it. Helped by a healthy dose of workaholicism, he made no time for a relationship beyond hitting the sheets whenever it was convenient. He wanted no complications or upheaval of any kind and thankfully none came his way. What did come his way was a long line of sweet feminine succor. There was Rachel, a doe-eyed business major from Houston. Born into a family of some ungodly sum of money, she still wasn't going for the free ride. When she was in town, she and Jake spent most of their time together in bed, with the television on but not watching it. That television was always on. One day in the middle of the Seventh Posture, the picture tube finally exploded, yet was never replaced. When they broke it off, Jake got a new TV.

After Rachel came Julia. Julia was a minor blip on the Jake screen. Not really worth mentioning except that shortly after he stopped seeing her, she got a part in some cable series and he couldn't turn around without seeing her picture plastered all over town and on every magazine cover. As another Metro Bus slowly passed him by, with her pearly whites blazing, he'd feel an ever so slight shiver under his right ear which he'd scratch distractedly. That would have been way too much work, he thought, with the relief of a freed death row inmate.

Then there was Monique. Monique's complete lunacy was a dilemma for him. Why? Because she had one of the best bodies, physician-assisted or not, that he had ever had the pleasure of taking to his bed. And quite limber too. One should never underestimate the added nuances a limber body graces to the art of love between a man and a woman. Monique was a NYCB prima ballerina, a US gymnast, a Chinese gymnast, a Chinese circus acrobat, a French-Canadian Cirque du Soleil trapeze artist. She was all of that and more. If he had found her at the bottom of the bed twisted into a pretzel after a few blissful hours, it would have come as no surprise. Having sex with her was like taking Pilates. Someone even commented several months into their affair that he seemed "longer." Not taller, just longer. "Hmmm" he mumbled as he looked down at his arms and legs.

Monique outside of the bedroom, however, slowly began to emerge as a really different and unfortunate story altogether. Her predilection for lying grew tedious. At first it seemed like harmless fictions, fables that were not worth the energy it would take to actually listen to them as they changed positions. She would tell him about these strange far off places where she had unusual experiences that seemed at the time, say, over sushi, very entertaining although he knew they were utter shit. Then she began remarking under her breath when they were out in public about various people around them. In line at the movies. Shopping for vegetables at the Hollywood Farmer's Market. That guy over to their right, no don't look, remember the story about her fiancé? and well this guy was best friends with Serge, when she broke it off in Geneva, remember? The one I told you about that confessed his undying secret love that he'd nursed all these years knowing that Serge was never right for me? Well he's over there by the tomato plants. Staring at us. Let's go.

Way too many of these stories started to tumble down the Monique pipeline, complete with private detectives and Saudi sheiks and after awhile, multi-orgasmic or not, it got to be too much. She took it really well. He figured her stories were probably in syndication around town and ending it with him wasn't pulling the plug on anything else she had going.

Jake's main concern, as we know, was work and right now it was to revise his menu before the upcoming awards season began. He wanted to have a selection that was a little more interesting. He figured that the huge press onslaught that would be generated starting in September and run unabated until it crashed into the summer movie season, could carry some pieces about Cupcake. He decided to try to figure out how he could switch out at least half of the cupcakes even if he had to keep the bland chocolate/vanilla crap for the cupcake ninnies. He decided to give Jill a call.

"Hey it's Jake. Put Jill on, willya?" The phone was handed over.

"Hey Jake."

"Listen, I'm working on the new menu and I want your input."

"Cool. What are you thinking about?" There was the din of yet another crash in his ear.

"Jill?" He could tell that she'd put her hand over the mouth piece and was yelling something at staff.

"Jill?"

"I'm here. Sorry about that." The mouth piece was covered again and he heard the faint echo of what were surely stern words with staunch pauses in between. Then "I'm here Jake. Go ahead."

"Well, I need you to think about the trends in restaurants right now. And what's being served right now at A-list cocktail parties."

"But Jake, you do cupcakes."

"Yeah? Do me a favor and do a little research on your end and we'll talk more about it in a couple of days."

"You're not coming in for a couple of days?"

"What are you crazy? I just mean that's when we can talk about this."

"Oh. So when are you coming in?"

"I don't know. You can reach me on my cell. Bye."

"Bye Jake." **CLICK**

Something was up, Jill thought. That woman with the giant purse must have messed with his head. Not that he didn't have a heart, Jake was a sweetie, but how could *that* woman break it? From what she knew, it just didn't seem possible, but never mind. Jill was glad he hadn't talked to this Ellie person because he might not come back for a week and she needed him in the store today. Jake just wasn't the kind of man to let a woman get to him, is all. But maybe she was wrong.

CHAPTER FOUR

Foods of the moment....Let's see, Jake inhaled deeply and started to think about what people were eating. He had stopped by Pike's, a small lunch-only restaurant in the Culver City District that a friend of his owned for a quick bite and cup of coffee. He sat outside in the back and dug into one of their signature dishes, sweated sweet red bell pepper slices with crushed pecans, crumbled gorgonzola toasted on pumpernickel and smushed like a panini, with a fruity Spanish balsamic and a nutty Israeli olive oil drizzled lightly. He liked them to add a smear of French whole seed mustard and he was good.

"Forget the coffee, give me a beer. Thanks."

Now let's see...braised pork, polenta with raisins, rustic, roasted, cheesy. Food seemed intense with flavor right now. Strong and earthy. Mainly it was due to the fact that autumn was approaching, but fussy and delicate still wasn't out. Not by a long shot. Pumpkin? Must think. Apple? Gonna have to, he groaned as he took another swig of his Grolsch. If Joseph Stalin was holding a gun to my head and told me right then and there that if I didn't eat a cupcake with apples in it, he'd have my brains blown right out, then what *apple* cupcake would I choose? Jake liked to play this game with himself. What comes to mind? Bloody brains. No, come on Jake, focus. Okay, in quotes, "applesauce cake"….with bright orange, marigold petals on the frosting, drizzled with a dash of brandy and set on fire. Jake took another bite of his sandwich, when his friend Mitchell came over, his white apron covered in grease and…

"Is that blood, dude?" Jake asked, pointing his elbow at him. Mitch looked down at his apron and grinned. Stoned.

"Yeah." Mitch said in his raspy alto.

"Dude, is that your blood?"

"No. It's Karen's. She cut herself with those new knives we got last week and I wiped some of it off the counter."

"Uchhh. Spare me the details of your sex life."

"Huhuuhuuh. But no seriously, she cut herself kind of bad this morning. Those knives are wicked sharp and I told her "be careful" man and she was just blazing through this onion and splash! It was *intense*."

Although Jake knew all about the grotesque realities of the chopping block, it was putting him off his lunch. He raised his hand for Mitchell to stop.

"Okay dude, sorry. What's up? I haven't seen you in a while."

"Work is all. I'm trying to get a new menu, well not a whole new menu. Just a few new items together."

"I understand. Totally."

"So let me ask you something."

"Sure dude. Go for it."

"If you HAD to eat an apple dessert…"

"What do you mean HAD to eat an apple dessert?"

"You know, if your life depended on it?"

"I don't think apples are that serious man."

"But if you had to."

"I like apples Jake."

"Just go with it Mitchell. Humor me."

Mitchell tugged at his short goatee and looked up to the left and then to the right. He scratched the top of his sun-streaked blonde head, squinted his hazy grey eyes and rewound the rubberband holding his pony-tail. And then he said...

"Apple pie man. Keep it real."

Jake wanted to reach over the table and backslap him with his panini but of course he knew that Mitchell was right. Anything too complicated would go over with a thud. It was the shackles of the cupcake ninny mob clanking again. Not that Mitchell was a ninny, he just understood and accepted his audience. He knew that there was a fine line between a customer who appreciated adventurousness and one that backed out of the room slowly. He had, so far, been a good judge of that, introducing more experimental recipes for the short term and changing the menu regularly. But he had a hard time with the plain fact that there must be tried and true comfort foods for his core audience. That's what they come through the door for, not for irony or experimentation. Cupcakes are about being safe and innocent and always celebratory. When you're eight, they're party to some of your best times. Cupcakes are as close to a soft drug as a little kid can get, as well as being beautiful and messy. For a little kid, they are decadence itself and Jake always wanted his to allow the customer to successfully tap into those memories every time, so that they would come back again and again. For the fix. He wasn't ashamed. Basically he was a dealer. Dealer and a healer. Aren't they all?

He hoped to settle on four new ideas that Jill and he could work out and get ready at the store. If he was to go "totally fall comfort," he could do an apple, a gourd, a spice and a cranberry. Blech. Jake felt the bile rise. If he could go "insane" he would do a cream cheese swirl cranberry with dried sugared clementines, okay now we starting to get somewhere, a light pumpkin mousse shot into a yellow cake, a boring all-spice with cream cheese for the ninnies and lastly a.....hm-mmmm...and lastly a spiced Mexican hot chocolate infused cake with an airy buttercream chocolate frosting. Well, I'll run it by Jill and see what she's got. I bet she'll be toast.

Two days had passed since Jill had last spoken to Jake. Of course she was toast, she was always toast, but not so fried as to prevent her from doing some hard thinking of her own. Not solely about cupcakes, mind you. The brown purse car-rying woman too, of course. It's really not as if she cared so much about Jake's love life, she preferred not to know about such things. But she had never to this day seen him act so pe-culiarly. Women came and went like trends and one doesn't invest too much in trends, especially if you're not into them. Or something like that. Jake was clearly, to all who knew him, not into the slow and steady race winner (i.e. nice but boring plain looker), and never had been to her knowledge, so it did, she had to admit, make her pretty curious. Especially since afterwards he seemed so focused on the menu and then disappeared for two days. He didn't return the calls she left on his cell, so she assumed he needed the space. Why can't a man be more like a woman? she asked to herself as she made out her monthly supplier's list. Her list wouldn't cover ev-erything, it never did, but it helped keep them fully stocked, especially when she and Jake were in there for hours working out recipes. She knew one of those marathons was just around the corner and a lot of fun, actually. He was without question a gifted baker, although he didn't do too much of it anymore. There was a reason why that company worked, besides good management and branding. These cupcakes were fucking excellent. Most in L.A. weren't. The space was a well-designed or the cakes were cute and that's where it stopped. They basically were no better, if not quite a bit worse, than what one would find in a supermarket. Except for a very few. Cupcake, she thought proudly, was one of them. And she, as she brushed her black hair back into a neat bun, was partly responsible. That hag, Her Sweetness, had some pretty good ones too. Jill had heard some buzz about a new bakery that had opened to good reviews in Brentwood. Sugar Peaks. Or The Creamy Squeeze. Some corn-ball or pseudo porno name like that. She would have to send someone over there to bring back a selection for inspection. That's always fun, especially when they're bad, which they usually were.

CHAPTER FIVE

Jake came into the bakery early in the morning, all be it, a few days later than expected. He was radiant and smiling which threw everyone off their game because, for some reason, they were expecting him to be sullen and quiet. But Jake was never these things. He was one of the glow-y people. Jake's "down" would pass for "up" by most people's standards. Even the medicated would be grateful to feel "down" Jake-style. If his "down" could be made available by prescription, it could save a lot of lives in this town.

So there was Jake shining like a beacon with a bag full of ingredients for his bake-a-thon.

"Hey" Jake announced as he set his purchases on the long table.

"Hey Jake" came the responses from around the room. Nadia popped her head out from around the front and shot him a peace sign.

"Where's Jill?" he asked. "We got some stuff to go over."

"She went out a little while ago. She'll be back soon. I think she went to get a paper. Something about a new bake shop." José coughed and wiped down his waisted apron.

"Go wash your hands." Jake ordered. Off went José to the bathroom. Jake turned back to face Tony.

"A new bake shop, huh? Where is this new bake shop?" Jake arched his eyebrow and looked for the coffee.

"I don't know man, I think it's west of here. Oh look Jill's back. Um, I'm gonna go back….." Tony started to walk back to what he was doing.

"Yeah, thanks man. Jill, what's this about…."

"Fucking assholes." She took the section that she had already separated from the newspaper and handed it to him. "They got the cover of the Food section and they're barely open. Helena Michaelson wrote it." She stood there staring at Jake to hurry up and start reading so she could start her rant, this much was obvious.

"Jill, relax, okay?" He shook out the section and saw a pretty large color photo of a patently insipid young woman with her finger jammed into the speckled frosting. Underneath it read:

FINGER FOOD

Special Report by Helena Michaelson for The Herald

Brentwood – Who says you can't go home again? Nobody here, at the recently opened Sugar Peaks, the latest in a growing local phenomenon of bakeries that specialize in cupcakes. Bette and Jonas Adler, a brother and sister baking duo who have been working as industry special event caterers over the years, finally threw in the towel and decided to do what they love best. Cupcakes. That's right, those little, in this case, not so little, desserts from the wonder years. Their huge display cases are full of those lovely special surprises in an array of flavors that could tempt even the most jaded LA foodie.

When opening their shop, the Adlers didn't need to worry about financial backing as they are the children of Jerry Adler, one of Hollywood's most successful producers. His credits include "Kiss Your Heart Goodbye" and the Oscar-nominated "Outcast."

"We both got tired of the party scene before we graduated from Bev High" says Jonas, a tall, gregarious blonde with piercing green eyes. He was wearing a tee shirt which read "I'll take a cup of cake," low-slung, faded blue jeans and pink plastic clogs. "He's right" added his stunning sister. "I went to NY to model for awhile but god I couldn't stand being touched all the time. I came back in less than a year and we decided that what we, Jonas and I, really like to do is bake. Although I'm a couple of years older, when we were growing up, you know we were all over the place following Dad, anyway we spent a lot of latch key time in the kitchen with staff and we learned how to bake pretty early on." Bette is obscenely gorgeous with long black hair and her tall, lanky frame is poured into black designer cords, a black cashmere tank and deep purple Havianas.

To be sure, I tasted a selection of their goodies and I must say they are some of the best in town. I was positively transported to fifth grade, a very good year if I remember correctly! Except for the math! Make sure that you have the lemondrop cupcake and the fudgepacker. Sugar Peaks is open Tuesday through Saturday from 11am-5pm.

"So what?" said Jake.

"So what!" exclaimed Jill. "Those two silver spoon.... They got the cover!"

"I know Jonas and he's a pretty decent guy."

"Oh my god!" Jill threw her head onto the worktable and rolled it from side to side moaning. By the staff's estimation, a pretty good show was starting.

"Seriously. Those two work hard, they don't have to, you know. Meaning they don't have to work AT ALL" said Jake.

"Don't tell me. You went out with that Bette girl" she rolled her eyes in disgust.

"So? She's a nice girl. You would totally like her." Jake smiled serenely. "Good for them. Look, I see no reason for you to be upset by a stupid puff piece. We could use a few of our own actually. Now let's get to work. I wanna show you something."

With that Jill knew that the subject was closed. But she couldn't help get in the last word.

"The fudgepacker?"

Jake took the contents from his bags and spread them across the work table.

"What's all this?" asked Jill.

"I wanted to run some ideas by you, remember?" replied Jake. Her irritability was starting to rub off on him. "Remember on the phone, research? Well, let's do some research."

"Sure Jake. Let's see what you got." Jill knew that she had better ease back into a cheerful and helpful mood, like immediately.

He laid out cream cheese, dried cranberries, a can of pumpkin filling, apples, a variety of nuts, heavy whipping cream, spiced Mexican chocolate blocks, Dutch cocoa and clementines. She held up the orange can of pumpkin filling. He didn't take the bait.

"Everything thing else we got here, I'm pretty sure. These are just things to mess around with, nothing's set, you know."

"Looks interesting. Tell me."

CHAPTER SIX

Jake began to review the thoughts that he had been kicking around since they last spoke. The bakery, now open, was starting to get crowded. Mostly in the store this morning were the industry suits who wanted a two thousand calorie breakfast that they could hold in their one hand while they ripped out an asshole with their cell phone in the other. Jake didn't much care for these customers but they always showed up once everyone else knew that a place was hip. Exceptionally slow on the curve, they followed after their wives, mistresses, girlfriends, secretaries and daughters. Yet however long it seemed to take, they always found their way to the extremely cool destinations. Take your baked good and go, Jake thought. Robertson had already been crawling with suits and macho toughs, jay-walking with their baby blue plastic shopping bags. Almost standing in the middle of the damn street, waiting for valet in front of the Holly, they felt compelled to let *everyone* in on the fact that they had just had lunch where all the ladies who lunch lunch. He had accepted that when the first scouts arrived, sniffing and gaping and pawing with confusion, that more would follow. He just didn't want them to ruin the atmosphere with loud abrasive questions and finger pointing. They must be watched, he had decided. Somehow these Alphas would have to embrace their inner feminine yet again, as they had in nail salons and beauty treatment spas, or they would certainly kill his business. But in the meantime, this morning, they kinda *were* his business.

"I think it's in <u>How to Cook A Wolf</u> where MFK Fisher describes laying mandarin orange sections on top her heater in Paris until they were dried out. I want to try that out here with the clementines" mumbled Jake.

For a brief moment, Jill felt herself lose her orientation and had to grab the side of the table for support. She wasn't quite sure what was happening to her, she blinked a few times and swallowed hard.

"Jill? Jill? Are you okay?"

Up until this moment, Jill had never heard the words "MFK Fisher" uttered out of the mouth of any heterosexual male. Never heard the phrase "mandarin orange sections" "dried out on a Paris heater" in any combination. The books written by one of the patron saints of all things foodie, French and existentially weighty, were crammed into the library of every girl chef and baker she knew. Before Julia, before Alice, there was the life-altering MFK, who had written several books on her life and tragic loves and the foods she discovered along the way. Jill, although she admired Jake's know-how and charm, had always thought of him, if truth be told, as a philosophical lightweight. Never had she imagined that he read more than a newspaper, magazine or hand mirror.

She felt something strange come over her and shook her head a few times to rid herself of it.

"Sure, Jake. I'm fine. I just got a little woozy, for a sec. I'm alright." In truth, that funny feeling hadn't gone anywhere. She was tracking it as it lodged somewhere above her stomach and went up and down, back and forth from her navel. It was warm. The dizziness subsided thankfully and she focused on Jake who was staring at her concerned. "So, clementines Jake? How do you want to dry them out?"

"You scared me for a minute there" Jake smiled. "Maybe you need to take it easy for a little while. I can work on this stuff while you take the afternoon off. If you're coming down with something you should have yourself checked out or at least get some rest."

"No really, Jake. It's okay. I'm perfectly alright. It must have been the canned pumpkin filling." She knew that only in a moment such as this, could she get away with that crack.

"Cut me some slack, pumpkins aren't even available." Jill shut up.

So for the rest of the day, the two of them went about formalizing the recipes for the cupcakes that Jake had been talking about. He, with his head full of nuts, yucky apple-sauce and heavy whipping cream. And she, with this funny, warm and tingling zig-zagging. It distracted her from what he was saying exactly, but as the time passed, became rather pleasing.

The applesauce one stayed...it was moist and nicely sweet without being overpowering. The cream cheese cranberry might work really nicely but the clementines had to go. Sorry Mary Frances Kennedy. The spiced Mexican chocolate was a bore. Out. The sweet pumpkin mousse rocked. Jake wasn't going to only appeal to the plebian cupcake eater if he could at all help it. They would have to take the applesauce as a peace offering or otherwise just fuck off. They would most likely settle on these three unless Jake came up with something else or Jill came up with anything at all. He noticed that she wasn't really a fountain of ideas and frankly was a bit let down. He could pretty much always count on her to not only be an excellent critic but to also have ideas of her own that were very good. He didn't realize for a moment that she was faking her physical and mental state and had been working with him in a cloudy daze for hours. Odd, since he had spent enough time in kitchens with staff at various levels of intoxication, but he never suspected that Jill was buzzed. Jill wasn't aware that she was buzzed either. She thought maybe she her blood sugar was low.

"So let's get these recipes written up and tomorrow, let's try not to forget, we need to discuss the upcoming season. We need some press in the Herald ourselves. And soon."

Jill nodded her head as she grabbed her bag and car keys.

"Sure Jake. I'll see you tomorrow. Good night."

"Good night. I'll see you."

On the way home she stopped at a nearby health food store and picked up a variety of immune boosting drinks and fizzy powders, some Japanese green teas, organic brown rice and leafy greens. She had the health bar prepare a protein drink with supplements and drank it in the car. I don't know what's wrong with me but I'm gonna beat this thing, she thought. There's too much work to do between now and Jesus, May.

CHAPTER SEVEN

Jake decided, after all that hard, albeit productive, work that he would actually go out that evening. He rarely went to parties, but his friend George had made him promise a long time ago to go to this thing and he had said yes, god knows why. George Fleming was an events planner, which was a good person to know in this business so that must have been the reason. He had a growing list of young edgy clients who got plenty of press coverage, and a solid list of boring old ones. The young ones wanted the impossible, with practically no budget and the old guard put you to sleep with their architectonic bouquets, stinking with tiger lilies, gilded faux bamboo chairs and that never ending basket of bread. But they paid very well indeed and that was vital. Every once in a while, usually as awards season began, George would, just for himself, throw a party or two of carefully chosen fabulous people to reinforce his presence on the scene. They were visually innovative without being gimmicky, of course, and people seemed to enjoy themselves as witnessed in the endless photos sent to editorial by 3 o'clock the following morning.

George had been asked, so indiscreetly, by way too many people whether or not Jake was going to be there tonight. It's not like there weren't enough good looking men to go around, but since Jake was not one to show up at every single party, wasted and barricading himself in front of the photog from *Them* magazine, he was a party desirable. He had an air of mystery about him. George secretly hoped that Jake would come because his very disinterest would make his arrival a personal coup. What's more, it would be good for Jake because what's wrong with the tiniest smidgen of press? Besides he's my friend, so where's the harm in any of it?

It was 7:30 and the final touches were being worked over like a bad perm. The ubiquitous red-carpet-for-absolutely-no-reason was spread and waiting to be trod upon and stabbed mercilessly by razor sharp stilettos. Some Gretchen, Stacy or Molly, in her soiled little black dress, who never in a million years thought she could be so lucky to get all the way here from Dumbfuck, Illinois, was vacuuming the last remains of cigarette butts out of the immediate entrance way. The ancient spilled wine and champagne stains could be seen pretty plainly in broad daylight, but only when you were standing right on top of them. However, it would be dark and awfully crowded with people paying far more attention to the cracking off of their heel; the busting of seams around their derrière; the flapping of mink eyelashes where the glue wouldn't stay stuck, and that disturbing cool breeze around today's rack of extensions. Breasts would be too busy heaving, faces painted bright and happy would be melting, heading South, and beads and sequins would be flying off dresses like bb-guns discharged. The only ones safe from all this sartorial danger were the horrified children left behind at home, in the waiting arms of their nanny, who would have to explain, yet again, as the door was closed behind them, why mommy and daddy looked like that.

Into this satyrica, walked Jake. He hadn't really cleaned up and he didn't much need to. He could basically wear a Prada suit with a good pair of Italian loafers and call it a day. Which isn't at all what he did. He walked into the party wearing the same clothes from this afternoon: jeans, a t-shirt with a few food specks hanging on and his running shoes. George had taken over one of the WeHo restaurants that was going to become something else in a month or two but wasn't yet, a space for whom the next lessee hoped was between incarnations of hip epicenterdom. He had had the entire space draped in a gauzy fabric that wouldn't show spills and made everyone's complexions look really sweet. There were small bunches of brightly colored flowers poked into clusters of cacti, set in elongated, rectangular gilt vases, which were all over the place, but glued down so that no one could knock them over or try to steal them. For the ladies would had to lean and couldn't sit lest their dresses explode, he had 36" steel bar stools with high backs. These where set around small matching tables in silver, which allowed everyone else, costume permitting, to sit around or just gather. He found some fairly decent Venetian-esque mirrors which he placed on all the walls, salon style and with lighting no brighter than 300 candles so one could kind of see what one was doing, but soft enough not to scare an onlooker. The restaurant emptied out onto a wide patio for the people who wanted to drink seriously, smoke, or at least sit seriously and spread the legs. He had canopied this area too, but not so much that you couldn't see the stars and breathe in the cool night air. For this, everybody liked George. He did try to make one feel as comfortable and confident as humanly possible at this sort of contrivance. And contrivance paid his bills, so don't knock it.

A young woman stood in front of Jake with a clipboard and too much paper, frantically trying to remember her alphabet and flip pages at the same time, when out popped George.

"Jake! Oh my God, come over here this instant Jake Wellington!" With her confidence restored, she quickly flipped over to 'W.' George had done it again.

Jake turned around to see George flying from across the main room dressed in a damn impressive suit. It was a charcoal/navy blue pinstripe with a light blue dress shirt and blazing orange tie. Savile Row.

"Oh my God, Jake, I can't believe you're here! It's so great to see you!" enthused George.

"Hi George. I haven't seen you since, when was it? Last week?"

"I know," he shrieked over the sound system. "It's been an age! You look wonderful, but you always do! Oh my God, there goes someone I'm dying for you to meet. Give me one second." He made his index finger signal "one." George sped off after a tall blonde in a white chiffon dress with wide red velvet ribbons tied at the shoulders. Jake thought she looked good from where he was standing. George, and the woman that he had just accosted, came back over.

"Jake, I would like to introduce you to Fiona. Fiona, this is Jake. Jake Wellington" gushed George.

"Hello" said the tall blonde with a little too much subtlety.

"Um, hi."

Fiona was quite beautiful but frozen like a bad slurpy. Not Jake's type at all. What was George thinking? She must be involved in some similar line of work.

"Jake, Fiona has just relocated to LA from Rome and I thought that you two should meet. Fiona, Jake is the most *divine* baker, you are going to just *die!*" gushed George, some more. Fiona looked appalled.

"*You* are a *baker?*" sniffed Fiona.

"I own a bakery. Sometimes I bake. Do you?" asked a bemused Jake.

"Never" replied the statuesque Fiona from Rome.

"Fiona, that's not Italian, is it?"

"No" was her answer.

George could see immediately that he had made a colossal mistake. He had forgotten what terrible snobs those blonde Romans can be. It must have been the Irish name that threw him off. He should have known better what with that accent. Jake shot George a look telling him that he was milliseconds from walking away when Fiona said.

"So, Jake is it? Are you familiar with a shop called Cup-a-cake? My little assistant brought me one if I remember. I had been cross with her. She had done something very stupid, it is so very boring. Anyway, the little monkey presented me with these small cakes. Do you know to what I am referring? I had never before heard of such a thing. The little cakes. It was very charming; she was so upset. Can you bake like that?" she purred, readying for her attack.

"Yes, Fiona, I am familiar with that bakery. It's mine. Excuse me. It's been a pleasure, but I have to see someone at the bar. George?" With that Jake tipped his head slightly in parting, shot George another look and walked away. Fiona was still trying to process what had just happened.

Being extremely good-looking, Jake wasn't used to such unpleasantness. He stepped up to the bar and quickly threw back a whiskey and soda. George slipped beside him and before Jake could put down his glass the apologies erupted.

"Oh my God Jake! I am so sorry! That horrible woman! I swear I must have confused her with another Fiona." George began. "What a bitch, Jesus Lord!"

"Don't worry about it. It's okay. Everything's fine" Jake set down his glass and looked at his watch. "Listen, I need to talk to you about business so can you do me a favor and call me in the next week or so?"

"Of course Jake! Oh my God! Let's do some business!" George was about to bust his guts all over the bar top.

"I'd love to stay but I've had a long day and like I said, let's talk soon okay? Bye."

"Bye Jake, and I'm sorry about that moment back there." Jake smiled and made his way out onto the street. Young girls with tight head ache inducing chignons were trying to work their walkie-talkies when a stunning man in the dirty jeans and crumb-y t-shirt sauntered by. They held the static in their hands and smiled appreciatively.

CHAPTER EIGHT

Jake stood leaning against his balcony's wrought iron latticework and looked out over the city. The distant street lights spread out before him twinkling, while he listened to the soft whoosh of the occasional car speeding or the skidding of an SUV full of drunks. It was two in the morning and he couldn't sleep. Jake thought that maybe being outside for awhile would help, but it was making him more alert. He briefly entertained going for a quick swim but remembered that the pool wasn't heated and that would suck completely.

What a waste of my time, he thought, looking back at how he'd spent his evening. What he didn't realize was that he at least had the good sense to leave once bored or put out. One drink, one chat, good-bye. Think what better times would be had, if in Hollywood, one did that more often? Don't crane your neck searching for someone more interesting, there isn't anyone. Go home. Now that he was wide awake, he decided to walk back in and approach the dreaded telephone's message light beeping in the darkness. He had put if off for weeks without meaning to and well, it was something to do, right? Feh.

Jake started to listen, praying that most would turn out to be wrong numbers or were otherwise irrelevant.

BEEP: Jake, this is Anna Linley, I got your number from Sean.

Who? thought Jake. Delete.

BEEP: Jake, heeeeeeey! How the fuck are you doing? This is Gomez.

Delete.

BEEP: Jake-o....

Delete.

BEEP: Jake Wellington, this is your mother, darling! Why haven't you called me? It's been two weeks. Call me or I'm coming out there.

Call mom. Delete.

BEEP: Hello this is a message for Jake. Jake this is Ellie. You don't know how hard it's been trying to find your number and I hope that this is right. Please call me. I need to talk to you. My number is 310-467-7877. Thanks. Bye.

Jake pressed "save." He had hundreds more but they would have to wait. He wasn't gonna call her, at least not right away. But he did write the number down on a scrap of paper and deleted the message.

What good was having a telephone? A telephone only allowed people that you didn't want coming into your life to do precisely that, come into your life. So Ellie had called his land line and she'd come by the store. Not a coincidence. What's next? He went to make sure his door was locked. If I didn't have so much work to do I would go on vacation, re-appeared his escapist fantasy. Knowing that he wasn't going anywhere, he decided tomorrow he would paint out his name on his parking spot instead.

Somewhere he'd read that when you're getting ready for something new, the past comes back to make sure you're good and done with it. Said Past wants to make sure that it learned you right before you can move on. Otherwise you have to do summer school. Or worse, repeat the whole year, get left behind by all your friends, and get labeled a retard. He probably read it in one of those dumb magazines lying about in a waiting room. It made him a little nervous because he wasn't even thinking about something new, much less dealing with Ellie Calder. He'd learned the lesson for God's sake. But a nagging thought popped up inside his head..."maybe I'm full of shit." Well I can't figure this out now, I'm going to sleep and back to the bedroom he slumped with his telephone message light flashing "395."

The next morning he got a call from George.

"Listen, Jake, you know how sorry I am about that heifer! I thought she was an heiress, a tycooness of some kind....well she's just an account executive! In advertising!"

"That's funny, man" laughed Jake.

"No seriously. People like that don't get onto my guest lists." George hollered into the phone.

"George."

"Okay, I'm calm. Listen, meet me for coffee in ten minutes at Le Confabulation and we can go over stuff."

"Okay. Fine. See you in ten."

"Ciao bello." **CLICK**

When Jake drove up to the meter he saw that George was already walking into the café. He had on a trim grey suit, oxblood loafers and a small porkpie tilted to the right. Somehow

George's anglophilisms worked and yet didn't. And yet did. *Anglophilistinist. Anglophilistinism.* Jake was counting out his quarters with each new non-word. *Anglocentricphilistinism.* Okay that's only an hour. Well that's all I've got and I'll be damned if I use a credit card so this will be one cup of coffee with oh here's another quarter...*Modus anglophilistinicus.* He looked at the oncoming traffic in both directions, unlike most people, and then crossed the street when there was enough time to get to the other side without being killed. Upon seeing Jake, George came back outside.

"We can sit inside or out" stated George.

"Let's sit outside, I don't have a lot of time on my meter and I want to make sure that I don't get a ticket."

"Oh I know, West Hollywood is like $50 or some crazy shit like that" said George although he was pouting on the inside because he wanted to sit and look at the nice wallpaper.

"Over there." Jake strolled over to a small wobbly table with two chairs. The woman behind the table was smoking profusely. "Maybe not."

"Look, there's one over there," George pointed. "That couple's leaving." George clasped his hands together in gratitude. "And you can still see your car!"

They settled down, ordered their coffees, George ordered a toasted sesame bagel with cream cheese on the side and jam, strawberry, two packages. Grape, if they don't have strawberry. Marmalade, if they don't have grape.

"Well George? What gives? And please don't mention last night again."

"I wasn't I swear I wasn't!" he made the sign of the cross and the boy's scout salute. "The thing is Jake, the thing is is that I've been thinking." He paused and glanced up from his cuticles.

"Yes. Go on."

"Yes, well. The thing is that, well you and I both know that you're completely fabulous and I just think that you should really get your name *out there* and have a *much* more visible profile." Jake didn't say anything. "And well, I don't know what sort of business you had in mind when you mentioned it last night, but I think that we should consider doing something together. Like an event." George looked at him with the stare of 'take no prisoners' label-branding know-how.

"An event?" asked Jake. This is exactly what Jake didn't want to do.

"That's right. An event. Nothing campy or anything like that. That is soooo done. And God knows you can do those weddings and showers and bar/bat mitzvahs until your dead, but god Jake that is so fucking BORING!"

"Um, actually that's how I make my money."

"God, I'm sorry Jake. You know what I mean." Jake didn't know how to take that. "Jake why don't you have a publicist?" asked George, trying to veer him off the subject a smidgen.

"I've been meaning to get one," he took a gulp of coffee, "but so far everything has gone really well by word of mouth and I'm not really happy with the idea of giving away 10 grand a month to accomplish what I already do for free."

"You have a point. But...." He poked his jelly-loaded knife at Jake. "You need to broaden your base with more high powered events, not just bored hausfrau 90210 style. AND you need more upscale publicity. You need a personal profile in one of the big glossies. I mean god knows I love a bored bev hills shopaholic as much as the next girl but please, enough!" George crunched into his bagel that sent toasted shards all over the place. "Sorry" he tried to say with a mouth full of danger. Ducking to avoid grape encrusted shrapnel, Jake smiled and looked at his watch. He had time.

"So what do you propose? No offense but you do events not profiles."

"I know that, listen. I happen to know that Jennifer Hargrove is leaving the New York editorial offices of *Extreme Leisure* to take over the LA offices." George's eyes flashed in triumph.

"No offense George but that sounds like a demotion."

George took another explosive bite and chewed contemplatively until he could swallow it all and it was safe for everyone.

"That used to be the case, Jake, but times they have changed. You'd be surprised. LA is hot Hot HOT. Those New York bitches are clawing each other's eyes out to get assigned out here. Those two times a year gigs set their asses straight. Besides there was 9/11 and gosh casual clothes are so much better out here and the 80s are back! Isn't it fabulous?!" Jake didn't follow.

"So, your plan is...."

"My plan is simple. I want you to meet Jennifer, she's coming out in a few days and I want you to sweep her off her feet."

"George."

"Listen. To. Me." he poked his fork at Jake three times. "I'm setting this up, don't worry, it won't be like that blonde Fiasco woman."

"Fiona"

"Whatever. I promise on my mother's grave, this will be perfect. You need a big full cover spread and then I want those cupcakes in a movie!"

Jake laughed so hard he spilled his coffee. The other customers turned around afraid to see that someone cooler might be having a better time than they were.

"Listen. Call me when you set it up. But if this turns out to be a mess, you are in big fucking trouble. I gotta go." Jake slurped the last of his coffee and threw a tip onto the table.

"See ya Jake." George smiled. He felt very good about this. *Extreme Leisure* was going to be extremely interested, he was sure.

CHAPTER NINE

"I want to add five spice to the sauce, Jill" said Jake absent-mindedly.

"Come again?" Jill was in the back loaded down with supplies and didn't understand what he was talking about.

"I want to add Chinese five spice to the apple sauce cupcake batter. I've got to do something with it so that *I* would personally want to eat it" he tried to explain more precisely.

"Oh, that sounds like a good idea. I'm sure that it will sort itself out into something really amazing if we allow it some breathing room." Jill put the last of her bags down with a deep sigh and Jake wondered if this was sarcasm.

"You think so? You don't think it's too stupid and obvious?" asked Jake again.

"Nah... It's a cupcake Jake. Hey...that rhymed. We don't want to seem complex, even if we are. God I'm talking like a self-aware male." Jill was killing herself.

"Ha ha, you're really funny Jill. Really, really funny."

Jake liked talking with Jill. He liked working with Jill. She was so practical and no-nonsense; not that she didn't have her female moments. She was the sister that you actually liked; the one that you let hang out in your room whenever they wanted and with whom you never fought. God I'm being really lame, why won't my head shut up? thought Jake. She was right, though, it would work itself out and be great. Just give it some time. He was also revisiting the spiced Mexican chocolate but this time only as a frosting. He hadn't run it by her yet, he wanted to think about it for little while longer. See if it wouldn't come together better in his mind.

"How are the orders looking? I'm gonna have to reprint the menu at some point when we're a little further along. What am I saying? We have to decide this week."

Jill went over the upcoming orders with him. They've got the Perry event but not the bat mitzvah which was fine because the former would be way bigger, like five hundred cupcakes. Perry would get press too which was good. She mentioned a few dozen of their usual meat and potatoes orders, the standard 3 and 4 dozen for birthdays and dinner parties. They didn't get the wedding. She could tell that he had had some sort of a panic moment just then and by reviewing the order book with him, he had been set back on an even keel.

"Have the Perry people told us when to deliver?" asked Jake.

"Let's see here, it looks like 5:30pm on Friday the 23rd. Oh and what's great about it is that they just want a variety with no special instructions."

"Awesome."

"Do we have any white paint around here?" he asked.

"I think in the utilities cabinet, why?" Jill thought this an odd question.

"I'm gonna paint my parking space."

"What's it gonna say?"

"Nothing."

"Well okay. I leave you to that." Jill went back to the pile of supplies she had hoisted up on the work table.

"No, not right now. Look, let me help you with that" offered Jake.

"I got it. You don't have to."

"No, I insist, it's a lot of stuff and we need the space anyway."

Jill started to get that funny feeling again. Damn. It was definitely pleasant but really annoying at the same time. She was getting super self-conscious which she didn't like at all. She was smaller than Jake and found herself inexplicably trying way too hard to keep her distance which was a. totally weird and b. totally impossible. She thought Jake was starting to look at her funny. She was going to mentally repulse that feeling away with sheer force of will starting right now.

Jake noticed a peculiar look come over Jill. She was squinting her eyes and furrowing her brows while she was putting supplies away. He could have sworn he heard a grunt. He watched how she backed away from the table somewhat and not come quite so near when he was picking up stuff or leaning over it. This started, what, five minutes ago?

"Jill are you alright? I thought that you went to the doctor."

"Huh?"

"You're acting weird again" said Jake.

"Am I? I don't feel weird at all. What was I doing?" She decided to play dumb.

"You have a funny look on your face and you're getting in my way kind of."

"I'm sorry, I think I need new glasses."

"Jill, you don't wear glasses."

"Oh but I do. Just not here. I think I'm gonna need to wear them all the time." Jill was sure that he bought that one.

"Oh, okay. Well get them soon."

Jill tried to force away that annoying warm serpentine feeling without it making noises or it showing on her face. She was not going to deal with a bizarre distraction like this while she was working for god's sake.

When they were done, Jake went to the utilities storage area and saw that way in the back were a couple of bashed up cans of white paint. He stepped through the clutter and took one can, found a screwdriver and some old stick for stirring. It took him awhile to find a sponge brush but there were a few lying around by the tool box. He took it all outside with some old newspaper and put the painting materials down so that he could move his car back a couple of feet at least. He got out and careful not to splash any paint, opened the can, stirred the paint back to a solid creamy white and with the brush slowly dabbed out his name. A roller would have been faster, but this would have to do. In a few minutes, say 30, he had nicely covered his name with none of the letters showing through and no drips. It looked like any other parking spot in the lot.

He put everything back and washed his hands. When he went back to the car he found in the passenger seat Ellie's phone number that he had written down on a scrap. Now that he was safe from possible stalkers, should he call her? Was he fucking crazy? But it did sound kind of important... oh forget it, I'm out of my mind. He threw the scrap into the back seat and went back into his store.

CHAPTER TEN

George called him before the week was out.

"Jake, I've got it all arranged" he didn't try to cloak the triumph in his voice.

"What have you done exactly, George?" asked Jake.

"Why I set up lunch with you and me and *Extreme Leisure* for sometime next week. You're available I pray to God!" There was a tinge of hysteria coming through the cell phone.

"Um, well I wish you had run this by me earlier. I got a huge order that has to be done on time, no excuses, George. I can't just leave the shop right now."

"Do not, and I repeat, do not try to get out of this one Jake. This is trés important. You can't sell your soul for this kind of meeting Jake. I'm serious. A soul's not enough collateral."

"Alright, Jesus. What is the big deal anyway? It's just a magazine for bored rich people." He loved to send George's head spinning. If only he could see it when the neck started to crack.

"Wake up sister, you're of no interest to bored poor people!" Sa-napp.

Jake laughed at that retort. George could put him in his place now and again when pressed.

"No listen, we've already picked the restaurant. She wants to go to Pike's. She's been hearing about trendy Culver City." George choked on those last two words.

"No that's cool, I know that guy. Give me a day and time so I can let the staff know exactly when I'm not going to be there, you know, when they need me the most."

"I'll call you back." **CLICK**

George called back in a couple of hours with the day, the time and the clothing instructions he knew Jake would completely disregard.

"We're going to meet at Pike's at 12 sharp next Tuesday. Write that down, Jake."

"I'll see you then, George. Call me if there's a change."

"Oh, there'll be no change, Jake."

Like most events planners, George had a tendency towards being too controlling. Jake was not going to wear clothes that he didn't want to wear for Christ's sake and if something came up, that was too bad. He had a business to run.

On the way to the business that he was running, he decided to go to the gym. He hadn't worked out in over a week and was sure they would bust his balls when he walked in the door. He drove over to Latitude and tried to find parking. Luckily someone was pulling out and he just waited with his signal light flashing. He had flipped down the mirror to see if he looked as worn out as he felt when he saw a familiar face looking at him through their side view mirror. Oh shit. God DAMMIT. It was Ellie. She had finally caught him.

He decided that he wasn't going to show recognition. He then decided to break the eye contact, if that's possible with mirrors, by focusing intently on putting the car in reverse. He looked back at her side view and saw that she was still looking at him. He looked back. She smiled. He stared. They could play this game in the parking lot all morning but cars were backing up behind him. He had given her enough room to back up, which she did finally, but then signaled that she was going to come over. She pulled the car to the side, allowing others to pass and just as he suspected, got out while he was parking. Damn, damn, damn, he thought. Holy shit fuck fuck. By the time he had slowly and calmly got out of the car and gathered his gear from the backseat, she was upon him.

"Jake!" she said with a happy smile. She looked radiant the way you always do when you've been sweating. But to be fair she looked pretty good, the three years had been good to her.

"Ellie!" said Jake trying to sound pleased and calm. He leaned down to give her a hug. Her hair smelled of the gym's private label shampoo.

"I'm so glad to run into you! I've been trying to reach you *forever* Jake. I even called a number somebody gave me who said it was yours. Did you get my message?"

"I'm really bad with checking my messages, Ellie." It wasn't a complete lie. "So it's great to see you! What's up? You said that you've been trying to get in touch with me? Is everything okay?" Jake asked trepidatiously.

"Oh, no I'm fine. You look good, Jake. As always." Ellie was grinning a little too much like a sly house cat for his liking. Something's up here, he thought. Why doesn't she get to the point? She could tell that he wanted to be on his way. For whatever reason he wasn't digging this parking lot reunion.

"So Jake, I hear you have this great business and I don't know if you know this but a lot of my legal work involves capital investments....." Jake cut her off.

"Listen Ellie, it's great seeing you, really, but I'm *so* late. We can't stand here in this parking lot, but why don't you come by my shop and we can talk there. Come by anytime." God dammit fuck!

"That's sounds perfect!" said Ellie.

"If you stop in around 4 or 5 it should be quieting down a little and we can either talk there or go somewhere close by." He could not believe those words were coming out of his mouth. She went to quickly hug him but it was awkward and they kind of shouldered each other with a few misplaced, badly timed pats. He looked away.

"I'll come by sometime real soon. It was great seeing you!" She walked back to her car. Jake wanted to make sure that he had all his things with him, but right now he wasn't so sure that he could walk. After a few steps he realized that he could and was, so he went, though somewhat unsteadily, into the gym.

He didn't know what to do first. His trainer, Mike, saw him and waved him over.

"Where the hell have you been man?" said a fairly trim guy who could pass for an east coast tennis instructor rather a trainer in a ridiculously overpriced Hollywood gym.

"I know, I know. I should have been here every day since the last time you saw me. But, uh..." Jake was still having trouble formulating concepts and articulating them.

All of a sudden, he was kind of tired. "I'm just gonna take it easy today and I'll be in tomorrow. Okay?"

"Sure Jake. Take it slow." Mike went back to his client doing the reps in his absence. He bent over to check his form and looked back up to give Jake a wink and thumbs up sign. Jake didn't see the wink since he was trying to walk straight to the lockers and not crash into anything. He came out and did twenty minutes on every machine in the place. He would have gone another round but he was much steadier now and ready for the sauna. He pumped for another five minutes and then called it quits.

Wrapped in a towel he entered the empty sauna room. He sat down and picked up a discarded newspaper only to lay it back down on the bench again. This was the moment that he had been dreading. No amount of exercise would stall the cyclone of confused and jumbled thoughts that would come crashing upon him as he soon as he leaned his head back against that hot wall.

CHAPTER ELEVEN

Fuck me, he thought. Jake knew that he could not spend too much time in that steam room. Fifteen minutes and then he would have to go take a shower. He had no intention of falling down any obsessive mental rabbit holes in 212 degrees Fahrenheit. Even if the Finns did prepare their dead for burial in places like these, he mused, no one's going to be preparing me. He tried to think about all sorts of stupid stuff like that to keep himself distracted. He'd work his monkey mind until it could fight no longer and beg defeat. But not just yet little one, said the monkey. Yes, he had finally run into her. And he thought, it even had a sickening air of synchronicity about it. But he had handled himself well and kept moving. He wasn't demonstrably rude, just completely cool, like always. "Like always," she had said. Yeah, like always.

He blinked his eyes a few times, looking around and decided that no matter what time it was he had to get to the shop. He took a fast ice cold shower, got his things out of his locker and dressed. He'd be at work by 11 o'clock at the latest. He prayed to God that she didn't drop by this afternoon.

He parked in front of his now blank parking space and entered the bustling kitchen. He could tell that the line in front went out the door and down the sidewalk. That's what I like to see, he smiled. His staff was working at a frantic pace because they had to keep the display cases full and they had the extra load of special orders. Jill was in the front speaking to a customer so he waited, not appearing in the shop area. His current situation had a brought with it a weird rock star trip where he had to remain a sight unseen unless he wanted to be mauled by crazed cupcake bacchae. There had already been a few occasions when he had stepped out to a screaming. So we'll just stay back here until Jill turns around. Did she just say "shoo?"

When Jill came back she was sweating. Jake didn't like that. It didn't look good for business if you were wet and dripping. And you're not supposed to be shooing flies or customers for that matter. He quickly gave her a cool damp cloth to mop herself up with.

"Thanks Jake. God, they're animals today" Jill said.

"Anything I can do to help?" No way was he going out there.

"No, thanks. It's actually calming down a bit" sighed Jill. "Some limos were out there before we opened and thought we'd make an exception...."not"....and then there have been those disgusting paparazzi walking back and forth on the sidewalk for the last couple of hours."

"Are you shitting me?" asked Jake incredulously.

"I would never shit you Jake." Jill said earnestly while she mopped.

"Who did they think was here or soon to arrive, I wonder?"

"I have no idea, but it's not like you can tell them to leave. They stay on the sidewalk."

Jake peered out the window as well as he could from where he was standing. What he could see, was a line filled with the usual undersized women with oversized sunglasses and ever more oversized bags. No celebrity would deign to wait in such a line, so he knew not to look for any.

"Hmmm," he said. "I don't see anybody. Who came by in the limo?"

"You know I don't follow that stuff. I have no idea. Some underage girl with a bad dye-job and even worse jewelry" said Jill.

"That could be anyone Jill" laughed Jake.

"Well then it was Anyone, most definitely" replied Jill. "The lonely Miss Anyone with her gallant driver in tow, poor dear."

Jake spent all afternoon at the bakery. He called his graphic designer to let him know that some new signage and stationery orders would wind up being a rush job but he would text him the info asap. He and Jill finally worked out the kinks for the new cupcakes. They had settled on the personally loathsome, but tasty to everyone else, five-spice applesauce with buttercream frosting, a simple vanilla white cake with the Mexican hot chocolate-based frosting, and the pumpkin mousse shot into a fluffy yellow cake with a caramelized crumbled pecan topped buttercream. They were all pretty simple. Jake was feeling quite sick about it. But they were delicious and that he had to admit, whether he wanted to or not, and perfect for the season. The colors were right: yellow, brown, orange, red. They could also add these to the mix for the Perry event.

Once again, throwing himself into his work, he not only kept himself on top of his game, he effectively avoided the tendency to get upset over things about which he could do nothing. Most people would have replied, had he mentioned such issues out loud, "Join the fucking club, Jake. Try dealing." But Jake never talked about such things, to anyone. Jake was like every other so-called lotus eater who, unlike other crowded city dwellers, were not impassioned opiners, did not gesticulate violently with their arms, did not raise their voices, nor spew obscenities unless they were behind the wheel of a car.

He and Jill worked compulsively for the remainder of the week. The staff was a little surprised to see him there all the time and had to be more careful not to slip and spill things all over the place like they usually did. They weren't a particularly raucous group but it was definitely a much improved mechanism with Jake around. He soon pushed the encounter with Ellie to the way way back of his mind and Jill was so busy she never noticed her body or what it was doing down there anyway. These two people preferred to be completely out of touch with their emotions. It was just easier that way.

CHAPTER TWELVE

Unfortunately for Jake, at the very moment that he had buried Ellie to way way back of his consciousness, she arrived at the shop. He had told her that things were fairly quiet by 4 or so, thus giving him no excuse to beg off due to the workload. He was actually leaning up against one of the stainless steel work tables laughing with Tony, one of the older bakers, when she came through the door. Tony hadn't been there the day everyone had crammed to see her standing out on the street so he didn't understand why the whole place became silent as the grave. Jake had been recovering from the last joke when he saw her and stopped short. He put down his coffee mug and went over.

"Ellie, you came for a visit. How are you?" He quickly walked her out of view of the staff and into the store room. Thankfully for Jake there were just a few customers in at that moment, although soon there could be a tea-time deluge.

"I'm great. Listen where can we sit down?" she asked.

"Well there aren't really tables and chairs, so why don't we go for a walk? I need to get out of here. I've been inside for hours." said Jake.

"Okay, that sounds nice, let's walk."

Jake held the door open for Ellie and the two of them turned to walk up the street. Ellie was wearing wide legged sailor trousers and flats and a rather nicely fitted leather jacket. She had changed her bag but it was still pretty damn huge. He didn't remember her being a sophisticated dresser but, whatever, people change.

"It's good to be outside" Jake breathed deeply and stretched out his arms. He had just caught sight of their reflection walking by a store-front window and had a disarming flashback to the days when they were together. "So what did you want to talk with me about?"

"You know how I mentioned earlier about my work? I handle the legal end of quite a bit of capital investments these days. I've read about your company, Jake, I... well first off congratulations!" she grinned.

"Thanks" said Jake.

"So anyway....I've read about your success and I wanted to ask you if you ever considered outside private investment?"

"Truthfully Ellie, I don't know very much about it. Why do you ask?" They had gone about a block and a half and he was ready to turn around and go back.

"Well, private investment companies contribute capital to businesses that they think have growth potential. Your company gets a push to the next tier and the private investor gets a return on his or her contribution." Jake actually turned around at that last word and waited for her to figure out that their stroll was coming to an end.

"Ellie, I don't really know how I want to grow my business and I don't think that I want some outsiders poking their noses in it." He sounded a little annoyed. From behind they heard the tune of an ice cream truck. On poppers. They turned around and saw one of those sexy pink Escalades. It was Sasha's. Fuck.

"Well I'll be damned. So there goes one of those fuckers."

"What?" asked Ellie.

"Sasha's" he pointed. "Sasha's is competition. They've hooked up with High-Bean Gourmet Coffees. I'd only heard about them until now. God I want to tag that car."

"See Jake, competition is everywhere. You know that High-Bean is going coast-to-coast, right? Look, the company that I work for doesn't have to have any say in your business choices. You could probably draw up any kind of plan that you wanted. I'm just suggesting that you have the sort of company that is interesting to investors and like I said, you could take it to the next level. Don't you want Cupcake in every major city? How do you think that happens?"

Jake had never considered expanding beyond two more bakeries locally. This was heady stuff. Going national? Why, he could have his own cupcake nation. Holy shit.

"Jake?" Ellie nudged him with her leather clad elbow.

"No, I'm here. That's a lot to process and I don't know if I want to become some kind of enormous corporate entity. You're gonna have to let me think about it."

"That's fine Jake. Here's my card." Ellie dove in deep and retrieved her card holder in less than a couple of seconds, much to Jake's astonishment. He'd expected that they would be standing there for another ten minutes before she got down on her knees and emptied her purse's contents on to the sidewalk. Instead, she simply handed him her card which read: GLOBAL INVESTMENT CORPORATION, INC. Ellie Calder, Legal Counsel. How original, he thought.

"Thanks" he waved the card and then put it into his back pocket. "Let me think about it for awhile and I'll get back to you. It was good seeing you Ellie." This was where it ended.

"Jake. Hope to hear from you soon." He leaned down and gave her a proper hug this time, sparking another completely uncomfortable flashback. He could remember now how their bodies used to fit together. Something that he didn't want to remember. He asked her where she was parked and she pointed in a southerly direction. She turned to face the crosswalk and said goodbye while Jake turned around and made his way back to his bakery.

By the time Jake returned a few minutes later, Jill was already inside.

"So I hear Ellie came by? How did that go?" Jill was curious to be sure.

"Okay I guess. She wants to get me to sign on with outside investors and put a cupcake in every city in the WORLD!" He raised his hands in the air like a daemonic cupcake industrialist in league with Al Qaeda.

"What?" Jill was confused.

"Yeah, that's why she's been showing up. She wants to grow me."

"And you said...."

"And I said that it was a lot to process and that I'd have to think about it" said Jake.

"Are you nuts!" Jill shrieked. The customer buying cupcakes for a dinner party stopped midstream in handing over her credit card when she heard the yelling coming from out of the kitchen.

"I **have** to think about it!" said Jake. "I don't know anything about this company she works with and this means that I have to hire a lawyer to look over *her* lawyer mumbo jumbo. We could lose everything. We could be eaten. We could wind up being so screwed that we want to be eaten." Jake explained. Jill had just heard "we". He had never said it in those terms before, ever. Maybe it was a slip. But it made that feeling come back for sure.

CHAPTER

THIRTEEN

In the darkness Jake reached over and found her warm body which responded immediately to his touch. They slid over to each other and Jake stretched his arm across her back. It was soft and smooth. She began to run her tongue along his earlobes and took his hands up to her breasts. She loved for him to fondle her breasts while she straddled him. He reached down and pushed his hard cock into her and pushed up high with his ass. She let out a slight grown which was drowned out by his. For a while he squeezed her breasts and pulled on her nipples while she rode him slowly. She loved this and could go on forever but knew that if she didn't vary the rhythm, despite her pleasure, he would come and that would be that. She ground into him pushing his penis as deeply into her as she dared until she knew she had to stop. She kept his hands on her nipples but pulled off of him. She loved the look of his cock and had to decide whether to continue to admire it or let him admire her breasts. She decided to fondle her own breasts as she slid down the bed and began softly kissing his throbbing penis. It was beautiful, shaped perfectly. She could play with it, lick it, rub her nipples all around it, suck hard on the head, but ultimately it was going back home, inside. He flipped her over and entered from behind. His cock hit perfectly and with every thrust she groaned louder and louder. Soon he was pounding steadily and she had no problem with that. He slapped her ass a few times and pinched it really hard. He bit her shoulder and bit her nipples over and over. He finally grabbed her hips and focused solely on deeply pushing and grinding until they came together. She threw her head back and he pulled out, turned her over underneath him and plunged back in for the last strokes. He shot for what seemed like two whole minutes.

Jake woke up with cum all over his lower belly and nob. "Shit." He had dreamt that he was fucking Ellie. He got up and walked into the bathroom to clean up. The lights in the bedroom were still on and he could see that the sheets were alright, well no, they weren't. He'd have to change the sheets now. He rubbed a damp cloth over the bed linen since he wasn't going to deal with any disapproving looks from the dry cleaners. Well, $200 sheets need the cum taken out of them too, sorry. He went to the cabinet and got a new set with cases and proceeded to remake the bed. He was still kind of hard from the dream. That hadn't happened in a really, really long time and it just made things worse. It was so vivid. Seeing her had triggered something inside and now he had to be reminded of the fact that they used to have great sex. Great sex. He forgot how much he missed that when they first broke up. Well he was just going to have to have great sex with someone else. It shouldn't be too difficult. He turned off the light and went back to sleep with a sad groan.

A Cupcake in every city. This was too much. Really too fucking much. Jill seemed to think it was a good idea, but he would have to think long and hard about it. First he would need to see a detailed investment plan from this company of Ellie's before he'd even consider it. He also had to find, like he told Jill, a trustworthy business attorney if and when he decided it was worth pursuing.

She was right though, competition was all around him. He may be sitting pretty now, but for how long? So far, he had done great without PR or a business manager, but he only had one store and one set of employees. Sooner or later the model that worked so well for him, would work just as well, if not better, for someone else. Who's to say they wouldn't push him out of business? He had to admit that he'd never given it that much thought. He was busy, he was making a lot of money. Getting this store off the ground had been his primary focus for so long. And Los Angeles was the kind of town where you could enjoy huge profits with only one or two stores. But sometimes you couldn't ride the wave of trendy popularity and come out the other end solid when it passed. A business could tank so easily, which he wasn't prepare to allow happen. Nor was he prepared to let some competitor seize upon what he felt was his rightful next step in the rung of success. He had to do something. Besides was it any coincidence that the first time he saw those pink cupcake Cadillacs he was standing with Ellie prodding him to move it along? Sasha's had a brilliant idea, one that he hadn't thought of and they would be delivering to customers that wouldn't necessarily be coming to his store. He had to talk to Jill about this as soon as possible.

The next day at work he was waiting for Jill to arrive when his cell phone went off. It was George.

"Hello gorgeous!" said George. He'd obviously had his morning coffee.

"Hey George, what's going on?" asked Jake.

"I just wanted to remind you about our lunch plans with Jennifer Hargrove tomorrow" said George.

"What time again was that George?" knowing that would piss him off.

"12 o'clock sharp Jake! For God's sake where is your calendar?" he snapped. Jake could hear him attacking his cell phone with a ballpoint pen.

"Do you want to come by here or meet there?" Jake asked.

"I have to pick her up since she doesn't know her way around L.A. and God knows she'll be completely lost once she turns off Robertson. You know how they are."

"Sounds good. I'll see you at Pike's tomorrow at noon."

He could hear George start what he knew would be a rundown of demands regarding his lunching vêtements, but he ended the call with a quick squeeze of his fingertip. **CLICK**

Jill was late, something that rarely if ever happened. She told Jake that she had gone to the doctor for her annual physical and that he didn't seem to think that anything was wrong with her.

"He did say that since the cold and flu season had begun, I should be careful to not get run down, but that was about it" said Jill.

"Well, what do you think?" asked Jake.

"About what?"

"Do you think there's something wrong with you? Physically?" asked Jake again.

"I don't know. I guess I'm all right. I'm making an appointment with my Dr. Yeung." replied Jill. She told Jake about all the tinctures and tests that her Chinese homeopath would perform on her. Jake knew that she would wind up walking out of that office with a bunch of bizarre dried up things, half of which she wouldn't end up using. Even worse, if she did, she would no doubt stink up the kitchen with her horrible gas and stomach cramps and god knows what else. The bathroom would become a toxic waste dump and there were too many people in this kitchen to put up with that. He prayed that she didn't make that appointment. Continuing on with her esoteric health quest, she said if she still didn't feel right, she would go to her Korean acupuncture guy.

"I think that you should just go to the acupuncture guy" said Jake.

"Huh? How come?" she asked.

"Because I think you need to work on keeping your body in a state of balance. I think you should stick with a modality that focuses on harmonizing your qi rather than a temporary fix." Jake was impressed himself.

"I think your right Jake. Thanks" said Jill nodding her head in agreement. "That's exactly what I'm gonna do."

CHAPTER FOURTEEN

Although Jake sincerely wanted her to be in the best of health, now was not the time for Jill to be calling in sick. She probably did need some kind of on-going body work, whether acupuncture or yoga, it didn't really matter. But there was no way he was going to endure the havoc wreaked upon the western body by the **EHARIC** or The Eastern Herbal Alternative Remedy Industrial Complex. You do that shit at home, behind a locked door, on the weekends, with the windows open.

"So Jill, I've been thinking about this investment thing" said Jake to completely change the subject.

"Oh yeah?" Jill's eyes brightened.

"Yeah, I'm not *so* against it...for the moment...although I'm warning you, I will go back and forth on this one" he said.

"Go forward Jake. Never go back. *Always* go *forward*" Jill shoved her fist in his face. He smiled and pushed her arm away.

"Well I need some time. Then I'll make a decision" said Jake.

"Well, duh."

Jake snuck into the front of his store to check out the new cupcakes. The new signage was up and the announcement e-mails had already gone out to the mailing list. Everything looked as it should and just as he suspected the applesauce cupcakes were flying out the place. God, he shook his head in disgust. Before the end of the day he would make sure that he and Jill had messengered care packages containing one of the new cupcakes, a copy of the latest menu, and the business card to all local food editors and "city scene" websites, TV and radio media. Usually some local news station or public television program would send over a crew to do a piece and they would surely get press in the Herald's food section. During these packaging onslaughts Jake always regretted that he didn't pay for a publicist, nor have interns come in. But he had always been hands-on and never thought, until now, that maybe it was time for a change.

They decided to prepare all the paper materials and packing first and call the messenger to pick up first thing in the a.m. They would leave placing the cupcakes in their boxes until about the same time as shipping to prevent a messy presentation, as much as it could be. Of course, just stuffing boxes with paper took up what was left of the day and they had to be back the next morning by 5, 6 at the latest.

When the final set of "Cupcake" packages left with the delivery van, the entire staff watched while it drove away in a state of punch drunk delirium. Luckily, the store front was ready for business with very little trace of the baking Armageddon that had occurred so recently. Jake had had the good sense to bring an extra pair of clothes because in a few hours time he had that lunch appointment with George. Just looking at them, he knew that they deserved to be set on fire. George would flip if he showed up dressed in them. And whether or not he cared to meet this journalist, he surely wasn't one for self-sabotage.

At eleven o'clock he went to his car and brought out his ensemble. Well, jeans. He would stick with the jeans because well, he just was. To that he added a crisp Ralph Lauren dress shirt, his brown mid-thigh length Dolce et Gabbana leather coat and his beloved, bashed up suede Gucci drivers of an indeterminate color. When he walked out the back, his staff whistled their approval. After enduring a barrage of *puta madre*-s, *ay coño*-s, *qué bárbaro*-s and *ai papi chulo*-s, he looked over to see Jill looking dazed and dumb-founded. He left carrying two cupcake care packages for his lunch guests, got into his car, and headed to Culver City, making pretty good time.

Pike's had just opened when he came in. He was sort of embarrassed. If he wasn't friends with these people this would not be cool. Wondering what to do with the coat, it was not exactly blistery, he left it on for the time being. He waved to the chef's station and motioned that he was going to the outdoor eating area. One of the waitresses came out and wiped down the table and made sure all the place settings were there. He told her that he was expecting two people, a man and woman, who should just be sent over. He ordered a cappuccino and looked at his watch which read: 12:07pm. Perfect. He could rest assured that he wouldn't appear over eager. At best it might suggest that not only was he the master of his own domain, but also the master of another's. Cool.

At 12:11 George and Jennifer arrived and were shown to his table. George was wearing a loden green suit with dark brown hush puppies. He had a purple tie and wore a dark wheat colored dress shirt. His cufflinks were Balinese silver with a small turquoise dot in the center. He was all sparkly eyes when he saw that Jake had taken the effort to dress properly. George introduced Jennifer to Jake and the three sat down. Jake looked over appreciatively at this Jennifer Hargrove woman. She was gorgeous. It's not that he was expecting a troll, but he wasn't expecting this. All too often he was easily the most attractive person in a room, which is not always a good thing. Especially in a room full of girls. This was a very nice surprise, indeed.

Miss Hargrove had lustrous brown hair which sleekly fell down to the middle of her back. Her standard issue oversized sunglasses were perched atop her head and her eyes, a bright ocean blue. She wore a dark colored pantsuit, or course, not having yet broken her New York habits, skyscraper YSL pumps in a blazing red, which her short, manicured nails matched perfectly. She had large diamond studs, one modest diamond ring on her right ring finger, and two intricately carved and linked jade bracelets, probably inherited from a demented grandmother in Connecticut. She was by no means an adventuress, but hopefully she would find a style of her own out here.

Jake decided to start off the conversation by playing bartender and getting their drink orders himself. He went into the main dining area, let the waitress know and came back to meet two smiling faces.

"George tells me that you're going to be working in Los Angeles Jennifer, is that right?" Jake asked.

"Yes, I've actually taken the plunge and moved here officially" she smiled. "I've haven't even been here a week."

"Well, welcome to L.A." he smiled and looked straight into her blue eyes. He raised his water as did George and they all laughed. People come out here and think they're in a movie come to life for God's sake, he thought to himself. But she is cute.

They talked about the ususual pedestrian things that people from the City talk about when they first choose to live in Los Angeles. How you can go from the ocean to the mountains in under an hour. How they knew they had to buy a Thomas Guide and learn the city because the streets go on forever and there's just no urban center, blah, blah, blah. How it's just *so* big. How the sticky sweet scent of the night blooming jasmine wafting through the house at night was absolutely *divine*. They would craft a list of complaints to match the ones they honed in NYC in no time, but for now, the love affair was in full flower. Their eyes are dewy with fantasy and cinematic expectations. Although back home they'd barely turn an eyeball in the direction of a celebrity, here they would veritably salivate at the mention of one. It's just a matter of time before she loses all of her clenched-jar mannered chic and I am going to enjoy every moment of it, mused Jake.

The lunch consisted of a selection of small plates, an insalate with seared black pepper encrusted tuna, ginger and sliced grapes, a selection of ladyfinger-sized sandwiches that were spread with warm humus, a cold pasta olivata and lastly a small tower of stuffed zucchini blossoms with heritage tomato bruschetta on the side. George looked as if he was going to cry.

CHAPTER

FIFTEEN

To be fair, Jennifer Hargrove wasn't a clenched-jaw at all. Underneath a veneer of sophistication perpetuated by the east coast fashion industry, she was a small town girl from Michigan. It took her five years in Manhattan to destroy that former version of herself, which allowed her to enter the most staid weekend homes in the Hamptons. No one would wonder how the hell she got through the front door, nor direct her to where she could put on her uniform. She learned quickly to spare herself embarrassment by being quiet, giving the impression of a genteel Southern girl, which everyone on the island mistook for refinement. But like all small town evacuees, she became a native New Yorker by degree and sheer determination, until she was unmistakable from the real thing.

The problem with New York, however, was that if you didn't truly believe it to be the center of the universe, which wasn't easy for most Iowans or North Dakotans, it eventually left you wanting more. A scandalous thought to many, to be sure, because what more could there be to want? However to some, those incessant, infernal images of Los Angeles bouncing off satellites and saturating the video feed with all that Sun, all those Teeth, became ever more enticing when one compared it to endless concrete sidewalks and black soot coming out your nose. Certainly for Jennifer, after several obligatory trips to the Coast, it was time to make the jump. Everyone's so casual, she thought, betrayed by the excitement of her double helix model of mid-western DNA.

Slowly, over the years the definition of chic was changing and it wasn't necessarily east coast or European anymore. *Extreme Leisure* was aware of this, and to remain relevant, like so many in the industry, it was smart enough to give Los Angeles its due. Whether it could bear to or not. If French couture is just so much dinosaur meat after a comet shower; if fashion magazines can only sell with movie starlets on their covers; if people only want to read about what celebrities wear, than invariably, whatever stood for Hollywood style, such as it was, would have to be reckoned with. Whatever it was, it had taken over. Despite pages of copy indicating otherwise, women were not "dressing up more" nor were they "returning to a more formal kind of classic glamour". Sometimes it looked like the industry was hanging off of Hollywood's back, praying to be saved. To wit, it had colonized the Costume Institute's Gala, bombardier'd the Fashion Week and denim was certainly not going away despite all prognostications to the contrary. Los Angeles editorial offices were busier than ever and Jennifer was no fool, she jumped like a rat off a sinking ship at the first opportunity. If it was a mistake, she could go to another magazine or start up, and if worse really came to worse, she would go back to the City. She was still young. Sort of. Like every other editor who failed in LA, she could maintain her dignity with a list of reasons to which no one would ever object and she could go back to her former life, no questions asked.

But here she was, on a superb, perfect, sunny day, eating a divine lunch with this gorgeous....baker? She was sure that's what George had been telling her repeatedly. She remembered that one of the features writers at *Extreme Leisure* had done a piece on that downtown bakery Les Fleurs du Sud and had never stopped raving about it. The cupcake trend, had like most things nowadays started west and moved eastward, and this interesting fellow, Jake it was, was somehow an important trendsetter. A cupcake maverick. She nearly choked on her coffee but waved away George's concern. Frankly, she thought, it was absurd. But there you have it and this lovely man would clearly take phenomenal photos so she just might do that feature as George had suggested. This was not, however, the time to discuss any business. It was too pleasant, too heady, Jennifer felt as if she had drunk too much wine in the afternoon. She was glad that she'd had some caffeine to clear her head. Welcome to L.A. indeed.

Jake made sure that they both took their little boxes which he had moved out of direct sunlight for the duration. George and Jennifer were delighted, as everyone always seemed to be, when they received their own be-ribboned cupcake package. He never stopped being amazed watching people's faces televise their sense memory of the third grade. No more class for the rest of the afternoon! He half expected people to morph into their former selves: the goof, the goodie-goodie, the teacher's pet suck-up in braids and all the jumping and squirming in those old wooden desks. Never happened. Wished it would. He walked alongside the two as they made their way back to George's car and continued to chat at the parking meter for a few more minutes. George was beaming. Jake told Jennifer again that he was so pleased to have met her, since George had said such nice things about her and that she could find his card in the box she was carrying. In turn, she said that George should give him her number and that she would love to talk again soon. He kissed Jennifer lightly on the cheek and then turned to offer his hand to George. George looked almost crushed to receive only a handshake instead of a kiss, but get real. Jake waved his goodbyes and walked back to his car. It was 2:30pm.

He decided to drive back to the house to change out of his clothes. Jake didn't want them smashed or wrinkled any more than they had been already. Heading north, in particularly thick traffic for the hour, he thought about lunch and this Jennifer woman and when he would ask George for her number. He hated this part of the game. But it *was* a game, and it was meant to be *played*. By the time he reached his house, he seriously doubted that he would be going back into the store. He took his work clothes out of the back and unlocked the door. The telephone messages were back to 400. Shit. He knew that there may be an important call in there but he just couldn't bring himself to deal with it. If he could just get an assistant to get that number under 100. He took a shower, got back into his jeans and a clean t-shirt, and was sitting out on the deck when his cell went off. It was George.

"Hi George? Where are you?" asked Jake.

"I just dropped off Jennifer. She likes you Jake" said George full of innuendo.

"That's nice, George. I like her too."

"So when are you going to call her?" George was going full tilt yenta.

"Um I don't know George. Maybe she should call me." Knowing the heat seeking missile had hit its target, detonation was immediate.

"I beg your pardon!? She just moved here Jake! You're supposed be the one doing everything!" George was livid before he realized he'd been played.

"Really? I don't know, seems kind of funny to me, George." Salvo two approaching target....

"Funny? There's nothing funny about it Jake! Now you call her, I'll text you her number when I get back to the office. Call her in precisely one day. Are we clear, Jake?"

"Alright, George. If you're absolutely sure." Jake smiled broadly while he looked over the city.

"I'm sure. I've gotta go....this traffic is unbelievable. Don't these people work? Bye." **CLICK**

Jake never got his last word in.

CHAPTER
SIXTEEN

Jake couldn't think of what do with himself sitting on his lovely wooden deck, looking out at the not too smoggy skyline. Was he joining the ranks of those who couldn't relax? He wanted to makes some calls about Ellie's company, to try to get some information about them, but it was too late in the afternoon. And besides, he wasn't *that* motivated. Definitely tomorrow, maybe. He would call Ellie and tell her to go ahead with a proposal, but he wasn't going to walk into this blind. Now that he was home, he could go listen to the message machine, but no, that wasn't going to happen either. He could go to the gym. Nope. He wasn't going to get back in his car during rush hour. He decided that he should call Mitchell since he hadn't seen him at the restaurant today. He clicked on "Pike's" and let the phone ring and ring. On the seventh ring, a slightly smoky voice answered the phone.

"Halllo? Uhm, Pike's" the scratchy voice cleared.

"Mitchell?" asked Jake.

"Hello?" This was really bad. He'd have to give Mitchell the lecture on how to speak professionally on the telephone.

"Dude, it's Jake."

"Dude! Howaryaman?" Mitchell was coughing heavily.

"Look I came by today for lunch and you weren't there man. I wanted to introduce you to some people." Truth was he didn't even look for him.

"Dude, I was sooo busy in the kitchen. We got slammed hard, man. I never looked up. What time did you get there?"

"Right when you opened," Jake laughed. But we were in the back. It was nice. I wanted to thank you guys.

"Listen, no problem, we had reservations for two large parties in the front room, plus the regular lunch crowd, plus the counter. It was wi-cked." Jake could tell a joint was being passed around.

"Mitchell, this is not Boston. Nobody says that here."

"That's okay, man, that's okay. So when are you coming down again?" Jake could hear more whispering….here hold it…watch out….take it….shit it's out.

"Mitchell?"

"Sorry dude, I'm here."

"Um, I don't know man, why don't you and Karen come up here for dinner or something" asked Jake.

"Drive all the way up to Hollywood, man?" Mitchell seemed shocked.

"Yeah man."

"Well, let me run it by Karen and I'll get back to you."

"No worries, dude. I just wanted to say thanks for a great lunch." Jake knew that the next time he would see Mitchell would be at Pike's.

"For sure dude, later."

"Later." **CLICK**

Jake looked at his watch. It was 6pm. What the hell was he going to do with himself? He came back inside and sat at his desk. He decided to go on to his computer to make a list of things for Jennifer to know about, now that she was in Los Angeles. The city of the angels. George probably did this already but what the hell. This would kill five minutes.

GUIDELINES FOR THOSE NEW TO TOWN

1. Do not overdress. It will impress no one. Diamonds and cars impress.
2. Be aware of pedestrians. They do not know where they are.
2a. Do not stop and ask for directions, especially at a gas station. Nobody can tell you how to get to your destination. Always have a map and plan your trip before leaving your home.
3. Be aware that people do not look where they are going.
4. Much like no. 1. Drive slowly through parking lots, as people will walk down the center of the car lane for no reason whatsoever.
4a. People will walk right in front your car while you are backing out with their children and small animals. Look both ways at least five times.
4b. Skateboarders, bikers and runners do not stop at stop signs. Only the blind.
5. Get acquainted with side streets, even alleys, as soon as possible. There is no need to travel on the main roads unless you don't want to get anywhere on time.
6. People smile a lot. You are not considered normal unless you do too.

7. Change your wardrobe immediately. Focus on accessories and your body.

8. Get a proper pedicure and do not neglect it. Nobody likes gross feet.

9. Go to real grocery stores and prepare real food.

10. Exercise until it is noticeable, not fashionable.

11. The first friends you make you will no longer have one year from now. Choose wisely.

12. No one will give a straight answer to a direct question. Perfect your skill at effective conversation if you really need to know something. Learn to inquire about 'y' when you want to know about 'x.' Don't harsh the vibe.

13. Do not assume because you are better read, perhaps, or more articulate, that Los Angelenos are stupid or not clever. If you think that you are superior and have better game, you will be burned very, very badly.

14. People can use their bodies much like their cars as a weapon, this mostly concerns women. Be careful not to get hurt. A well placed elbow adjusting sunglasses or on the hip, works wonders. Consider purchasing a purse that looks chic and painful if struck by it.

15. Also for the ladies: the men leave a lot to be desired. Keep your NY boyfriend if possible. Or find another one out of town, say Europe or Asia.

16. You will have to look for your own cultural satisfaction. Take advantage of the universities.

17. There is no nightlife as one normally defines it. Entertainments are private. This is a private town in many regards. The best occasions happen behind the hedges. That's what they're for.

18. Like most blondes, most bimbos aren't. Not everyone that seems stupid, is. Except for maybe the men.
19. You can never use the word "awesome" too many times. You will discover other similar words; please use them.

He thought that would do for now. Perhaps a little too bold to send himself so he decided perhaps the best thing would be to send it to George to forward his 19 simple rules. Now it was 6:12.

Still at his computer, he went onto the web. First he did a search on venture capital and read as much as he could stand. Let's just say it was an eye-opener. He read all about the different categories of investors and degrees of financial involvement. He took special note of their general return expectations and the length of time they tended to involve themselves. He read about the dot.com failures which made him really skittish. In fact the more he read, the less interested he was in going this route. There was no way he would talk with Ellie's people without a neutral legal/financial advisor present. From what he could see the profit for a venture capital group was in the early stages of a startup and then funds are pulled out after 3-5 years and reinvested somewhere else. He could be royally screwed just like he thought. Perhaps the best outcome, if he indeed wanted to grow the company, would be by growing it beyond his competitors, hitting a brief plateau and then growing it again before they caught up. He didn't need Ellie. He didn't need to be in every city. Jake had no intention of losing control of his own company by being overly ambitious, or unrealistic and greedy. He was not going to crash and burn by overexpansion; wiped out to pay back investors whom he had never wanted in the first place. Fuck the Cupcake Nation.

He then did a search on Global Investment Corporation, Inc. That brought up 2,500 items. That was one mediocre name for a company, but he should talk, right? He narrowed his search by including "Ellie Calder." That brought up fifteen. It was New York based with offices in Los Angeles, New York, Tokyo and Dubai. She was one of a fleet of lawyers but only two were here in town. It did invest in companies, but none were in the food industry. He thought that was peculiar and would have to ask her about it. She had been with the firm for five years and from what he could see, she would not be the point person with whom he dealt most closely. That person would be in New York. The companies that they invested in were generally mid-sized, nothing as small as his. Not one. This was all very strange. He looked at his watch with a yawn, it was 10pm. He favorited a few websites and shut down the computer. Enough of this.

CHAPTER
SEVENTEEN

The following day Jake mulled over the information that he had reviewed the night before. He put a call into Ellie and got her office's voice mail.

BEEP: "Ellie, this is Jake. I wanted to talk with you about some things when you get a chance. I just have a few questions. Call me at the shop. The number is 310-897-4359. Thanks, bye."

He then called George,

"Jake! Hello! Wasn't lunch marvelous! Jennifer was so pleased! Now have you called her?" George was going to gush for days.

"George? George, listen....Do you know anyone in the investment field?" asked Jake.

"Why, no, I don't believe that I do. Why do you ask?" George was intrigued. Jake could hear that one eyebrow rise through the phone.

"I need to ask a few questions is all." Jake replied.

"Oh, I think there's a little more to this story....."

"Not really, I've been approached and I'm leery and I need some facts about the business" said Jake.

"By whoooooooo?"

"You know I'm not going to tell you that, George."

"Well you can't say that I didn't try. Sorry, but off the top of my head, no, I can't think of a soul, but I will let you know discretely if I remember. Now I must go. Call Jennifer." **CLICK**

No lead there. He couldn't just walk into a firm and schedule an appointment. Or could he? There were tons of them up and down Wilshire. Why was he even stressing? Because Ellie had put all that shit in his head about Sasha's conjoined with the High-Bean, the Adlers, Her Sweetness and god knows how many more coming up behind him. He needed to figure out who was his real competition and what he was going to do about it. Or he could he absolutely nothing and coast along on like he had been. George had better come up with somebody.

For the rest of the week, actually the month, the shop became a near unbearable den of hysteria as everything seemed to need his attention at the same time. The Perry five hundred was now. Jill needed to talk about the press calls and requests that were starting to come in. They needed to firm up some awards season pre/post party clients before he lost them to another baker. Ellie still hadn't called back and he had to talk with a business advisor who wasn't full of shit.

First things first. He rang Jennifer's office. It hadn't been one day, like George had ordered, but so what. She hadn't called him either. They could both use the excuse of too much work.

"*Extreme Leisure*. How may I direct your call?"

"Jennifer Hargrove. Jake Wellington is calling."

"One moment and I'll see if I can connect you. Would you please hold."

"Jennifer Hargrove's office. How can I help you?" Her secretary.

"Yes, this is Jake Wellington. Is Miss Hargrove available?"

"Please hold while I check." Bullshit. 45 seconds passed.

"I'm putting her on Mr. Wellington. Please hold for another second." One.

"This is Jennifer" It was Jennifer.

"Jennifer! Hello! Hi, it's Jake. Listen I am so swamped at work that I haven't had a chance to call you. How are you?" Jake was calm and friendly.

"Great. I've been swamped too. I'm just pulling out from under it, knock on wood" she laughed and groaned. Great minds, great minds.

"I feel bad because I wanted to call you so much sooner but this, is as you know, the beginning of a pretty insane period" said Jake.

"Well I'm glad that you found the time." She seemed sincere.

"I wanted to ask you if you were free to have dinner with me?"

"Gee, that's so sweet (**truth?**). I'd love that."

"Great. How is your schedule looking? Are you free this week?"

"Let's see" Jake could hear pages flipping. "I'm kinda tied up over the next couple of days but I'm free on Friday. Is that a bad day out here?" asked Jennifer.

"No, not at all. If you go to the right place, it can be quite pleasant."

"Well great then. Let's do Friday. How about 7:30? Of course you pick the place."

"Alright. Now should I pick you up at your place or do you want to meet somewhere."

"My place is actually a sad affair. Boxes and everything. Let's meet."

"That's fine, if you give me your e-mail, I can send you the address."

"Okay, it's jhargrove@el.mag.com

"That's great. I'll send it over tonight when I get home. I'm looking forward to Friday. Bye Jennifer."

"Thanks Jake. I am too. Goodbye."

Jake clicked off his phone with quiet satisfaction, ran his hand through his hair, he needed to get it cut. He looked up. Jill was staring at him. She'd never given him a look quite like that one. It was fierce; scary fierce.

"Jill?" Jill snapped out of it almost immediately.

"Yeah, yes Jake?"

"Are you pissed about something?"

"What?"

"You look pissed." She put her fingers up to her cheeks and felt around to check.

"Jake, why would I be pissed?"

"Don't know. That's why I'm asking."

"No Jake. I've got nothing to be pissed about. I am tired though. Listen we have to go over the press list." She seemed completely normal now.

"Can we do this after the shipment goes out? Is that okay?"

"Sure Jake. That'll be perfect."

He watched her closely as she walked away from him. She looked alright. Maybe she had a lot on her mind. They both went back to their duties, answering staff questions, dealing with the phone, checking on supplies and relaying back and forth information to each other on the status of orders as they were readied to be shipped out. The five hundred had to be baked alongside all the other smaller orders, using all the ovens and it had to be done in one day. Today. Jake would have to make sure that all the frosting was prepared this afternoon so they could begin immediately, then pack and ship. Once the order was out, he and Jill could sit down and go over the next set of hurdles.

CHAPTER
EIGHTEEN

Exhausted, Jake lay in bed drifting off to sleep when he woke up with a start. He hadn't picked a restaurant nor sent Jennifer an e-mail. He looked at the clock on the nightstand. 12:45a.m. Shit. He quickly turned on the light, tried to jump out of bed but instead got caught up in his sheets and fell out clocking his head. Untangling himself with half his torso on the floor, he finally stood up, threw the sheets away from him and stumbled out the room. He went into the office area to turn on his laptop. While he waited for the server to come up he decided on Haroun, a new North African fusion spot where the head chef was, no surprise, an ex. He knew she was superb; it had just opened and was getting great buzz. He went on-line and looked up their website, checked the address, the telephone number and the online reservations link. Before he clicked for Friday, 2, 7:30, he checked the menu just to be certain. It looked fine and he hoped that he wouldn't regret it since, never having been there before, there was a bit of risk involved. He was curious as to why he had no trouble making reservations, but quickly wrote down the confirmation number. He sent Jennifer an e-mail with directions, logged off and turned out all the lights. He went back to his bed where he safely pulled his bedclothes over him, bringing no further injury to himself, and turned out the nightstand lamp. That was a little too close, he thought and immediately passed out.

When he awoke the next morning, he worried that he may have made a mistake. What if this restaurant was shit? Why was it so easy to make reservations and so soon? He decided that if he could think of a better choice, he would make a second reservation just to be safe. After a few minutes he nixed that idea, thinking that he was being stupid. A few minutes later he went back to the original plan of safety in numbers. Jake, you're being a freak. Relax. Besides, he couldn't think of another place that he wanted to go to anyway.

He stepped into his bathroom and caught sight of himself in the wall to wall mirror. There he saw a red bump on his forehead above his right eyebrow. If anyone asks, I'm not going to explain it. Now that he remembered to, Jake looked around for a hand mirror to check the state of his hair. Jake was thirty seven so it, meaning balding, could start at anytime. His father lost his hair in his fifties, or so they say. He found a mirror at the bottom of a pile of junk in a drawer next to the sink and held it at variety of positions until he could see the back of his head. It was impossible to be sure. Did it look thinner? Did it feel thinner? He brushed his hair roughly with his hand, but looking down he didn't find any sticky follicle'd strands in the sink. There may be no obvious cause for concern perhaps, but it just didn't seem that thick anymore. Was it from all the stress? He was going to keep an eye on this.

He showered and dressed for work. Before he left he put in a call to Jill. She picked up after one ring.

"Hi Jake!"

"Jill, you're perky this morning? How are you?"

"Great Jake! I've been frosting cakes for hours. I think I've gone blind!"

"How's it going over there?"

"You mean apart from the blindness?"

"Jill."

"Well, before, when I still could see...we had finished" she was smiling, he could tell.

"Wow, that's fantastic. It's all done?"

"Yep, the guys are packing them up for delivery as we speak."

"Isn't it too early?"

"No actually, the Perry people called yesterday frantic about getting everything super ahead of schedule so they're thrilled. We did good Jake."

"Wow, well listen why don't you meet me for lunch? Get some fresh air, it's my treat for all your hard work."

"Oh my God, that's fabulous. Where and when?"

"Let's see, how about Red Helene's at 12:30? You got the front covered right?"

"Of course! See you then!"

Jake drove his car out of the garage and down the hill. He picked up a coffee and wondered what he should do with himself since he hadn't supervised the party shipment and didn't really want to go to the shop just yet. He could go to the gym like he promised Mike, but if he didn't turn his car around soon, the chances would be highly unlikely. He could go to a shopping center and look at books. He could find a farmer's market and look at produce. Jake wondered if his life was empty, lacked purpose and utterly meaningless. He was noticing that he was super touchy these days, kind of raw and he didn't know what the cure for it was. Maybe it was his mid-life crisis arriving early and uninvited.

Truth be told, he was sensing a feeling of rudderlessness and panic when he wasn't constantly in motion. If this Ellie set-up was legitimate, and not a scam, it may only make his little work "problem" worse. Jake was beginning to realize that he needed to find a means of grounding himself, to stop spinning around in circles. All he did was work. He always felt good, but then, he was always working. If he had a little as two free hours his heart would start to pound. The telephone didn't help at all, it just made him more prone to, dare I say, anxiety. From a man with no cares in the world? Something must be wrong. He decided to turn the car around and go to the gym.

CHAPTER NINETEEN

Of course, before the thought was a minute old, Jake had pulled his car to the side of the road and let it idle. Again he decided against doing what he had just decided to do. Instead of the gym he could go back home to swim, but the pool was still unheated. So what would he do until noon? Go to the bakery. I have to accept the fact that I have no life, he thought. I need a life.

When he arrived in the shop, his staff looked up surprised to see him.

"What?" he asked.

"Nothing, boss, we just weren't expecting you until this afternoon."

Jill came from around the partition between the kitchen and the store areas and greeted him with a look of equal surprise.

"So you're surprised to see me too? I just saw you guys yesterday if I'm not mistaken?" Jake said that a little too harshly. Staff tried to look busy. "Jill let's go over the press stuff now."

"Sure Jake, I'll be right there." She came over with a stack of papers and sticky notes.

"O.K. Let's take a look. Tell me what's most important."

Jill laid everything out on the table and tried to decipher her own mess.

"Miss Helena Michaelson wants all the new cupcakes messengered over to the Herald and then will call for a telephone interview. However, she may want to come to the shop with a photographer" said Jill.

"Pig. Have they gone out yet?"

"Yeah, they're gone.

"Good, next."

Jill cleared her throat. She didn't understand what could have made Jake so cranky. He was the mellow one and she the up-start. No way was she going to start being reasonable. You can't change the roles at whim, just 'cause.

"KWTW's "Let's Eat"'s programming director called. They also want to do a piece for this Sunday's show. That's a telephone interview. That would be later in the week."

"What else" he exhaled.

"The weeklies haven't called. One of the morning shows, "Wake Up Los Angeles," wants to send a crew over or have you come in."

"Is that it?"

"Well Channel 6's "The Food Dude" is also sending a crew."

"So we got two TV spots, one radio, and one daily?" asked Jake.

"Yep, there may be more, the packages went out just a day or so ago, right?"

"Did anyone go with the deliveries to the Perry group?"

"No Jake, remember they sent their own truck. We told them to keep them on the cool side until about an hour before set up and to call if they had any questions. I also asked them to send j-pegs of the display once the tables are set. They said that they're going to tier them and there's a florist there so it should look pretty cool." She could see the crinkles in the corners of Jake's eyes start to smooth out.

"That's a great idea Jill. Thanks for taking care of that."

"So are we still going to lunch?" Jill asked.

"Yeah of course, why wouldn't we be?" Jake looked taken aback.

"Well you looked like you had a change of plans, the way you came in here and well I don't know. Forget it." Jill was going to spare him her Helena Michaelson/Red Helene pun/crack since it wasn't even funny, it made no sense to her and she was just too tired.

Jake took a quick peek out to see how the front looked. Frankly it needed to be cleaned up a bit. Even though he knew better, there was no one in front, so he quickly wiped everything down and then sent staff to mop the floor quickly and rinse down the front window. Luckily he didn't get caught by a single cupcake groupie, got no photo requests, nor accosted by some horrible person, like, I don't know, Ellie, say. He was gonna call that bitch but not today. Today he was taking his manager out to a nice lunch and had a date for this evening. Today he was going to relax and try to get the grip back that he once had so surely.

When it was 12:15 he and Jill went to lunch. They took Jill's car because she really could not comfortably fit in such a small sports car. (**obvious lie, she is a midget**) But truth be told, she didn't like the way Jake drove. She had a huge black SUV that may not drive as fast as a Porsche, but it could certainly crush it. That gave her a great deal of satisfaction, as it did the thousands of other drivers of over-sized vehicles.

They drove off in the bright mid-day sun and even though it was officially fall, she had to turn on the air conditioning.

She didn't like this weather really. It was hot and cold at the same time. You didn't know whether to have hot or iced coffee. Thongs or shoes? Tank top or coat? It would surely make you sick in a day or two. People compromised by wearing the coat and the thongs drank iced tea and got the cold. Or was it some weird hay fever? Or maybe 2012?

Red Helene's was surprisingly not crowded for once. Probably because Jill and Jake got there on the early side for the usual lunch time crowd. All the tables would be filled within the hour. They served an anglicized Chinese menu set in a Taking Tiger Mountain By Strategy décor. The color saturated images of rifle toting women in regiment blue shorts and bright crimson ballet shoes leapt and grand jetéed off every wall. Other than the Maoist wallpaper, there was nothing authentic about the place which was most likely why they did such a brisk business. It was everyone's favorite hometown chop suey joint whether they'd left it behind in Kansas, Far Rockaway or West Palm Beach. The surly wait staff could turn over a table in a New York lunch hour, i.e. twenty minutes. Instead of an iced matcha yerba buena boba, they offered their famous (and Al-Anon discouraged) noontime whiskey sour with an umbrella or the unnaturally foamy piña colada with powdery bits of piña colada mix floating around in it. What dish went with a lumpy cocktail during one's lunch hour was entirely at the customer's discretion. Red Helene's liked to connive its customer back to the older, deadlier way of eating and living, much like Trader Vic's but without the geriatrics.

"God I love red toe shoes Jake, don't you?" asked Jill as she sipped her sidecar.

"Uh, sure I guess."

"They're just fantastic. I wished I'd taken ballet but I have fat ankles" mused Jill.

"Jill." Jake wanted her to focus a little more.

"Yes Jake."

"Take it easy with those sidecars. They're super sweet and will make you sick if you're not careful."

"Uhmmmmm," she groaned nodding her head as she continued to drag on her two little cocktail straws. She patted her napkin to her lips. "I know Jake. It's a work day."

"Right. And I wanted to talk to you about something."

"Work?" She ran her fingers around the top of her glass wondering where the waiter was so she could get another. And eat too, of course, she was starving.

"Organic."

"What Jake?"

"Organic. Tell me I'm crazy but if I don't jump on this we're gonna be screwed."

"Organic...."

"Cupcakes." Jake was beaming with a slight cast of paranoia in his eyes.

"Organic cupcakes...... Well, you certainly know how to surprise a girl." Where was that bartender?

"Isn't it obvious? And I just know," he smacked his hand down on the counter which made her jump, "I just know that that Miss Michaelson is going to bring it up in the interview so we have to already be on it. Am I right?"

"I don't know about that, Jake, but sure, I think we should go for it." Jill let the words "vegan" and "gluten-free" remain silent.

"Humph. You just wait. Anyway I want cupcakes by the end of next week. Where's our waiter?" Jake looked around impatiently.

CHAPTER
TWENTY

When they got back to the bakery, both were gassy and a little looped. Jake tried to keep moving because really a kitchen is too cramped quarters under certain circumstances. He did his usual afternoon peep out the front and obviously that direction was a no go. Jake went out back by his car where there was much improved air circulation. He checked his messages and saw that Jennifer had called about one hour ago. She dialed from her direct line so he got through immediately.

"Jake?" she answered.

"Hi! How are you? Are we still on for tonight?"

"Oh, absolutely. I'm looking forward to it. By the way that cupcake was to die for! George was right!" she said. (she got that cupcake ages ago)

"I'm glad you liked it. I'll see you at Haroun at 7:30. Bye, Jennifer."

"See you."

God, was this the stage of dating he hated. Nobody talks like that. He hoped that it wasn't an indication of their evening together. The afternoon's drinking hadn't helped. He was woozy. Maybe he should go to the gym. Scratch that, he thought, I'm gonna take a swim in my freezing pool. That and have an espresso.

Jake went back into the kitchen, his gas balloon depleted and the population's safety restored, at least for the moment. He got a bottle of water from the refrigerator in hopes that it would help and not create the reverse effect.

He borrowed Jill's laptop to do more research. This time he looked for what people thought an organic cupcake was. Disgusting, clearly. Something foul and misshapen and meant to punish. Why did these bakers have such an aesthetic and culinary affinity towards dirt? Well he would not be a part of that, no sir. He was going to make organic cupcakes that would be awesome. It would mean another press shipment but so be it. That was fine.

"Jill if anyone asks about what we talked about...." he whispered. Jill had no idea what they had talked about being a cocktail lightweight. She was trying to shake off her buzz by busying herself at a frantic pace around the store.

"Could you be a bit more specific Jake?" Jill looked up from the utensils she was washing in soapy water much to the surprise of Nate who actually did that job.

"You know.....the (cough) new idea I mentioned at lunch." Jake said measuredly.

"I'm still at a loss, I'm sorry..." She had to concentrate and not play with the pretty bubbles. "Oh, oh, oh! Yes! Of course! Now what were you saying?"

"If anyone brings that "subject" up, tell them that we are working on it and it will be incorporated into the menu shortly and to stay tuned" said Jake.

"Well of course Jake. What else *would* I say?" replied Jill, looking at him as if he was being stupid.

"Well okay as long as that's settled. I have to go back to the house. I'll talk to you soon."

Jake made excellent time driving back home, even for a late Friday afternoon. When he opened the door the stuffiness struck him full in the face and he quickly opened two of the larger windows. He got a bottle of water from the refrigerator, he was feeling less sluggish, but not great, and went into his bedroom. There he took off his clothes and got into his swim trunks. He paused in front of his full length mirror and stood looking at his body for a long time. He still was fit and toned. There were no suspicious fatty deposits that he hadn't noticed before. He could use a hair cut and clip those toe nails. He flexed each arm, nothing wobbled. He was on thin ice, pushing forty, and he knew that this would just get harder and harder to maintain. Before he had a panic attack, he took the water, his sunglasses, a towel and some sunscreen outside and threw them on to one of his many deck chairs. He prepared himself for the blast of ice when he cut through the water and touched the bottom of his pool.

When he came up for air he gave out a squeal, actually, it was more like a scream. He went back under praying that he could warm up as soon as humanly possible. In between strokes he shook and chattered, but Jake managed to do five laps and eventually began to feel alright. He knew that if he stopped moving his body temperature would dip almost immediately so he did two more laps and got out of the pool. Ran out of the pool. Ran into the shower, adjusting the nozzles to hot and slowly cooling it down as it began its rise to flesh scalding. At last, he was awake and clear headed.

Jake went into his closets and picked out a well worn chocolate brown cashmere turtleneck (don't worry, he's really hot, he can rock it) and a pair of jeans. Tonight, he was going to enjoy himself. He grabbed his black ski jacket just in case it got cold but would leave it in the car. He sat down on the bed to put on his brand new black Heschung boots with side buckles, unfortunately those were going to hurt. He took them off and put on some leather thongs. This meant clipping those toenails after all. Which was fine. He shaved quickly, without drawing blood and smoothed on a tiny dab of Kiehl's in case it started to sting. He put the eau d'Hadrien *Homme* back on the shelf. Let's not over-do things, he thought.

By the time he got to Haroun's she was already waiting. Shit, he thought.

"Jennifer, hello" he kissed her on the cheek. She smelled wonderful. "I am so sorry, I hope that you just got here?" he inquired. She was wearing her hair in a long braid under her left ear. She had on a knee-length black jersey, that screamed "date dress", but complimented it with a beautiful persimmon dupioni silk wrap and small gold hoops. She wore work place heels, but these were a little kittenish. Cute, he thought. Not that he knew as much as you might think about women's shoes. But all and all she wasn't without hope.

"Uh, Jake?"

"Yes Jennifer?" he raised his head and smiled.

"Why are you looking so intently at my feet?" she asked a bit concerned. If he was a fetishist, she was going to nip this in the bud immediately.

"The shoes, I can't tell who's the designer. I'm sorry, that's really rude."

"No, no, not at all, I don't even remember myself. Nobody interesting. I think I got them at Bloomie's."

This scintillating conversation was interrupted by the waitress, a tall Japanese woman in a black tee shirt and matching trousers. She showed them to their table and presented each with a menu; Jake with the wine list.

"So Jake, that list you sent George ..." Jennifer started.

"Yes?"

"I thought it was very interesting. I showed it to a friend of mine who moved out here a couple of years ago."

"And?"

"She laughed a lot. She thought it was good and wanted a copy."

"Um." he said.

"No, no, I printed it out. It's not going to fly across the internet unless someone wants to take the time to type it in again."

"Okay, so I guess then it *won't* happen." Jake laughed.

Is he laughing at me? she wondered. I'm going back on the sauce, he thought.

The waitress returned for their drinks orders and they both stuck with white. It took ten minutes to find those wine bottles, but after they were opened and poured, the waitress took their orders. He was going to get the grilled lamb with the minted couscous and coriander confit. She wanted the small filo dough balls filled with whipped rosemary infused potato crème and fried for just under a minute. These came drizzled with a cucumber sauce and served with a spicy tangine.

They clinked glasses, sipped their wine and looked at the table, each other and smiled, their glasses, the candle holder, the curtains, the others diners, back at each other once more and smiled again. What does one say at this point, really? Why something stupid.

"So, Jennifer? How do you like Los Angeles, so far?" Inside his head, he groaned silently, sending off a internal shock wave of disgust. I cannot *believe* myself sometimes, he thought. I'm cool. I am cool.

"Um," she took another sip of wine. "It's so new to me to tell you the truth Jake. It hasn't really sunk in yet. Frankly, I don't even know what I'm doing." Please don't descend into a sloppy self-pitying drunk he thought, afraid that she couldn't handle her liquor and that he have to call a taxi, etc…

"I've never rented a house before and I'm just sort of pretending to know how to take care of stuff without a super" she explained. Phew, he smiled. "It's a really sweet cottage from the 20s up in the hills. It's not big, but it will do for the time being." What was it about New Yorkers and Hollywood architecture from the 20s, he wondered.

"Do you think it was a gangster's moll's house?" he asked.

"Oh my God, Jake, what made you ask that!? That's exactly what the realtor said it was." Jennifer was astonished. Go figure.

When the food arrived it looked heavenly. Their plates were sprinkled with little flower blossoms that didn't blow off when set down on the table. Jake's had a pyramid of couscous with raisins and fresh mint which supported slices of grilled lamb, nice and pink and rubbed with cardamom, nutmeg and honey. Jennifer's stuffed filo was crunchy and soft and sweet and the tangine was mildly spicy with added pickled lemons, almonds, cinnamon and prunes. They were so delighted to be served and have not only something to focus on but something delightful too. The food relaxed them both and they ordered more wine. He was smiling broadly when he happened to turn to his right, just in time to see Ellie getting up from her table and coming over.

CHAPTER
TWENTY-ONE

"Well I'll be goddamned?" he put down his glass.

"I'm sorry?" said Jennifer.

Before he had time to say anything, Ellie was at the table.

"Jake, what a surprise!" she exclaimed. She had left her dinner guest with a somewhat anxious look on his face. Jake looked grim and Jennifer looked baffled.

"This is a surprise. Ellie I'd like you to meet Jennifer. Jennifer, Ellie's been giving me business advice of late." The two women looked at each other pleasantly but with reservation. The 'please to meet you's' were exchanged and they both looked back at Jake to say something.

"Gee Ellie your date looks awfully lonesome over there. Gosh."

"Oh Dave? He's fine. Listen why don't you guys join us?" She waved at her abandoned dinner date.

"Well actually Jennifer and I have a lot of catching up to do, if you guys don't mind, but it was great seeing you. Let's talk soon okay?" Jake spewed the words out in one breathless salvo at Ellie, who looked vaguely disappointed, but what could she say?

"Of course, I just came over to say 'hi!' So, 'Hi!,' she waved with her tiny hand, "you two enjoy your dinner." 'Bye' went the tiny fingers.

Jennifer had that serene look on her face of a woman who's too controlled to reveal her true emotions, in this case, mainly negative. She went back to her meal, which was delicious enough to ease her out of a burgeoning crummy mood. She grabbed her glass and took a gulp.

"Thanks," he raised his glass as did she.

"So obvious question, who was she?" Jennifer put her fork down.

"She's a local business attorney and she's trying to encourage me to accept capital investors."

The tightness around Jennifer's mouth softened and she faintly relaxed her shoulders from out of her earlobes.

"But that's sounds great. We should have had them join us" she said.

"No, I don't think so. I don't know that guy and she's being really dodgy and I don't think I really want to go that route financially to tell you the truth."

"Why ever not, Jake?" she looked stunned.

"Because they'll want their money back, and this is my baby and I don't want to lose it to speculators. I need to know a lot more about it and Ellie's too flaky."

The waitress came to clear away their plates and talk about dessert.

"You know what, we're actually gonna pass on dessert, but we'd both like coffee and the check, thank you." The waitress nodded while balancing plates in her hands and walked away officiously.

Jennifer went back to the investment topic.

"Well, I can see your point but I wouldn't reject it because you don't trust her. It might be a really good move, just with a different operation."

"Maybe, it's something that I'll have to mull over awhile." They both drew from their glasses trying to create a kind of pleasant atmosphere, despite not having all that much to say before that Ellie interruption. Or after.

"Jake, I wanted to tell you that my senior editor is flying out from New York next week." The coffees were set down and the check placed on Jake's side of the table. He opened up the billfold and threw in his American Express. Titanium.

"Is that good?" he asked.

"Well, yes and no. She comes out around this time every year and although her focus is mainly on celebrities, I want to sell her on the idea of a food personality feature." She looked up at him, then paused to take a slow sip of coffee. It was strong and good. She was not going to sleep easily. But she knew that already.

"You didn't explain the 'no' part. Or *was* that the 'no' part?" Jake smiled.

"I guess it was" she laughed. "She's a nutcracker if you know what I mean and I don't want her to be mean, that's all."

"Well, I appreciate your concern and but isn't it more important that she not be mean to you? Frankly, I don't know the woman. If we meet, and I don't see why we would, she must be used to people being equally unpleasant. I'm sure she couldn't care less. I'm sure actresses on the Disney channel are more horrible than she is."

"Oh, I don't know about that."

"You haven't been out here long enough yet. But seriously, why do we need to meet?"

"Well, if she likes the idea, she'll most likely take over the article and conduct the interviews herself."

"Don't worry about it. Let her do what she does."

"Inevitably, I will." She only half-smiled.

With the bill paid, they gathered their things and went outside together. Jake asked if she'd like to go have another drink somewhere else, but she declined. She gave her ticket to the valet and Jake waited for her car with her.

"That was a wonderful meal and thank you so much for suggesting this place" she said.

"I'm glad you enjoyed it. Next time you pick." He smiled. She smiled back and her car rolled to a stop beside them with the door popping open. He paid the valet and helped get her into her car all the while wondering just how North African his breath was. When she was set and safely belted, he leaned in and kissed her lightly but full on the mouth. Twice.

"Drive safely. Goodnight."

"Goodnight, Jake." She smiled and drove off.

When he walked back to the valets they were looking at him appreciatively. One gave him a nod and a thumbs up. I wonder what their spread sheet for tonight's dates looks like, he mused to himself.

"What were my odds?" he asked.

"I'm sorry?" said the taller of the valets.

"What were my odds? For tonight?"

"Strictly confidential, sir, you understand."

"Someone lost some cash then."

"The night is young, sir, the night is young."

Ok, that was really strange. He was walking back to his car, he'd parked on the street, when he could see little Ellie out of the corner of his eye. He thought she was about to call out his name, but he hopped in and drove away so fast he couldn't have heard it if she had.

He had never expected to sleep with Jennifer tonight. They weren't horn dogs together which was kind of nice. Different. Different to be interested in a girl you didn't want to fuck the first night. He actually wanted to get to know her better and if they never slept together that would be fine too. This was something new. This might actually be a relationship.

CHAPTER

TWENTY-TWO

Jake dragged his ass to the gym the next day shocking even himself. Spotted with his first step through the door, he waved off his trainer Mike, again, telling him that he had just enough time to run through the machines and then he absolutely had to leave. Again, he vowed, on his mother's grave, that they would start up their schedule soon. Real soon. 'Why do you have to lie to me, Jake, why do you have to lie....to me?' was the look on his trainer's face. Jake felt a little shitty.

As planned, he plowed through all the machines that he could get to, working each for 15 minutes and then flew into the showers. He hadn't bothered with his locker today; he just ripped his work clothes out of the bag, dried off, and stuffed the sweaty ones in a Target shopping bag that he crammed back into the gym bag. Changed his socks too.

Out the gym's front door he flew back to his car where he tried to reach George on his cell. George picked up with a delighted "Hello Jake!"

"Hey George. I need your advice."

"I love to offer my advice, Jake, you know that. Now, how can I help?"

"Who's the best florist in LA, George?"

"For what?"

"Excuse me?"

"For what social situation, hello?"

"Um, I guess "day after a date" flowers."

"A date? With whom?"

"Jennifer, who do you think? And I need her work address."

"Well, I don't know, you could be a slut for all I know Jake. Hold on, let me look it up." He gave him the address and suite number and made the following recommendation:

" 'Mignon et Doucement', but they go by just 'M and D'. They're off of Beverly."

"Never heard of them."

"Why does that not surprise me, Jake? Now how did it go last night?"

"Um, it was fine."

"Fine? What does that mean, fine?"

"I don't know her George. George are you wearing your wingtips?" There was a long pause and a clearing of the throat.

"Yes I am, Jake, why?"

"I can tell when you've got your wingtips on. Are you wearing your argyle socks, George? A traditional tartan plaid?" A second long pause followed.

"Well I can tell you that she loves yellow. Call me if you need to know anything else, I gotta get my other line."
CLICK

Jake waited to call this florist once he was in the bakery so that he could concentrate on driving. When he walked through the kitchen, he could see that the line out the door was the usual 15 people deep and down the sidewalk. He hadn't even done his press yet, which reminded him, when were those people coming next week?

First things first, he looked around for a spot which would attract the least amount of attention and could still get a signal. He moved up front a bit, only to be in the way of the metal carts. He finally went back to his usual spot near the coffee maker and dialed the florist's number, but also caught Jill's attention. He waved 'hi' and mouthed a completely unnecessary 'I'm on the phone.' Mistake, now she was curious. She grabbed some papers lying on the work table, which she began to shuffle around, then slowly but deliberately, began her way over to him.

"Yes, I'd like to send some flowers, please. Sure, I'll hold." Jake said as he watched Jill's slow-motion trek. When the M and D gentleman came back on the line he explained that he wanted a simple, elegant (words sure to insult any floral designer) bouquet to say "thank you for a lovely dinner last night" in yellow. No daisies, no marigolds, no gerbera, no French tulips, no.....the florist stopped him.

"Sir, have you ordered from us before?"

"No, but you come highly recommended" explained Jake.

"By whom may I ask?"

"No, sorry. That would be indiscreet of me."

"I understand completely. Well, I must say that we have a wonderful assortment of *truly magnificent* flowers. You will not be disappointed I can assure you of that quiet honestly. To whom shall we send the arrangement?"

Jake fumbled for the note upon which he'd scribbled George's information and recited it into the phone. Listening, Jill kept her back to him, staring into space. He continued with his telephone call...

"I know zinnias are out of season but listen, if a yellow flower isn't what's most beautiful, pick what's the most beautiful instead. Ok?"

"Of course, we'll j-peg you an image of it before we sent it for your approval. Is the number you're calling from alright?" Jill threw down her papers and walked briskly to the bathroom much to the surprise of everyone in the kitchen. One of the girls, allowing Jill neither space nor privacy, took off right after her. 'Shit, what the hell?' thought Jake.

"Sir? Is that alright?"

"Um, yes, that's perfect. Could we speed this up I think I have to attend to staff."

"I understand, but I will need a credit card number." Jake tried to yank out his wallet but his fingers couldn't accomplish the maneuver. After three tries he finally pulled it out, found his Amex and read the numbers.

"I got to go, call me if you need to know anything else." Jake hung up the phone, shoved his wallet into his back pocket and stood staring at the bathroom.

"Jake, what's wrong with her, man?"

"Like I know? I was on the phone. Ok, give her some space." He pushed through the kitchen's clutter and went to the bathroom. At the door stood Janice, one of his recent hires, who worked mostly in the shop but was helping out with the frosting today.

"She will naaht come owyuute Jake. Ah tried." She had a thick and sloppy Texas drawl and still hadn't figured out how to put her apron on right.

"That's ok Janice, you go on back to work. I'll take it from here" said Jake. Fuck an A, he thought. Shit. He knocked gently on the door. He couldn't hear anything. He knocked again.

"Jill, it's Jake, are you okay in there?"

CHAPTER

TWENTY-THREE

"Jill? What's wrong?"

He could hear faint sniffles, and then the water faucet turned on. He stood there for a while hoping that she would come out soon. He waved staff away as one by one, they were gathering at the restroom door to stand with him. Do you want her to feel like a complete ass?, he thought. He had waved the last employee back to their station when he heard the faucet turn off and a mighty blow into a Kleenex or more likely toilet paper. Jill cleared her throat and unlocked the door. Jake scooted away from the door only to conclude that that move was a hopeless one. So he turned back to the closed restroom door and stood there waiting. When Jill finally came out she couldn't look at him. She let out a muffled 'I'm okay' and walked back into the kitchen area. The guys gave her looks of concern but remained where they were. The girls, however, moved towards her offering thoughtful touches and soft words. Gilberto walked over to Jake and gave him a meaningful stare.

"What?" asked Jake.

"Don't take this the wrong way Jake, but sometimes..." he shook his head.

"What the hell are you talking about?"

"Sometimes you can be a complete pendejo. Sorry, man, no disrespect but I had to say it." Jake looked completely confused. "Sometimes boss, you are clueless." He thumped his own forehead since he hadn't planned on getting fired.

"Think about Jill for once." Gilberto shook his head and went back to work.

Think about Jill for once? Think about Jill for once? Jake couldn't believe his ears. What the fuck just happened? The day started out reasonably well, nothing great, and then it just skidded on to the embankment and burst into flames. Jake thought maybe if he just pretended that these most recent moments had not occurred things would right themselves into some sort of normality. Isn't. Wasn't. Didn't. Once it became clear that that denial tactic wasn't working, he clung to the tried and true female hormonal insanity excuse, but that didn't explain Gilberto who didn't suffer from the malady. He could see from out of the corner of his eye, Gilberto making eyes at him, trying to subtly stare a hole into the side of his face. Jake turned and eventually met his gaze only to find him now twitching his head in Jill's direction.

"Go over and talk to her man."

"What?"

"Ay coño. Talk...to...her." He jerked his head as gently as he could and turned his back to Jake. He was through with him.

Jake now really did feel like a pendejo. He knew all the guys were thinking the same thing more or less, the ladies too. Jill had gone back to her work but was ruddy eyed and had a stuffy nose when she spoke. No way was he going to walk past her and pretend that it was business as usual. No way was he going to go up to her and talk to her about work, pretending that she didn't look like she'd just finished watching her favorite soap star die in a hospital gown after only one week of happily wedded bliss. He had to go over there, take her outside and talk. So that's what he set out to do.

He approached calmly and forthrightly, like an employer is supposed to do. Except for the metallic cacophony of the baking apparatus, you could hear a pin drop. The staff was preparing themselves to listen to every nuance in Jill and Jake's imminent exchange and watch their silent body language with the two pairs of eyes in the back of their collective heads.

"Jill, when you have a moment. I need to speak with you outside."

"Sure, Jake. I can go now." She followed him outside into the parking lot.

The two filed out much to the horror of staff who thought that they had a front row seat. Now they would not be able to see or hear anything. Jake closed the door behind him. If he hadn't stopped smoking five years ago, this would be the time to light up. But the craving passed. Jake began.

"Jill, I don't want to pry into your personal business. You know that, right? But what just happened back there?" Jake felt that he may have just fucked that up, but it was too late.

"I know Jake, and I'm sorry. But I can't really talk about it. Not now."

"I understand, Jill, really I do. But you can't bring personal stuff into the workplace. You saw how disruptive it was. I don't mean to sound callous."

"You're right Jake. I was completely unprofessional. It won't happen again. I promise."

"Is there anything that I can do?" asked Jake with complete sincerity.

"Uhm, I don't really think so. No. But I appreciate the offer."

"Are you sure? You know that I would do anything to help."

Jill looked like she was about to come undone again. He was blowing it, he knew that much.

"So can we go back inside and get back to work?"

"Of course, Jake, and I'm sorry." Jake reached over and gave Jill a big bear hug and he could feel her diaphragm contract a few times, but there was no sound of sobbing. She pulled away and went back into the store.

Jake knew that that was not what she needed to hear but hell, he didn't even know what was going on. He did the best he could as an employer, trying to be both professional and caring. What else was he supposed to do? Give her the day off? Was she having a lady day? Maybe he should ask Gilberto. He followed Jill through the back entrance and his staff turned away from the door as quickly as their necks would allow, trying to make it look like they had been working all along. The girls in front popped back to the other side of the partition. The energized chatter became a study in casual insouciance. This going to be a long fucking day.

A peculiar chirp popped out of his phone which indicated that a message had been delivered. He opened it up to see a photo of a petite yet wondrous bouquet. "Miss Jennifer Hargrove's arrangement. Sent at 11:35am. We appreciate your business. M + D."

CHAPTER TWENTY-FOUR

Jake closed his cell phone not knowing what to do. He should feel good, but he felt like a turd. Had he had done something real bad? He knew that the "professional" speech that he'd delivered was "appropriate" given the circumstances. Being an employer required those sorts of exchanges. But without knowing what had caused Jill to become so upset, he didn't know if he had somehow made things worse. Jill gave him no sign to have any misgivings; she had pulled herself together and gone back to work. Her interactions with him and other members of staff were relaxed and eventually the incident was forgotten. There would be no drama in this shop, no intrigues or power plays; this was a safe refuge for cupcakes and the people who loved them.

The weekend couldn't come fast enough. Considering that it would be starting in a few more hours made it so much easier for Jake to bear the wait. He would spend time on his next project: the organics. Basically he would do what came naturally, follow his usual plan, come up with new recipes, but this time use only organic ingredients. It damn sure wasn't going to be one of those camouflaged by chocolate monstrosities. These were going to be his best yet. So when he got home, he knew that he was staying in, turning off the phone, which most likely couldn't hold any more messages and may have actually broken, and think it out. Lemon zest cake with pink lemonade frosting, strawberries and cream, sarsaparilla bundt with some kind of nutty frosting, sugared date cake with cherry frosting, tomato cupcake with chocolate frosting, a pear chutney cake with some kind of frosting, something with figs, something with rose petals, something with real maple syrup. He could feel rising up with in him the desire to go into some Asian fusion yin overload freakout. He knew that would be a hopeless endeavor, there could be no edemame, or mung beans or roots of any kind other than ginger. But maybe he could do something with black tea?

On Sunday he got together all of his supplies, what wasn't at the Hollywood Farmer's Market, he would pick up at the health food store. There he could find organic baking soda, all the organic dairy, organic jellies for what jellies he didn't make himself, nuts, eggs and flour. He brought it all back to the house and started experimenting. After a couple of hours he realized that he missed Jill. She was a perfect foil to his Frankenstein persona. He decided to call her. It rang and rang but there was no answer. He left a message for her to call if she wanted to come over to the house. She never called back.

By that evening he had five potential recipes which he hoped Jill could continue working out with him during the week. He knew that press would be coming, including that dreadful Helena Michaelson, and maybe this would be a good hook for them to have something to talk about in addition to the newest flavors. It would suggest that they were always doing what no other baker in LA was, something exciting, pushing those cupcake boundaries. His recipes were always a little different and maybe it was time for him to be making a bigger statement.

On Monday he came in with his list: the lemon zest, the fig incorporating rose petals, and an earl gray iced orange cake, sarsaparilla bundt with nutty maple frosting, and pear chutney with vanilla cream cheese frosting. He brought with him enough ingredients to make them all in house with Jill and see what she thought. Jake hoped to God she was over whatever she had come down with on Friday.

"Jill's called in sick" said Gilberto with a look of 'I told you so.'

"She isn't sick is she?" asked Jake. "You know she was talking about seeing a doctor and not getting sick. Is she sick?"

"I don't know man?"

"Well who talked to her?"

"Janice, I think. Yo, where's Janice at?" Gilberto looked around the kitchen. She came from the shop, looking frazzled with her apron wrapped all wrong. Again.

"Janice, come over here please." Jake ordered.

"But theah ah a tun of customahs" she drawled.

"Who's out on the floor?"

"Nahdia and Geoffray."

"They can handle it. First of all, fix your apron and wipe the sweat off your brow." Janice started to use her apron and quickly thought better of it. Her eyes locked on the paper towel dispenser and tore a bunch off to use instead. Jake helped her tie her apron properly so that the logo was centered with the strings in front. "Second, did you talk to Jill this morning?"

"Yes, Jake."

"How'd she sound? What did she say?"

"She said that she had come dowyun with that cold that's going arowund and that she didn't dauh come ee-in and get everyone else sick. She said to caw-ll her at home if you needed anythang but that she was staying in bayyud."

"Okay, thanks Janice, you can go back." That accent. His head hurt.

Jake took out his cell and dialed Jill's number. She picked up on the eleventh ring.

"Haalo" she muttered under the bed clothes and into the phone, and then had a fit of some kind.

"Jesus, Jill are you okay? Can I bring you anything?" asked Jake. He was concerned but a little repulsed.

"That's so nice of you Jake, but I'm so tired. I really need to sleep. Call me later." She hung up. She sounded drunk.

"She's really sick," said Jake. He looked around a little panicked. "Where does she keep that agenda?"

"I think she took it home with her, man."

"She did what?" Now he was upset. He went over to the area where she kept the planning calendar. It wasn't there. "Somebody's gotta go over to her place and get it. We have press all this week." Nobody said anything. He may be the boss but he knew what that meant.

CHAPTER

TWENTY-FIVE

Getting his hands on the agenda was absolutely mandatory. He looked over her work area one last time to make sure that it wasn't there. He double checked the calendar in the company lap top and found nothing for the coming week. He signaled for Janice to come over again when she finished with her customer.

"Jake, is theyah anythang that ah can do?" she drawled like molasses that couldn't move.

"I'm glad you asked. We're going over to Jill's place" he said.

"But Jake, ah don't know wheah she…"

"Nadia does. Nadia, give Janice Jill's address. We have to go over there now."

Nadia put down a searing aluminum tray, took off her mitts and fished for a pen and slip of paper. She wrote down the address and checked with Jake to make sure that he knew how to get there. It was all the way cross town and would take over an hour at this time of day.

"OK, Janice let's go." Janice was so new that she was clearly the least essential person and therefore the best employee to take along with him.

"Let me warn you know that I have a very small car and that I am going to drive it very fast," Jake stated.

"Didn't y'all know mah daddy was a race cah drivah?" she grinned.

"Was?"

"He dyehd."

"God, Janice, was it racing? That's awful."

"Naw, cansah. Daddy was a smokah. But thanks ahl the same. Ah looove to drahve so let's see waht this baby cayn do. I'll watch for the pó-lice."

"Janice, we're in a city."

"Jake, that's ahlright. You just drahve." She buckled herself in and he could have sworn that she was looking for a helmet. He put on his seat belt and put the car in gear.

"Purrs lahkah little kitteh. A little kitteh with grate beeg clowes." Janice grinned. Jake was wondering how exactly she got into the cupcake business.

He was not going to be encouraged to get a ticket because of crazy speed racer to his right. He kept Nadia's address and barely legible directions on the dash board and his speed within reason, despite Janice's obvious disappointment. But speed within reason for Jake was twenty-five miles per hour faster than any other driver. They arrived at Jill's apartment building in 30 minutes, going deeper and deeper into the smog. He got out with Janice and went to the intercom. He wasn't going to go in but he wanted to at least get to the door. The paper said '#5G' which took awhile to find since the buttons were next to the last name, first initial. They pressed the button after 'Ingram, J.' and heard a familiar raspy "yeah?" followed by a disturbing coughing fit.

"Jiyull it's Janice, ah need to pick up the work agenda, can ah come up?" There was a click and a buzz. Janice looked scared. Jake whispered a 'you'll be fine, go on' and while Janice opened the front door he stayed put. She would have asked for the appropriate biohazard gear but well, it would be rude to arrive unannounced dressed that way. She hoped that she could just hold her breath long enough to get what she came for and leave. Hopefully, Jill wouldn't be in the mood to chat, or touch her, and maybe she'd just leave it by the door and go back into her apartment. Janice would have to wash her hands vigorously when she and Jake got back. Maybe Jake could stop on the way so she could get a shot of ginger juice or three.

The elevator stopped with a lurch on the fifth floor and Janice stepped out with the same hesitation and looked for #5G. It wasn't to the left, so she headed in the other direction and saw an open door. Germs are just poring out of that place, she thought in disgust and covered her face. She grabbed the sleeve of her hoodie and knocked lightly on the open door whispering "Jiyull?" All the lights were off, the place was thick with body heat and no ventilation. She didn't want to take another step further in when Jill suddenly appeared with a glass of water in one hand and the agenda in the other.

"Oh my Gawd, Jiyull."

"Yeah." She started to topple over with yet more coughing.

"Let me take this, and you go on back to beh-yud. Do you all want us to pick up anything wahl we-uh he-uh?" she asked, praying she'd decline. Jill wagged her head no, and stumbled back to her bedroom waving her hands in what must have been a gesture to say 'I'm going back to bed, thanks,' or 'good-'bye or 'git.'

"Thanks, Jiyull. Feel bettah. Cawl the storah when you feel lahk commin ee-un. Bah nayow." Janice closed the door softly and ran for the elevator.

Jake was waiting exactly in the spot where he had been standing when she went inside. He stepped back as if she was contagion. With care, Jake grabbed the book and opened it to this month to check that all the information was there. It was, thank God. They returned to his car quickly, threw the germ-ridden notebook in the back and after having strapped themselves in, he leaned over to open the glove compartment. Opening it, he cracked her knees, but more importantly, he found a full bottle of the anti-bacterial gel which he handed her to use and asked for it back to use himself while driving. She was impressed by that last bit. Daddy never did that once behind the wheel. Might have saved his life.

Janice had her ginger root shot and bought a Wisconsin ginseng ampoule just for good measure. (Jake would not let her get the goji berries.) With the business agenda safe, they returned to the store to see the line of frosting devotees being appeased and pastry carts ready to be emptied. Reviewing the calendar, Jake saw that the Assistant to the Herald's resident Food Diva would be calling. She would be outlining ahead of time exactly what form Ms. Michaelson's condescension would take: whether via telephone, in situ or an appearance with entourage and staff photographer. Channel Six's "The Food Dude" was sending a crew; "Wake Up Los Angeles" did, in fact, want him in studio. If this agenda was still correct, no dates were set beyond "sometime" this week. People would be calling. As for the other newspapers, they could take care of themselves, they had copy and photographs. Jake was not about to call Jill to ask her if this information was current. He was going to wait until she felt better and called in herself. If she missed this week, he would certainly miss her but he would be all right.   The store would be ready by Wednesday for any filming or still photography.   Now that he was revving into a hyper-organized state, he decided that he'd ask Janice to take his message machine and transcribe everything for extra credit. He was feeling quite accomplished, taking care of all this shit, when someone said from behind

"Ooh Jake, you got woman trouble."

CHAPTER

TWENTY-SIX

Fuck me, Jake thought. He could hardly believe what was staring back at him. Jennifer and Ellie were standing in the store front eyeing each other with suspicion. That's when they weren't looking at him, each with their own unique take on feminine eyeball plaintiveness. He couldn't leave; he was standing right there and was expected to do something, like respond. Ellie was vying for his attention by trying to make her eyes appear bigger, while Jennifer adjusted the strap on her hobo bag and pursed her lips. Who to talk to first? He could get rid of Ellie or risk offending Jennifer. He'd just answered his question.

"Jennifer! What a nice surprise. Hold on a minute, okay, we're having a bit of a crisis right now!" Jennifer smiled in triumph and Ellie wore the look of the defeated and the dumbfounded.

"Ellie! I'm sorry that I haven't been able to speak with you. Weren't you supposed to call me? Unfortunately, now's not a good time. Can it wait?" he asked with all the good natured charm he could squeeze out of his sphincter muscle.

Ellie smiled brightly and said 'of course, Jake, I popped in because I kept on missing you, but of course it could wait, we'll be in touch.' She turned to Jennifer to nod a dismissive goodbye. Jennifer was playing with her cell phone. Faced with such an effrontery, she walked out the front door, with a bag (half her size) in hand.

"Jennifer, I think she's stalking me!" said Jake. He didn't look like he was kidding.

"Oh Jake, come on!"

"Seriously, she keeps on showing up and I don't know what to do anymore!" Jake figured he could be the *demoiselle* and she could be the *knygt erraunt* for a change. Gender roles were in flux these days, fuck it.

"Now Jake, don't you think you're exaggerating just a little bit? You need to calm down. Don't get yourself so upset." Ah, she's buying it.

"No. I don't. I need some air." Jake grabbed her hand and pulled her through the kitchen and out the back door. He sat on one of his fenders while she stood there getting ready to light a cigarette." Jake looked horrified.

"You're not going to smoke that are you?" he asked.

"I hadn't planned on writing with it" she replied smartly.

"It's going to ruin that lovely skin. And kill you" he said contemplatively.

"Fine. Put this on the list of things I hate about L.A." she said waving the unlit stick at him.

"What, you hate L.A.? So soon?" he was disappointed.

"Jake, it is really different. I don't understand it."

"Oh, that reminds me, I forgot to put the five second rule on my list."

"What?"

"Yeah, when the light turns green, people don't hit the gas for roughly five seconds, sometimes as long as seven."

"OH MY GOD JAKE! I mean, I'm not the best driver, clearly, but what is *that* about?" She had to smoke that cigarette now. He'd provoked an emotion out of her but she was going to get rid of the pesky thing. Still, he stared her down until she put the cigarette back into the box and the box back into her purse, and closed it.

"Well..." he cleared his throat. "I used to think it was Los Angelenos being dumb and slow but it's Los Angelenos being smart and not getting killed by the idiot in the SUV gunning through the red light." He explained waiting for her reaction. He saw the light bulb flash above her head.

"Ohhhhh. That *is* smart."

"See. Anyway, that woman, Ellie, who you've seen now twice? Am I right? Well, she'd been lurking around and maybe I am being paranoid, but she's starting to freak me out. I'm going to have to figure out a way to get rid of her."

"Jake, maybe she's a needy customer." Jennifer suggested.

"Huh, I never thought of it that way." Jake was tapping his grizzled chin in contemplation. He wanted to ask her if those little grey hairs were growing in again. "But she's not a customer."

"Thanks for the flowers, by the way. They were lovely and they made everyone in the office completely jealous. You have excellent taste, Jake. Oh and my editor's coming out soon. I know she's going to take over the piece on Los Angeles food trends."

"You already know her tricks. Why the concern?"

"I'm just warning you" she said.

"Warning me? What do I have to be afraid of?"

"Afraid, no, I don't mean that. I'm just telling you 'fyi' that she's a piece of work. You may never meet. It depends on what I write and then how she wants to destroy it."

"What you write, huh?" For some reason, this seemed like an appropriate moment for Jake to kiss her. He drew her close to him and was impressed that she didn't topple over in her Louboutin boots. The heel on those babies were insane. He kissed her lightly and then parted her mouth and kissed her again. She was surprisingly strong and pulled him towards her to a standing position. They kissed again and Jake was happy to realize that there was chemistry between them. He had been a little worried. He separated a bit so his eyes could focus and ran his hand down the side of her throat and squeezed her shoulder. He was eyeing her right breast but chose to leave it alone for the time being.

"I hadn't planned on taking the afternoon off, but..." she smiled suggestively.

"Me neither, I'm completely swamped inside." They kissed again, this time more passionately and she could feel his arousal against her jeans.

"Well," she licked her lips. "Let me get back to work and finish what I have to do there and you do the same. We can have dinner tonight? Sounds okay?" He kissed her lightly on the lips.

"Sure, where?"

"Your place."

With that she broke away and took her keys and her cigarettes out of her bag.

"Text me how to get to there and I'll come by around 8? That sound okay?"

"Come hungry" Jake smirked.

She smiled again, got in her car, placed her sunglasses in position and drove off. She was beginning to understand the LA look. But it would take time. Instead of waiting while the hand on the clock spun around, he went back into the store ready to face a burgeoning nightmare. Unfortunately, neither Jake nor Jennifer had spotted the other burgeoning nightmare, Ellie, who had been standing across the street and out of view, watching everything.

CHAPTER
TWENTY-SEVEN

Back inside, Jake reviewed once more the agenda's notes. Tomorrow would be the beginning of a crazy week to be sure. He would call Jill also and perhaps send a care package round to her apartment. Hopefully she would answer the phone. As for today, it was shot for baking 'organic' as far as he was concerned. He would begin tomorrow, for the first time, in he couldn't remember how long, without Jill's input. It would be like when he was first starting out.

On the way back to his house, he stopped by the grocery store. He didn't need to buy much, because if he had judged the situation correctly, they were not going to be eating much. He got two bottles of an old vine syrah, some handmade ravioli, whole cream, Irish butter, portobello mushrooms, a golden honeydew, proscuitto, a small piece of parmigiano-reggiano, heirloom tomatoes, ice-cream and fudge brownies from the bakery counter. He tried to keep it simple. He found some decent looking grapes, fresh figs and some peachy chocolate roses that didn't have that nasty freezer burn on their petal tips. No way was he buying red, that's so obvious and rather sad.

When he walked into his place he opened the windows in the sitting room to air it out. He put away all the groceries, quickly dusted and vacuumed. He changed his bed linen and coverlets and brought in a couple of gardenia blossoms from the garden to float in the silver Jensen bowl on the nightstand. He made sure nothing was lying around that shouldn't be and if it was, hid it. Everything looked presentable, not precious, but not stinking of bachelorhood either. He took a rather long shower, shaved and changed into a clean pair of underwear, jeans and t-shirt. He checked to make sure no hairs were protruding where they would not be appreciated. He got out his cologne, but put it back. He got out his lotion, but put that back as well. Smelling soapy and well-scrubbed would work nicely with the home cooked meal. The theme would be fresh, clean and intercourse.

Jake went into the kitchen, having found his thongs, and looked at the floor. The entire place needed a quick wipe down and quick because there was to be no sweating. He did the floor and the counters and then went outside to cool off while the floor dried. After about ten minutes he went back into the kitchen and started to bring food out the fridge. He set his dining room table. Jake had a collection of sterling silver water pitchers and he put the roses in three smallish ones, setting them on the table with no candles. The cutlery, he had found in Massachusetts at a flea market and they had been a bitch to ship, he remembered, but worth it.

He looked at the clock, it said 7:45. He opened the wine to be on the safe side. He started boiling the water and did all his chopping. The doorbell rang. Perfect. He felt his stomach flip and sweat burst out of his pits. Not good. Be cool. He went to the door and opened it upon a truly lovely sight.

Jennifer. She'd brought red wine and her hair was down. She blushed and smiled, he kissed her and brought her inside the house.

"Wow, Jake your house is lovely" she said admiringly, surprised at being impressed.

"Thanks. I'm really happy here. Let me take your coat." Jake pulled off her short and shiny Burberry trench and much to his surprise she was wearing tight, low cut blue jeans, a loose cashmere sweater as a thin as a t shirt so you could see she had a beautiful brassiere with the tits to match, a pair of Zanotti sandals and understated diamond jewelry everywhere.

"Wow." Jake said. "You look stunning." Please don't flip you hair, don't bat your lashes, giggle or otherwise ruin what's beginning to be a perfect moment for me. God you have low expectations, he thought to himself.

"Well thanks, Jake. We aim to please" she smiled modestly and pulled her hair behind her ears. "Can I help you with anything? What are you making?"

"Just ravioli. I forgot to ask if you were allergic to anything." Jake asked now.

"Me? No. That's so sweet of you. No, I can eat anything, as far as I'm aware. Oh, before I forget, my editor called. I would like to set up a meeting. We can have lunch if you're not too busy."

"Oooh, next week is really a bad time for me. We'll have to play that one by ear, but I'll do what I can. Would you like your wine or mine?" He brought her into the kitchen after having hung up her coat and got two wine glasses from the cabinet.

"I see you opened a bottle; let's start with that." He poured two glasses, handing her one and clinked the rims.

"Cheers."

"Cheers."

"Let me finish up dinner, it will only take about half an hour. Why don't you take a tour of the house and outside.... the cd's are stacked over there by the stereo. It's pretty easy to operate but let me know if you have any trouble." He hoped that her hands were clean.

"Okay." Jennifer took her wine glass and went off to check his place out. He had several French post-war era prints, but other than that nothing on the walls but mirrors. No bad posters, no bad paintings, no bad sculpture or lousy photographs. She liked that. There was very little clutter. There were a large number of books, which didn't surprise her. The furniture included some mid-century, some nice repros; all and all, eclectic and comfortable. His house may be big, but it was inviting, not a showpiece. She stepped outside to see a wide and pretty expansive view of the basin. She could smell not only the flowers in his small garden but all the gardens wafting up the hillside. The pool glistened as she walked along side it to the back. There was an array of fruit trees, potted succulents and trailing roses, some oil lamps and a fairly decent sized lawn which ended with a stepped stone retaining wall. She came round the other side of the pool, tossing a fallen rose into the water and let out a sigh of deep contentment. She was so right to leave New York. Who could not love living here?

She came back into the house having emptied her glass and placed it on the kitchen counter. Jake looked down to see that her sandals were off her feet. His ravioli was almost done. He was working on his sauce. She stepped over to where he was standing and kissed him deeply. He returned the kiss and stroked her back. She knew better than to distract a cook, so off she went to the living room to put on some music. She found a George Shearing, some west coast jazz from the early 50s, a Jobim and slid the discs into the cd player pressing 'shuffle'. She kept the volume low so that it wouldn't be intrusive and sat down to watch him cook. I hope I don't fall asleep, she thought. Jennifer was not familiar with being fine and mellow.

Jake quietly finished setting the table and told her to have a seat. He poured her a second glass and set the bottle down.

"Let's eat!"

CHAPTER
TWENTY-EIGHT

Jennifer pulled her seat up closer to the table, while Jake began bringing platters out. First came the golden honeydew and figs wrapped in proscuitto. Then the stuffed ravioli with cream sauce, shaved parmigiano-reggiano, sautéed tomatoes and mushrooms. They smiled at each other as they took a sip from their wine glasses and dug in. Jennifer and Jake didn't speak after the first couple of bites. They ate. They drank. It was just as he had planned, simple and unassuming, but fresh. The dishes weren't meant to be savored but gobbled down despite the desire for each bite to last. Juicy and tangy, sweet and salty, creamy and spicy, one fork full after another. Like two little piggies at the trough. But Jake liked to see that in a woman. And he certainly did not object to it in himself. Neither he nor Jennifer showed the slightest restraint in the face of good food. Whether refined or reformed, it was hard to tell, but they were both hedonists regardless. Thank god the napkins were absorbent.

With their plates practically licked clean, Jake took them away and brought out the second bottle of wine or was it the third? She waved it away.

"I've had more than enough, Jake, but thank you." He poured himself a glass, which turned out to be from one of those that he'd bought, thus it was only their second bottle, thank you very much, so relax.

"That was wonderful Jake" she said. She had the glow from eating a satisfying meal as opposed to the constipated stare from the desperate need to unzip her jeans, so that her belly could flop out. Jennifer didn't have a belly, but nevertheless.

"Can I ask you another question about your list?"

"Sure." Jake looked up from the sink where he was stacking dishes.

"Why was there so much about driving and pedestrian behavior? I mean, there was more of that than anything."

"Well" he said, wiping his hands on a dish towel and setting it down upon the counter. "I was trying to give you a head start on behavior that you probably won't see in any other city. The stuff that's unique to Los Angeles. Human nature is pretty much the same, you know, character, ambition, greed. That stuff I didn't see the point in addressing." He came back to his seat to join her.

"But why cars, Jake?" she still didn't get it.

"It's a car culture. It makes a city different. Wheels. I don't know, it's hard to explain. People are wired to roll, they are not walkers, they don't interact with each other like in other places. That throws a lot of new people in town off. In NY the man on the street is totally on a par with vehicular traffic, despite how absurd that looks to an outsider, and still he's conscientious and saavy, here he is road kill, and yet he is oblivious, contemptuous and thinks at the very least that he is indestructible. People are peculiar, as you may have noticed. Now are you ready for dessert?"

"Let's wait a while longer. Well where are all the dead bodies, then?"

"Just look for the candles, flowers and teddy bears. Do you want to go outside and sit by the pool?" he asked, fearing he was boring the shit out of her. He was starting to bore the shit out of himself.

"Yes, that's a great idea! I love your back yard. I want a back yard!"

Jake took the wine and she took the glasses (oh, maybe just one more) and they went out and sat on the lounge chairs by the shimmering turquoise water. He lit some of his brass oil lamps and went back inside for a couple of throws in case it got too chilly. She wrapped hers around her shoulders and sat back with a look of sweet contentment.

"It's really nice here Jake. Thank you so much for inviting me. That's the best home cooked meal I've had in a long, long time." Jake took her glass and set it down, filled. He sat on the side of her chair and kissed her. He hoped the wine had killed the scent of garlic and onions in his mouth. If it hadn't it was too late now. Maybe he had some of that peppermint ice-cream left over. He'd have to go check. On and on his mind prattled about food and odors and the refrigerator and dishes in the sink and he realized that he was not even present in the moment of a kiss. And now it was over. Let's try this again, he thought. He cleared his mind of all the useless chatter and kissed her fully, thinking of nothing. He was working on his Zen approach to French kissing. It must have worked because the next thing he knew she had pulled him on top of her with that unexpected strength again. His mind started to roam over to the wine bottle and glasses and what if they tipped over when she grabbed his ass and gave it a nice tight squeeze. She pulled the throw out from between them and laid it over his back. She wouldn't throw it on the ground. So he threw it on the ground.

The great thing about those loungers is that they comfortably hold two people and you could totally do it and they wouldn't self destruct underneath you. He couldn't unbutton her blouse because it was a sweater. He couldn't take off her sandals because she was already barefoot. So he focused on her jeans which slid off to reveal one of those Italian thongs that's nothing more than a rubber band in an eye-scalding color. He leaned over to kiss her stomach and then her thighs and spread her legs open when she stopped him.

"Can't your neighbors see, Jake? Let's go inside."

She jumped back into her jeans. He took the bottle and glasses. Jennifer took the throws and following his lead, walked into the house and on to the bedroom.

CHAPTER
TWENTY-NINE

Jake placed the glassware on his dresser and took the throws out of her arms. He sat on his bed and drew her to him.

"Let's see those panties, again" he said, helping her out of her clothes. He didn't want to tear at her sweater but he did want to see the contents of that bra too. Jennifer slid out of her jeans, stood up to show her whisper of a thong in a shade of chartreuse that could make your eyes bleed. The hedge was nicely clipped and trimmed, he could see this through the green triangle of dental floss which he slid to the ground and out of which she gamely stepped. She knelt down on the soft shag rug which lay beside his side of the bed and helped him out of his jeans. He was already fully erect, always a nice thing to see, she thought. She smiled and gently stroked him from the shaft to the tip a few times just to watch his penis get harder and the veins start to pop. He gave up on the sweater and laid back on the bed while she set about taking him into her mouth. Careful not to scrape him with the molars, she eased him in and out slowly. She spread his legs further open with her hands and continued for a few more moments. She pulled her mouth away and his prick bounced up to his navel. Jake tried to sit up on his elbows but instead chose to rest fully on his bed and wait for her to join him. She took off her sweater folding it neatly and placed it on the bureau. She let him see her bra, a sheer balconette with most of her full breasts protruding. Removing and setting it upon her sweater, she turned to face him and smiled. Jake reached out his hand for her to grab hold of and she crawled up fully onto the bed.

Once she was beside him, he cupped her breasts, flicking her nipples. He sucked alternating with a light pinch with his thumb and forefinger. They were soon standing erect and she gave out a soft moan. He continued to kiss her between her breasts, down her belly then opened her legs and kissed her inner thighs slowly. By squeezing and kissing, he knew that in little to no time, that she would be wet. He lifted her up by her ass and licked her clit with upward strokes. He drove the tip of his tongue into the little bud of it waiting for her moans to follow more rapidly. He squeezed her ass while she lay there groaning and waiting for his tongue. But instead, he took his cock and slipped it inside her. They both let out a groan as he pushed as far into her as he could. He drove long and hard strokes, as long as he could make them and then she flipped him over. Again with the muscles, he thought. She doesn't look that strong. Holding his arms down, her breasts and hair in his face, she ground her hips around in wide circles until his head started to move from side to side. He sat up and grabbed her hips to control the rhythm knowing that he was about to come. She stopped. She pulled him out and slipped back next to him and let him enter her again. Jake twisted her hips so that they were scissoring when the grinding began again. He pulled out almost all the way and slid back in again, slowly, very slowly until he knew he couldn't hold off any longer. Sensing this she grabbed him by the ass and pushed him deep inside her, changing the speed to a steady pound. He came deep inside her but he wasn't altogether sure that she did.

After a few minutes, he pulled out and lay down beside her in the fluffy sheets. He was smiling and spent. He stroked circles around her breasts.

"Jennifer, you didn't come did you?" he asked.

"Jake, we're not through yet." That made Jake a little nervous; he didn't know how much stamina he would have tonight. And he had to work tomorrow. Shut up, he said inside his head.

"We're not?" he tried to look decadent instead of unsure and a little panicky.

"You want to, don't you?" Jennifer started to look a little concerned herself.

"Sure, just give me a minute. Let me catch my breath." Words no woman really ever wants to hear.

He kissed her and lay back down again wiping the sweat from his brow. He knew what she was thinking. I may have left one coast for another, but here's another one of those one shot wonders.

"Let's get some dessert and bring it back to bed." Jake offered brightly.

"OK, what are we having?" She stood up and came over to his side of the bed, helping him up too. He looked like he could use a nap, poor baby.

"Oh, I got ice cream and stuff. Come on." They padded in their nakedness over to the kitchen, where he got two spoons, two bowls and napkins which he placed on a tray. He took the peppermint ice cream and nuked it in the microwave for 20 seconds or so and scooped it into the bowls. He smashed some fresh, pitted cherries that were in the fridge and put a few in there. He took the bag of brownies from off the top of the refrigerator, where it was getting warmed up a little bit and mashed it. Taking the fudge crumbles, he spread them over the ice cream as well. Jennifer's eyes were glassy and not from an orgasm.

"Do you want syrup or nuts or something else?"

"No, that looks great; it's fine just like that." She looked a little feral.

"OK, back to bed." He kissed her and returned to the bedroom balancing the bowls carefully as he climbed back onto the bed. She joined him with equal care, trying not to unsettle the tray as they proceeded to sort out what was his and what was hers. They emptied their bowls in due haste and if it wouldn't have been such a bother for seconds, they would have had them.

Thankfully, for Jennifer, the sugar overload was just what Jake needed to go back and finish his job. He deftly cleared the bed of the tray and kissed her until their lips were no longer cold and minty. Jake stroked her body with his hands over the blankets as he knew they were icy from handling the spoons and the bowls. He stroked and kissed her until they were both warm. She smiled broadly as he threw off the duvet and the top blankets. Jake pulled her hair away from under them so as not to get yanked and kissed her behind her earlobes and on down her neck to her left breast. Jennifer arched her back as he slowly began to knead her nipples to erection. Her excitation excited him, the way she turned her head into the pillow case or grabbed at his waist. He turned her onto her stomach and lifted up her haunches so as to enter her from behind. Jake could touch everything from this position and knew that he would get her off. He nibbled at the curve of her nape and massaged her clitoris until again she was very, very wet. He continued to use his index and middle finger to massage her nipples while he slowly ground into her. This time she was losing it. Jennifer's arching back seized up underneath him while he continued his thrusts. He pulled out and massaged her moist clit with his cock and eventually dipped back inside, never leaving her nipples unattended. He continued this until he heard her give out a large gasp and slammed her back into him. He flattened her down onto the bed and thrust until he came a second time. She was immobilized with a satisfied grin, which from his position he couldn't see. But the grin said well done, my lad, well done.

CHAPTER THIRTY

Around three in the morning, Jake found himself staring at the ceiling. This really is not a good time for insomnia, he thought. He reached out to Jennifer and put his arm around her. She was snoring softly. As his opened eyes grew accustomed to the dark, he watched while she cuddled up under his arm without waking. He lay his head back down and tried to go back to sleep, but he knew that it would be a long night. He inhaled the scent of her hair and closed his eyes.

Strangely, when he opened them again, it was morning. He had slept fitfully, mostly like due to a new partner in his bed. Now he felt groggy and out of sorts. Jennifer was already coming out of the bathroom and putting on her clothes.

"Good morning, sleepy" she said.

"Good morning," he yawned. "How did *you* sleep?"

"Like a log. That's pretty unusual for me, to tell you the truth. How about you?"

"Alright I guess." Jake replied throwing his legs over the side of the bed and standing up like a cripple. Dressed, she walked over to a still naked Jake and gave him a kiss and a squeeze. He stretched like a cat and then suddenly groaned in pain.

"You poor darling. I know just how you feel. Tons of coffee is the only remedy, I'm afraid."

"I think you're right."

"Shall I make some?"

Jake didn't want to sound rude so he didn't say anything for a few ticking moments.

"Right. I understand. Well, I have to get to work. Now where *are* my sandals?" Jake felt bad. He didn't think of this as a one night stand nor did he want her to think that he did. And he didn't want her to think of it that way. But frankly, he didn't know what it was, other than sex and a meal. A Happy Meal, if you will. He quickly found some underwear on the floor and went after her. When he reached the living room, her sandals were on, her hair back in a pony tail, and her jacket and purse in hand.

"Thank you Jake for a lovely night." She gave him another hug. Jake held on to her feeling ridiculous standing there in his underpants.

"I'm glad you came over." He replied with confidence and manliness. They proceeded through the 'awkward walking to the door after the first night of sex together' segment relatively smoothly. Jake tried somewhat successfully to keep his body out of view of the neighbors when they kissed goodbye.

"Call me." she said, regretting it the second it came out of her mouth. Jake just waved and nodded, which only increased her discomfort. Two of the saddest words in the English language. God I hope I didn't sound *that* needy, she thought. Am I needy?, she nervously wondered as if she'd forgotten her deodorant. Jake, on the other side of the door, noticed the hole in his underwear as he started to take them off. I don't think she saw that, he reassured himself and went to take a shower.

He knew that he would have a lousy, but very busy day, which was a shame because the evening had been great. He stood under the shower nozzle for what seemed a long, long while yet finally relented, stepped out and dried off. By the time he got to work, the staff was in a panic. This morning was not starting out as well as he had hoped.

The first words to great him when he got to the store were:

"Helena Michaelson called, she's going to be here to interview you and take photos around 11am."

"Great. I *love* Helena Michaelson." He reached for his first of many cups from the coffee maker and turned back to look at his kitchen. Everyone stood frozen staring at him.

"Has anyone called Jill?" he asked. He heard a little bit of mumbling which he took as a 'no'. He reached for the phone and put in a call. After several rings she picked up.

"Hello?"

"Jill, it's Jake. How are you? Are you alright? We were so worried."

"I'm feeling better. I guess I really needed to sleep."

"You sound better. Listen, I'm assuming that you're taking a sick day today. If you feel better tomorrow, maybe you can come in. But only if you think you're up to it. I absolutely *do not* want you coming back to work sick, do you understand?" Jake was waking up.

"What's going on Jake?" she asked.

"Huh?"

"What's going on today?" she asked.

"Oh nothing special. Same old, same old. Now can we bring you anything? How's your cough? I think it sounds better today." In all the years she had known Jake, he was sweet, he was thoughtful, but he was never, ever a mother hen.

"Is there anything you're not telling me about? You know I'm gonna find out."

"Why would you say that, Jill? Did you take your aspirin this morning? You don't still have a fever do you? Did I ask you that already?" She sensed that he was shitting some sort of a brick.

"Jake, I know something's up. You haven't heard me cough once since I picked up the phone. I'm coming in." Jill hung up. Just as soon as she had done so, she was felled by another bout. Jill was grateful for having the bed underneath her when it struck.

"Jill's coming in." he said still holding the phone in his hand.

"Thank fucking God" Jake heard from somewhere behind him. Signs of the Cross were quickly swiped and every face looked innocent.

"Thanks. Thanks a lot." He poured himself another cup of coffee and proceeded to inspect the place. Everything looked good. The floors and work tables were clean and gleaming. The front was in order, although he couldn't help but grab a cloth and a bottle of spray cleaner and swab everything over. The front window was fine but, of course, he still felt the need to buff the door pull and ask that the front floor be swept again. Jake checked over everyone who would be seen by their guest, to make sure that they were dressed properly and with no noticeable stains. While he was fixing Janice's apron for the third time, he got on his cell phone and called the florist. Balancing the phone on his shoulder, he ordered a slightly larger bouquet to be sent to Jennifer's place of work. Yes, he was on file. Yes, he'd like to send a note. It should say…(something nice, not stalker-like or lame)…"Thank you for being such a lovely dinner guest, Yours, Jake."

"Awh, that's swee-uht." drawled Janice. With that, he dropped his cell while trying to center her belligerent front apron tie. Jake reached down to pick up the phone and hit the 'end call' button, but the battery was gone. He crouched down to find it and snap it back in. And that's where he heard of Her arrival. Like a bad spaghetti western, standing in the shadows of a swinging saloon door, stood the infamous Herald food critic, Ms. Helena Michaelson.

Helena breezed in with her assistant and photographer cluttering up the entire front bakery. Customers were jettisoned out of their own personal space, not only threatened by the thought of losing their place in the cupcake line, but worse, losing their cupcake. And for what? To make way for a movie star? No. TV? Cable? No and No. This entourage enveloped only the most important food critic on the West Coast. The lone Fate who held the string and the scissor for any regional chef, baker or restauranteur, is all. Her face wouldn't be recognized, nor would she want it to be, for she enjoyed a more significant form of celebrity. She was maybe just an acolyte; but it was of a nearly aristocratic pedigree. The lineage of the *extraordinarily unattractive female cultural arbiter*. The *connoisseuse*. The *maligned female aesthete*. Following in the footsteps of the Diana Vreelands, the Elsie de Wolfes and the Elsa Maxwells, she was a monstrosité de bon goût. These high priestesses whose masks must fall away, test the mettle of those who dare to brave the altitudes. These horrors, with their jacked up noses and too wide eyes, their shocking facial asymmetry and unmanageable coiffures are the living ontological proof of the divinity of beauty; those who assure us of its existence by embodying its polar opposite. They are its most faithful and ardent handmaidens. And not very nice.

As she looked about her, she gave out the teeniest suggestion of a judgmental sniff. Something like the sneeze of a gnat. Her assistant understood this to be her cue to begin proceedings, while Jake stood up, slightly agape at the mouth having gone all pillar of saltish at the sight of her. It's not that he hadn't met her before; but she did take some getting used to, even for the initiated.

CHAPTER
THIRTY-ONE

"Helena!" exclaimed Jake, taking both she and her staff aback. So bold, so familiar. Not what Mme. was expecting at all.

"Jake how are you my dear?" She gave him permission to kiss her on both cheeks and so he did.

"I'm so glad that you could make it today. Please let's go through to the back." Ms. Michaelson turned to the Herald photographer and told him to take some shots while they conducted the interview. Then, with a wave of her arm he was dismissed.

Jake led Helena and her assistant to the back of the kitchen, which was not actually an office, but would do in a pinch. He had a desk from some eco-friendly Albanian designer, so it just appeared sleek and minimalist, rather than practically useless. There were only two chairs, which was perfect since the assistant understood her place all too well and stood against the wall in silence. Helena perched her brittle derriere in the chair that he had stood behind as she sat down "daintily," if that's the word, while he flopped down into the other, pushing the hair out of his eyes, his first of many deliberately, disarming gestures.

"So Jake, darling, tell me. What are your feelings about today's cupcakes?" Is she for real?, he wondered.

"Well Helena," Jake looked about while framing his words and then slowly focused direct eye contact on this food Medusa. "I have to tell you, although my impulses tell me otherwise, I try to focus on simplicity. It's a cupcake."

"Yes, I know Jake dear, but why do you think it's creating so much interest? After all….." she leaned forward and exposed her crepey, ruddy décolletage.

"Well I do think that every now and then when things get complicated…the world is kind of a scary place right now, and I guess it always will be….anyway….people are seeking innocence. They're looking for the absolutes. And as daft as that sounds, for Americans, a cupcake is pretty much as innocent as it gets." He pursed his lips a bit and bit the bottom one saving a slow sidelong glance for last. He would have looked for the chapstick for a slow lower lip application, but this was working well enough. Jake could do "slutty whore" good.

"Quite."

"So, I'm offering innocence and comfort, at a very reasonable price. It's simple and takes the customer to a place they remember very fondly."

"Proust's tea-soaked petites madeleines, perhaps?" she cooed.

"Perhaps. But these memories have no pain with them. There is no jolt into an emotionally wrenching past, no bittersweet nostalgia when you eat a cupcake. No Speak, Memory I'm afraid. Cupcakes are joyous. Like being on the playground or when class broke early for a party. I'm giving people those memories. Or rather, they are finding them here." He paused for a moment. "Shall I bring you a few samples to taste while you're here or would you like to take them with you?" Jake softly touched her hand with one finger. Helena looked like she was ready for the fainting couch but soldiered on, intrepid reporter that she was.

"Well a girl has to watch her figure but I will bring a few back to the staff. You know they work so hard." Jake caught her assistant's eyes rolling up into the back of her skull.

They reviewed all the basics. When he started and why? Who were his best clients? How he couldn't possibly divulge that information. What was his guiding motivation and inspiration? Was he attached or single? Who were his favorite movie stars and had he dated any? Who were his favorite designers and what was he wearing? What did he think of the other local bakeries?

Jake answered a few and dodged the rest. Most of this information, at least what was pertinent to her article was in the press kit sitting somewhere on her desk back at the office. Helena had gone all pink, so he was fairly certain she would be kind. Unless she was the sort who hated to feel desire for things she couldn't have and retaliated.

"Let me get you a selection that you can take with you, all right?" She nodded and blushed. "Come." He helped her out of her chair and took her hand as they walked into the kitchen. He knew that she had been in more kitchens than he had seen birthdays but he did the usual kitchen tour bit and his staff acted their parts nicely too. He went over and picked out a large purple box and folded the tissue paper down in the bottom. He then took a sampling of everything that was still warm from the kitchen and laid two of each into the box that held a dozen. While Helena stared at the process like a young woman buying her first set of La Perla lingerie, Jake removed a Cupcake emblazoned golden seal to close the box and put it in its purple bag. But this one was huge. He'd especially ordered the MK Olsen size after seeing Ellie. Ugh. Ellie. Forget about her for the time being would you? Breathe out.

Jake took the bag and walked out the store with her and the assistant, asking where they had parked.

"But wait, we need to take a few pictures of you for the article, dear." Since the staff photographer had been outside taking shots of the store a crowd had gathered at the sight of an expensive camera with hefty lens. He suggested to Jake that they go back inside for the rest of the shots since it was getting out of hand on the sidewalk. So Jake posed in the kitchen, at the counter and beside his signage but from inside the store.

"I think I got it" said the photographer.

"Thanks man. Listen come by later and I'll hook you up. Let Helena's assistant know too, just come by anytime." The photog's eyes lit up. For the first time today he was being treated like a human being. This Jake's a good guy.

"I'll take you up on that, man. Thanks alot."

"Sure, no problem."

"Take it easy." After the man talk, Jake followed him back out to where the ladies were assembled.

"Helena, always a pleasure." He kissed her again on both cheeks and gave her a long squeeze. He shook the assistant's hand and gave her a quick nod. She did not quite make it out of her professional assistant fog of resentment, but managed a vague smile therein.

As Helena sped off, Jake was in the back office area with his next cup of coffee. He planned on taking a break and cleaning up a bit more, when he was jolted out his chair with the door banging open, a loud fusillade of coughing in tow.

"I'm here. What'd I miss?" and having said that, Jill erupted into another thunderous attack.

CHAPTER
THIRTY-TWO

"Jill! I told you to stay home!" Jake yelled as he looked at the spilled coffee on the floor. He put down the cup and went into the bathroom to get something to clean up the mess. "You know I don't want anyone sick in here! You are contagious!"

"No I'm not!" Jill yelled back. She sounded as if her tears were about to make another appearance. Jake came out of the bathroom and began mopping up his third cup of coffee with shaking hands.

"Look, Jill. Don't think that I don't appreciate your driving all the way over here. But you need to get well before you come back. I know it sucks laying in bed feeling badly but you just have to do it." Jill *was* welling up and went into the bathroom and shut the door.

"Fuck" said Jake. What is with her? I don't make my employees cry! I am a not a shitty boss. I am a nice boss. As regular as zombies at sundown, here came his employees trying to crowd their way into another tiny space to see what they could do. If Jake hadn't been so exhausted and fed up he would have swept them all away with a hairy eyeball, but he just couldn't deal with this shit right now. Some of the girls knocked on the door for Jill to come out but she was racked with another coughing fit and they retreated from the door in due haste.

"Jake. Man, you gotta get rid of her. We can't have any *gripa* around here, man" said Gilberto pointing at the door.

"You. Go." Jake pointing back at the kitchen. "In fact, everyone, out!"

"Ok Jill! Can you hear me! Jill!" Jill had stopped coughing and blew her nose at length. "Ok pull yourself together and come on out" he said close to the door. She came out, puffy with a wad of toilet paper in her hand which she intermittently coughed into or wiped her nose.

"I'm sorry Jake, I'm going *crazy* at my apartment. I thought you needed me." She burst into tears. Oh lord.

"Highly functioning people like you and I don't do 'sick' well. You know that" said Jake trying to comfort her and not get infected. She sniffed and nodded her head up and down. Jill was leaning in, seeking a hug but he just couldn't go there.

"So I want you to go back home and get back into bed and at the end of the day call me if you're up to it and I'll give you a run down of what's happening, okay? Is that a deal?" Jake felt like he was talking to a five year old. However old she was at that particular moment, it worked. She blew her nose, one last time, gathered her things and went out to her car.

Jake walked with her, keeping a healthy distance, and breathing as infrequently as possible.

"Now, Jill drive safely and call me when you get home."

"Jake are you holding your breath?" she looked horrified. Jake matched her look and returned it even though it was true.

"Jill, I think you need to go home, now. We'll talk later." He tried to make his diaphragm fill out the words with what little oxygen was left. "Roll up your window."

Jill did so with suspicion. She saw his nostrils flare as he deeply inhaled to refill his lungs with life-giving oxygen. He made the sign of the telephone with his pinky and thumb and mouthed "call me." She had to stop with the accusatory stare-down, so that she could find where her key went into the ignition and turn it over. She backed up the car.

"Drive safely!" he yelled and waved goodbye, hitting her fender lightly.

"God damn!" he said, with his head muffled in his hands and walked back in.

"Is she gone?!" asked two or three of his staff at the same time. Out from the front of the kitchen Janice yelled at them.

"Y'all otta be ashaymed a yo-selves. Not one awah ago y'all were beggin' her to git ovah hiah and now y'all want her gahn. Thaht's a shayme." She looked down at her apron strings and re-tied the bow perfectly. I couldn't have said it better myself, thought Jake.

"Yeah," said Nadia. "You guys suck."

"All right everybody. We've had more than enough excitement for one morning. We've got work to do. Who's up in front?" Now that it was over, staff went on back to their responsibilities and Jake went to the store front to see about the line and make sure that the display cases were indeed full.

"I need you guys to fill this whole section over here and clean up the place." He was in drill sergeant mode, something nobody liked at Cupcake. It would be a sad day until he snapped out of it. Which judging by his needing a fourth cup of coffee was not going to be for a while. The line was still long, but at least there was no paparazzi walking by looking for things to shoot. Hopefully things were going to calm down. He decided that at the very least, he was going to calm down.

He put a call into George; it had been a couple of days.

"George."

"Jake! I'm so glad you called!" George's enthusiasm was a little jarring.

"George, what are you doing today?" asked Jake.

"The usual, I have an event tomorrow, so I'm just going over stuff. Why?" asked George.

"I wanted to know if you could get us into Man-icure this afternoon. I have to get out of here for awhile."

"What a fabulous idea. Let me make one more phone call and I'll call you right back."

Man-icure was the first mani/pedi salon for men in Beverly Hills. It had been doing a huge amount of business because, well, men liked to be with other men, no matter how cool they managed to act in a women's nail salon. It looked like an old school barber shop with chrome and leather chairs. Staff-wise, Man-icure tried to appeal to all possible tastes from which you could take your pick. It was a fancy Nevada whorehouse kind of nail salon. You could look down at a bosomy tattooed cleavage or read the paper. You could pick a big beefy bruiser to take a whack at your feet with the thai stone chakra massage. You could have dainty German Heidi doll simply clip your big toe while you played with your cellphone. It was a full service salon but without the femi color palette. Mani-cure was clubby. The lesbians of Beverly Hills were *huge* fans.

George called back in ten.

"We can go at 2:30. I got four so we can do mani and pedi together. Oh Jake, I'm so glad you called! What fun!"

"I think I want a mask too."

CHAPTER
THIRTY-THREE

George and Jake lay in their matching leather soaking chairs, with their limbs slightly splayed. Both wore masks made with bentonite to draw out impurities, mashed papaya and strawberries for the fruit acids, milk for the lactic acid, and honey for moisturizing. They'd been shaved and hot toweled and now with their facial masks in place, the attendants set about to care for their hands and feet. Talking at this point was strictly out of the question but George tried to open his mouth a couple of times only to realize it was useless.

"You must relax and allow the mask to cool and harden" ordered a chap with the crew cut and crisp barber's jacket. Why don't you hit me, thought George. It should at least be on the services menu. The two of them had so much to talk about but their mouths were forced shut. As a result, Jake was in the throes of relinquishing control, though he capitulated quickly to enforced relaxation. Although his body fought against it, once dominated, he fell asleep. George had no idea that Jake had nodded off under his creamy craquelure until he noticed the breathing. Oh well, nothing left to do but enjoy it, he thought and resigned himself to feeling wonderful.

For all its butch accoutrements, the stainless steel and leather and chocolate brown, Mani-cure was a girl at heart. Lower rung attendants brought over giant soaking bowls filled with flowers blossoms. Manly ones, like marigolds. Roman chamomile and orange blossom oils were poured into the bath and the feet were soaked and scrubbed. Once dried, the pedicure continued with a clipping, a pumicing and finished off with a small palm full of peppermint and eucalyptus oils massaged in a deep tissue fashion. Heavenly, thought George. If only Jake was awake to enjoy it. Must have had quite a night of it. Must inquire.

Once the feet were done, the attendants: George's, sporting a razored goth shag and a blue eyebrow piercing; Jake's, a bleached suedehead with that one beady eye, went ahead with the manicure. The masks had dried sufficiently and low rung attendants returned to hot towel the dried and flaking crusts off. At this point Jake woke up with a bit of a start, somewhat disoriented. He looked confusedly at George. George didn't think he knew where he was for a moment. Slowly, recognition and calm returned to Jake's face and he lay back again.

"Jake, I think you need a shrink. I've never seen anyone with your control issues get a mani-pedi. There I said it." George stared straight at the gleaming blue metallic barbell studs bouncing over on his hands.

"You think so? Really?" asked Jake. He was a little surprised to hear that.

"I know just whom you should see. She's great" said George.

"I don't think so, but thanks." Jake hoped he hadn't hurt his feelings.

"It's okay, Jake. You're just not ready. But one day you will be. And that's okay. I can wait. I'm here for you. You know that, don't you? Rome wasn't built in a day."

"George. Shut up."

George and Blue Stud nodded knowingly. Um-hum. His attendant's piercing arched with a little resistance, but it did go up.

The hands were soaked in mildly hot, soapy water and the nails cleaned of debris with the cuticles then cut back. Their fingers were stretched; their wrists twirled and their hands pressed back. Way back. A creamy exfoliant that smelled like peaches, those delicious, tart, completely artificial peaches, was smoothed over the hands with mitts to remove dead skin cells. Back into the soapy water their hands went again to rinse of the scrub. Then they were dipped into ice cold water. The boys shrieked. Lastly, the nails were shaped and buffed and to finish a light hand cream was rubbed into the skin. Nail varnish was extra and they both passed.

"George, I want a drink" said Jake.

"By all means. Where shall we go? Some place civilized or no?" asked George.

"No."

"I like how you think Jake. Let's go to The Cleft."

"George, I'm not going to a gay bar!"

"Shoot, right when things were going so well. Okay then, where? And don't even think of mentioning a sports bar."

Jake laughed. He could just see them with their neon plastic pedicure thongs propped up at the bar, while they drank Miller's.

"No, let's go to Phuket" Jake suggested.

"Excellent!"

In the olden days, that's to say the late 1980s, Phuket was a reputable Thai restaurant but having fallen on hard times by '93, losing one owner after another, it had ultimately become a bar. A dark and dirty bar. The walls were still painted black from when it was rock club and the booths remained from its incarnation as a restaurant. The stage had been ripped out to put the bar and that is where Jake and George each grabbed a stool. Addressing a tattooed blonde with dead eyes and something wrong with the mouth that couldn't be confused for a smile, George ordered a vodka tonic with lime, Jake a scotch and soda. A suspicious bowl of chex mix was tossed over to them and the drinks set atop dirty paper napkins. Eyeing the tats, George asked,

"Did you get those in prison?" Jake shot him a stern look to be quiet and took a long pull from his drink.

"God, what day is it? When is this week over?" Jake finished his drink and called the bartender over.

"Lemme have a Heineken."

"Sure love. Are you still working on yours, then?" She looked at George curiously.

"Yes I am." She walked away. He whispered over to Jake "she's British."

"I got that George, thanks." George paused but decided not to take offence and took another sip instead.

"So Jake, why are you so stressed?"

"It's a full week of press for me. Jill is out sick but won't stay away before she infects the whole store." He frowned. And then George did too.

"Well I hate to say it but, press is our friend and you'll do fine with or without Jill. Oh sorry Jake, that's my cell."

George reached into his jacket pocket and checked to see who it was.

"Oh look it's Jennifer! Should I take it?" asked George mischievously.

"Sure, tell her I said 'hi!'"

"Hello? Jennifer? Hi! What? Oh my God! Listen I'm in a bar with Jake! He says 'hi!' She says 'hi' back. Can I call you later? Okay. Bye-Bye!" He clicked his phone shut and put it away.

"So what's the deal with you two? Are you sleeping together yet?"

Jake choked on the beer which threatened to come burning out of his nostrils. The bartender looked up from her Sodoku puzzle book but went back to it as she saw Jake wouldn't require CPR.

"Jesus, George. A little subtlety perhaps?"

"I thought so! So tell me. Are you two an item?"

"George, no offense, but mind your own business."

"I thought so! I'm so happy for you Jake. She's a great girl!"

Jake couldn't think of anything to say because he knew it was hopeless at this point, but just in case, he warned,

"Listen George, we're just getting to know each other. I like her. She likes me I'm pretty sure." George nodded his intense agreement. "I don't want to talk about it."

George clapped his hands in elation and reached over to give him a hug.

"Oh Jake!"

CHAPTER
THIRTY-FOUR

In Jake's mind the week was unfolding like a slow motion thrill kill nightmare. Jill didn't come back in. She wouldn't answer the phone. Jake left about five messages but none were returned. She must be pissed off, he thought. She must think she's not appreciated. Well that is just complete bullshit. Thankfully, the radio interview went fine. The "Let's Eat" people were organized and unpretentious and the telephone interview lasted less than ten minutes. Easy. He hadn't yet heard from "The Food Dude" but Jill could take care of that when she returned. The public broadcasting crew came early in the morning which helped avoid upsetting the crowd and creating too much of a stir. Everyone was given their own goodie bag, including the camera crew, which contained three cupcakes, an amount, as far as Jake was concerned, which was two too many. But they seemed pleased and he didn't need another lecture from George about making nice with the press.

The stress of running the place did weigh on him without Jill. Even if it was just her moral support, which he knew it wasn't, she was palpably missed. He had prepared for it to be rough going. He had to be both the bad cop, Jill's job, and then the good cop, his job, otherwise he risked mutiny. So if he was sharp or cross, he used it in the context of the bait and switch routine, and added a 'go team!' finish. Kind of like a scary but indulgent alcoholic parent. It was working, yes, but for how long? It couldn't help but eventually freak out his staff, who may have started out being unconsciously manipulated, but would eventually wind up hostile and dysfunctional.

He conceived, he delegated, he coached, he cheered, he scolded, he coddled, he supervised, he executed, he paid, he thanked. It was pretty awful. He didn't cry though, not once. During this new, and hopefully short-lived, work set-up he remembered to bring in his message machine and handed it over to Janice.

"If you can transcribe these messages in a week, I'll give you $300." He prayed she'd accept.

"Whah, shoah Jake. Ah've alwayyys bee-uuun a free-und to the easy muh-nay." She seemed quite pleased. Some of the staff, busy on-looking and not working, seemed a little jealous, a little hurt. Weird. He'd have to think of some other menial tasks to extend towards them, if that sort of thing made them so happy.

On Wednesday morning, he had to be in the Cheetah studios no later than 6:30am. He didn't need a wake up call or a driver; he wanted this over with as soon as possible. He would get himself there on time. He took his Hugo Boss down vest from the car and met up with the "Wake Up Los Angeles" guest liaison at the welcome area.

"So we're going to go straight to Hair and Makeup and you're going to be on at around 7:20, okay?" she was officious and laid back at the same time, if that's at all possible. In other words, her glasses were Italian and rather severe, her hair in a tight pony-tail, her walkie-talkie barely hanging on to the waist of her low-rider jeans and a bit of her thong was showing. She wore running shoes and her nail polish was chipped in the new style, naturally.

"Okay, sure. Lead the way."

"Well hello there handsome!" leered two crew members as they made their way down one of several bunker-like hallways.

"Tom, Stew! Shut up! Go!" The liaison juggled her coffee, walkie talkie, cell phone and clip-board. How she opened the door to Hair and Makeup, he never knew, but she backed into the room and jerked her head for him to go to one of the chairs and sit down in it.

"Alex, he has to be ready by no later than 7:15. All right? You want some coffee?" Jake didn't know who she was talking to.

"Mr. Wellington?" she kicked the chair.

"Huh?" he turned and saw that she was talking to him.

"Would you like some coffee?"

"That would be nice, yeah, thanks."

"One Coffee, Hair and Makeup" she barked into her walkie talkie. "Anything else? Roll? Bagel?"

"No thanks. I'm good."

"7:15!" she said to Alex and left the room.

"Rrrrrarrhhh" said the stylist.

"Pardon?" Jake was ready to leave.

"Debbie. Girl, she's jacked up on Red Bull, coffee and peanut M&M's. Add that walkie-talkie and our friend over here's one *extra* crazy bitch, as you can plainly see." Jake couldn't tell whether this person was male or female, but it didn't matter, he was going to try to sleep with his eyes open. "I don't have to do a thing to you, sweetheart. You are per-fec-tion."

"Thanks?"

"Thanks Be to God, is what I'm sayin'? Okay? Do you go to church? No? Well, anyway, God loves you and I'm just going to comb through this hair. You do need it cut, you know. I can do it if you like? I'm just gonna use some powder to get rid of this shine. Do you want me to pluck those eyebrows? They're a hot mess. Lord have mercy. Umph."

"No thanks, I'm good." Jake said for the second time.

"That's good to know, honey. Yes indeed."

Someone barged in with a small Styrofoam cup of brown liquid. Taking the cup in his hand, Jake now didn't know what to do with it. Wasn't gonna drink it, no way.

"Can you put this over there…" he paused. "I don't much feel like drinking it."

Taking it out of Jake's hands, Alex's fingers caught a nice long stretch of skin.

"I don't much blame you. Between you and me, I don't think that it *is* coffee. There are a lot Scientologists around here you know." Holding his makeup sponge, Alex shot him a conspiratorial stare. "Yes, indeed. Uh-hum."

The door banged open again this time with a perky young woman in a fluorescent blue "Wake Up L.A." t-shirt. Jake was starting to feel queasy.

"Let's go. You're on in five."

"Good luck honey."

"Thanks." Jake followed the t-shirt through the internal hallway system until they went through a door, passed security, and stood at attention waiting for his cue.

The set was occupied by three people. Two women flanked a *very* middle aged man. The women weren't terribly much younger, but where he presented a somber newscaster image, they looked kind of hard and sluttish. Jake figured this *must* translate better on television. They wouldn't intentionally alienate their core audience of women with kids. The reasoning being behind the chicks, he assumed, was that if men came into the kitchen, they wouldn't bother to change the channel. Jake and the attendant waited through the commercial break and still longer during the next news segment and "repartee."

"I don't know if you two know this…"

"What's that?" the women said in unison.

"The hottest new trend for Los Angeles, and in fact for a lot of cities is *cupcakes*."

"Oh come on! I totally knew that already. Are you kidding me? It's *totally* hot." This came from the right side, the long haired redhead with 400 cc's of breasts.

"Well so I didn't know that. But, in any event, we have as our guest this morning the owner of one of L.A.'s hottest, we use that word here a lot don't we? One of L.A.'s HOTTEST bakeries. Jake Wellington of Cupcakes. Welcome, Jake!"

A crew member with audio in his ear whispered "go, you're on" and pushed Jake a little too roughly toward the left end of the set. It was pretty weird, no studio audience, all this *shmontzes* in an empty L.A. warehouse. Jake tried to keep his forehead from kneading up into a knot of pain, but instead remain open, pleasant and positive. He grabbed his seat and considered Botox.

"Hi." Maybe he was too mellow.

"Hi!" said the two hooches. They seemed to have no cross talk problem since they used the same words much of the time.

"So Jake. Welcome to the show."

"Thank you. It's good to be here."

"Ooooh, he's cute!" said the redhead.

"*Super* cute! Are you married, Jake?" asked the blonde. She was a little older with a bit more of a polished veneer, like a rock and roll wife who was forced to get a job.

"Girls, let's focus."

"Yes, Bob, cupcakes."

"Yes, cupcakes."

"So Jake, tell us how you got into this business." Jake reached for his oversized coffee mug, remembering too late not to take a sip from it, but stopped himself in time. He just let the brown liquid touch his lip and he quickly put it back down onto the holodeck.

"Well," he cleared his throat, "I always liked to bake and believe it or not, I had a girlfriend who used to tell me how great my cupcakes were."

"Oh we believe it!" replied the girls winking at each other.

"Uhm, anyway, I started a catering company and then after a year or two opened my own store that specializes in cupcakes."

"That's very interesting" said Bob.

"Very" said the girls.

"So how did you know it was going take off as a trend the way it has?" asked Bob.

"Well, that's the funny thing." The girls laughed heartily. Jake continued. "I had no idea. It was a complete surprise to me."

"You don't say?"

"Wow." they said it together with the accent over the same syllable.

"Well Jake here's been **kind** enough to send over some **cupcakes** for us to sample, **girls**" announced Bob, a little too heavy with the *sotto voce*. This always pissed off the show's producer. This is a morning show, she'd say. This is not the 6 o'clock evening news. We don't cover Afghanistan. We don't cover North Korea. A little more Hef and a little less Cronkite. A production assistant brought out the large platter with three of Jake's cakes on it. They hadn't been styled.

"Wow. Those look yummy, Jake" oozed the redhead.

"I can't eat that, that's at least 1500 calories! How many calories is that?!" the ex-wife looked frantic.

"Tell us what we have here, Jake."

"Well, that one to your left is an applesauce, the middle one is a vanilla cake with chocolate and the last one over there on the far right is a yellow cake with pumpkin and pecans."

"What'd he say?" asked Bob.

There was a collective production staff groan.

"I can't eat that!" the blonde shrieked. The redhead reached over and said

"I'm just gonna take a tiny little piece. Uhmmmmm. THAT is SO good Jake. The chocolate frosting? Oh my god! What's in it? It's REALLY, REALLY good! UHM!"

'Uh, well it's got Mexican cocoa pieces melted down? It's used in hot chocolate?"

"Wow." She slowly wiped the corner of mouth with her fingers and licked the frosting off. Bob was kind of disgusted. "Are we still on camera? Which camera are we on?"

"Well Jake, thank you so much for stopping by. The bakery is called, aptly enough, Cupcakes. The address is at the bottom of your screen, viewers at home. Thank you again, Jake. Jake Wellington. Cupcakes of Beverly Hills."

"It just 'Cupcake'" said Jake.

"And we're off!" said a crew member to his right. He stood up and knew not to even try to fly away. He tried that when he was ten and broke his arm.

"Jake, Oh My God those are *great*! Really!" said the redhead.

"We're back on in two minutes folks!"

"Thanks guys!" Jake jumped off the stage and followed the liaison out. He asked her which way to the parking lot and she found a lackey to do the honors. As far as she was concerned, she was finished with him.

CHAPTER

THIRTY-FIVE

Happily for him, Jake's dread of the upcoming week went largely unfounded, as it kept moving along fairly painlessly. He was a bit concerned about the silence emanating from Jennifer, but he had assumed that she would contact him once her editor gave her a chance to breathe. Jake was afraid that if he called it might appear that a. he was only calling about business or b. he was only calling about sex or worse still c. he was calling about business and sex. Jake felt that, in this instance, allowing her to set the pace was the right move. However, it had been several days and only now did it occur to him that he had misread the situation. Was he supposed to call? Had she been waiting all this time? At this point, she could quite possibly think he's a cad, an absconder of her dignity and sexual self-respect. He put in a hasty call to his personal expert on heterosexual relationships.

"Jake!" exclaimed George.

"Hey George, are you busy?"

"Not too busy for you. What's going on?"

"I wanted to ask you....has Jennifer....mentioned me.... at all....to you recently?" he paused wondering how stupid exactly *did* he sound?

"You're joking right?" said George sounding confused.

"No. Seriously. Has she said anything?"

"Well.....she asked about you. Why haven't you called her, Jake? You are being awful to Jennifer. You'll be lucky if she ever speaks to you."

"Cut it out. Shit. I gotta go. I'll talk to you later." Jake hung up the phone and dialed Jennifer at her work.

"Jennifer?"

"No, this is Ms. Hargrove's assistant. Who may I ask is calling, please?"

"Mr. Wellington. Mr. Jake Wellington." There was a pause.

"Hold on please." He heard the click of the hold button go on and off and on and off and on and off. She must be new.

"Hello? This is Jennifer."

"Jennifer, it's Jake." Silence. "Jennifer?"

"It's been a while Jake, I didn't think you were the type to dine and dash."

"Excuse me? I'm trying to reach Jennifer. Miss Jennifer Hargrove. I sent her a bouquet to her office, the second one if I'm not mistaken and wanted to make sure that it was received....." But the silence continued. After a few more seconds she broke it.

"I'm sorry Jake, that was completely rude of me. I'm having a shitty week. I shouldn't have taken it out on you. You've been an absolute dear." Phew. Or should he be hearing the strings from *Psycho* right about now?

"You scared me there for a minute. I wasn't aware that I'd done anything wrong." Jake could assume the role of the self-righteous pretty damn fast, even for a pretty boy.

"I'm sorry. How are you?" Jake described bits of his week so far and her chill thawed out almost immediately. She laughed pretty hard over his in-studio appearance.

"I'm sorry I missed that!" she laughed.

"I'm not. I felt violated."

"So how can I make up for being so awful to you? Can I take you out somewhere? You name the place."

"Well actually, I wanted to celebrate getting through the week by taking a drive up the coast. That's why I called. Are you game?"

"God I'd love to but I think I have to work over the weekend. Which reminds me. My boss is going to want to interview you."

"What?"

"I told you she was going to take my feature over. She wants to interview you before she flies back to New York on Sunday. So you can't go driving."

"Well when does she want to conduct this 'interview'?"

"Probably Friday afternoon. Are you free?"

"I guess I am now. Sure I'll be there."

"It's great exposure Jake. She'll ask you all the questions on my sheet that I've prepared for her...that's her conducting an interview, then I'll write the piece and then she'll destroy it. We can go for a drive after that. That is if you still want to." What does that mean? Ignoring his own confusion, he carried on.

"So you're weekend's shot?"

"Pretty much. I'm sorry. But I'm glad that you called and she's coming back into my office so I have to get off the phone. I'll call you with the time and location for our little meeting. That will be perfect, Mr. Wellington. We'll be in touch. Yes, thank you. Good-bye." Jennifer switched into her professional voice which was a quite a few decibels louder and rich with the eastern seaboard.

"Okay, talk to you later." **CLICK**

"Jake can I tawk to yuuu?" Janice's frozen molasses in January drawl was hard to take first thing back in the store. She looked extremely concerned.

"Sure what is it?"

"Well ah stawted the transcaription lahk yuu aiasked and ah need to tawk to yuu."

"Okay?"

Janice brought out a legal pad. She said that she had gone through so far about fifty calls. She was no where near the end, obviously, but, she didn't know how to say this, well at least twenty-five so far were from this one particular woman. Jake felt sick.

"Are they from a woman named Ellie?" Janice nodded her head yes.

"Well does she say anything that I need to know about right now?"

"No she just cawls and cawls. No message rehleh."

"Okay, well just go ahead and finish and we'll talk about it afterwards, okay? Thanks for telling me."

"Well, ahlright? Whaht ah you gonna do?"

"I need to see the whole list of calls. Then I'll deal with it. Please be discreet and not mention this to anyone, Janice."

"Of course, Jake. You cayn ahlways trust eeyun me."

Shit. Fuck. Goddamn.

"I still can't get Jill on the phone" said Nadia.

"Forget it for now. We can deal with that tomorrow. Hey! Did any body answer the phone today? When it rang?" Jake asked loudly around the kitchen. Everybody's response to the question was a blank stare. He picked up the phone and decided that he'd call Jill.

CHAPTER
THIRTY-SIX

He let it ring and ring. Finally after about fifteen rings the phone picked up.

"Hello?" It was a male voice. Very stern.

"Uh, Hello. I didn't mean to disturb you but I'm trying to reach Jill. This is her boss." There was a long pause. Jake felt awkward.

"Hello? Are you still there?"

"I'm sorry. Jill isn't feeling well."

"I don't mean to be rude, but who is this?"

"I don't see the need to answer that question. Jill will call you when she's feeling better. Goodbye." The guy hung up.

What the fuck?

"Does anybody know what guy would be answering Jill's phone?" Jake posed this question to the entire staff.

"I know her dad lives kinda close by" offered Gilberto.

"Dude, he lives in the *Valley*." laughed Tony.

"That's close."

Dad? Is that possible? No dad would sound that young. Or possessive. Or rude.

"Does anybody know if Jill has a boyfriend?" Silence.

Maybe when she got sick, she found herself trapped in some horrible abusive relationship scenario and this guy's holding her hostage in a stinky pink bathrobe. Jake decided that for the time being, he was going to leave it alone, but tomorrow, he was driving over there. If he had to, he'd call the police. Don't worry Jill, he thought, I'm going to get you out of this mess. He figured he shouldn't go over there by himself. Who was the biggest guy at the bakery?

"Who wants to go over to Jill's with me? There something funny going on over there and it might get pretty heavy."

"I'm there Jake. Count a sister in." Nadia was the only one to respond.

"No offense, Nadia. But I was thinking of one of the *guys*. I'm sorry." Nadia looked stunned.

"Jake, I'll have you know, I take kick-boxing. Nobody's gonna fuck with me."

"Um, no."

"How about you, Fred? Are you interested? Jill might really need some help." Fred was easily the biggest guy on staff. Weighing in at a good 265 lbs., he was enormous.

"Jake, as much as I'd like to help, it's against my beliefs." Now it was Jake's turn to look stunned.

"Fred, are you a Buddhist or something? I didn't know you practiced non-violence?" asked Jake a little bewildered.

"Buddhist? I'm not a Buddhist; I'm in medical school, remember?"

"Fred, you lost me." A navigational guide wouldn't have helped Jake at this point.

"Hello? The Hippocratic Oath anyone?" Raising his spatula and clearing his throat and expelling a tired, disgusted sigh, "And I quote...'*In every house where I come I will enter only for the good of my patients, keeping myself far from all intentional ill-doing..."*

"Patients? What patients, Fred? From where I sit, you're frosting a cupcake" said Johnny. Fred shot him a look of pity and went back to his mixing bowls.

"Enough! If nobody's gonna come, I'll just go by myself. That's fine! I'm sure Jill will be real proud of all you guys. Thanks Nadia. I'll tell her that you wanted to come but that I wouldn't let you."

"Thanks Jake. I'm available if you need me."

"Okay everybody. Back to work. I want this place cleaned up and that front line cut in half. Got it?" Jake clapped his hands together and tried to throw about an intimidating macho attitude. Might as well start practicing for tomorrow, he thought. He started walking around the kitchen, inspecting everything, leaning over bowls and into ovens. He pointing fingers a lot even though everyone knows that's so rude.

"Clean this area up."

"Put those utensils into the washer."

"The bathroom's a mess, who's responsible? You can't leave it like that."

"Somebody could trip on this, put it back where it's supposed to be."

"You need to make a bleach solution not just soap and water. Wash it down every two hours."

He tried to deliver this alpha bark with focus and 'intention', the way he'd seen on 'real' cop shows; and he thought that he was doing it pretty well. But he thought wrong. His staff needed no better convincing, that under no circumstances, should he go to Jill's alone. Boss is gonna get himself killed, yo.

"Jake, when you head out tomorrow, let me know, I'm coming with you." 265 lbs. was in.

"Yeah, count me in." 210 lbs. was in.

"I'll be there Jake." 200 lbs. was in.

"We'll go together." 195 lbs. was in.

"Thanks a lot guys. I'll let you know when it's time." Jake couldn't believe it. He knew he could be intimidating but he never realized that the big dudes considered him a peer. He'd never wanted to over emphasize his machismo, thinking that it was so unnecessary. But if you have it, you can't exactly hide it, this he finally understood. You need to lead. You're *forced* to lead.

After work he went to the gym, still flying with the adrenaline rush of his management skills. His trainer, Mike, gave him his usual "why look who actually showed up" face and came over.

"How are you doing Jake?"

"Good, real good. I know I didn't call but do you have any time now?"

"Sure, Jake, sure. Get into your gear and meet me back in ten. I'm finishing up in the corner."

Jake walked into the locker room and appraised the scene. Although no one else was in the room he felt a bonding. He felt strong and powerful. He put his work clothes and sneakers in his locker after changing into his sweats, and snapped shut the combination lock. When he came out his trainer was ready for him.

"Okay, Jake it's been a while. Let's take it nice and easy. You don't want to push too hard today." Jake was going to protest but he couldn't afford to hurt himself; he was too busy. So they did the old routine focusing on strength and some muscle building. Jake wanted a little sculpting but that's all. Biceps, abs, but that was about it. Maybe the glutes. He had a neck, but he wanted to keep it. He wanted to always be able to lower his arms all the way; no cupcake hands. Seriously. It didn't take him long to break a sweat and start breathing hard. Panting would have been a better word for it. It had been too long since he had last come in. But all that was going to change as of right now.

He remembered that he didn't have his towel when sweat started to drip down his face.

"I must have drunk more water than I realized today."

His trainer was a little concerned about his being so out of breath. So much so that he cut the workout short.

"Listen Jake, I forgot I have another client who's just come in. Do you mind?"

"Oh no, sure, go ahead, I'm just gonna do a few more reps and then call it a day."

"Great, I'll see you soon."

"Yeah," he gulped air and swallowed. He was done. When his trainer left, he waited for what he thought was a reasonable length of time before nearly falling off his apparatus. Once back up on his feet, he walked as purposefully as he could manage, to the door leading to the locker rooms without passing out or vomiting.

CHAPTER
THIRTY-SEVEN

By mid-morning the following day, the line coming out store was formidable, hardly manageable and a little scary. Jake received a frantic call from Nadia that things were blowing up like crazy and that she hoped to holy hell that he was coming in. Now. This is why....

BEAUTIFUL THINGS COME IN SMALL PACKAGES
Special Report by Helena Michaelson for The Herald

Beverly Hills -- As readers of the Herald already know, the cupcake scene, which I have been following since its inception here in the Southland, has been gaining ever greater momentum over the last year in particular. Today, there is no brighter star in its firmament than Jake Wellington, owner of Cupcake, a charming bakery located in the heart of Beverly Hills. What's more interesting, is that Mr. Wellington, who is both beautiful and utterly without pretense, has approached the baking of a children's comfort food with the sometimes foolhardy risk taking that one usually associates with the grandiloquent chefs of haute cuisine. Haute cupcakes you dare ask? The idea may seem absurd to some, but I can assure you that he edits his vision for mass appeal. Otherwise you might very well indeed find sugared violet petals atop your gingerbread spice cupcake with a saffron orange marmalade filling. But don't think that it wouldn't be scrumptious! Nothing is too risky for this baker who I met with recently to discuss his thoughts on his Art. The store is packed nearly every day to feed a virtual *army* of devotees, with a daily purchase turnover of over two thousand. He enjoys the support of a dozen staff members who bake some of the most delectable and intellectually engaging baked goods you could ever hope for. Although gorgeous enough to front any fashion cover, Mr. Wellington prefers t-shirts and jeans. A dedicated workaholic, I'm sure a career as a mannequin never crossed his mind, as his focus and intensity on his iconoclastic métier is razor-sharp. Of course, Hollywood is no stranger to this baker's delicacies, but to his credit, he will not speak of his celebrity client list. Nevertheless, it is a fact that he is on all the A-list menus, comfort food or not. And unlike any bakery in recent Los Angeles history, his line is *the* line. The most fashionable women in the city, whether they swallow a calorie or not, are seen at his wonderful bakery. It is my prediction that not only will he re-direct the flow of ideas about what makes a cupcake; his establishment will in future set the tone for what is "now" in fashion, art and design. This may appear to be a diabolically high claim on my part, but dear readers, be your own judge. I can assure you that I have seen and eaten the future and it is at Cupcake.

When Jake parked his car, the back door was already open waiting for him to come in. He'd spent most of the morning figuring out how he was going to spearhead the Jill rescue mission. He didn't know when the Herald piece was coming out, much less that it was in today's paper. When Jake approached the back door, a copy was quickly handed to him and staff members stood around him as he read in horror.

"Holy shit" he said when he had finished it.

"Dude, you don't even want to see the scene out front" said Johnny. Did he have to say the word "scene" like that? This was not the Sunset Strip, Jake griped to himself.

"Did anybody do a head count?" There was silence.

"Okay somebody, go out front and do a quick count. I need somebody else to do a rundown of what we need to restock and let me know immediately." Jake had barely stepped a foot in the door. He did happen to notice that his picture for the article was full color and his hair looked pretty good. Regardless, he stopped assessing his photogeneity and put the paper down heavily. There was no way, he could set foot in the front, he would have to rely solely on feedback to get through this day and all those that were to follow like it.

Johnny came back into the kitchen area from the store front looking as if he'd just been mauled in an animal preserve.

"I lost count at 125. I can't see that far down the street anyway."

"Bullshit," said Tony.

"Seriously, you can't tell what's a head after awhile." There was a long pause of disbelief. "Go out and take a look for yourself if you don't fuckin' believe me." Johnny challenged him while he tried to flatten down his hair and straighten out his apron that was wrapping around his waist in an unbecoming fashion. Nadia came up to a slightly freaked looking Jake and pulled him aside. Futile act, as all staff standing in the vicinity moved along with them.

"We have to restock everything before the next two hours. I'm gonna call the suppliers and see what they can do. If not, someone has to go to the grocery store. We're probably going to have to do this every day until this dies down."

"Nadia, actually I want you to call." Jake continued "Okay everybody listen up! If you haven't taken a look at the L.A. County Retail Food Inspection Guide lately, I suggest you do so sometime today. There's more than one copy. They are in the red three ring notebooks. Make sure that you review the guidelines and take it upon yourself to bring something that you think is not right to my attention. I'm pretty sure that with today's article will come an unscheduled inspection. We have to keep our 'A'."

Jake went back over to Nadia who was just hanging up the phone.

"We can get everything delivered in the next three hours at the soonest. And they've changed the delivery schedule so we'll still probably have to go to the store and get stuff."

"Can you take care of that for me, Nadia?"

"Sure Jake I'm on it."

Jake knew that everything had just gone into overdrive and would remain that way probably until next Monday at the earliest. As the day moved steadily along the lines remained ridiculous but they were able to keep up with the demand. But the phone orders alone were enough to kill his staff. Luckily he had the room, the storage capacity and the staff to make the transition at a moment's notice. Otherwise, he would have been completely screwed by good press. Nice. He really needed Jill and he was going to resolve this situation as of tonight. He would get to the bottom of it. He had a manager's life to save.

CHAPTER
THIRTY-EIGHT

But before Jake could get to the bottom of anything he had to contend with his cell. It also, wouldn't stop going off. The problem with press is that once you get it, everyone you know, and even those you don't, has to call and tell you. He may just have to turn it off, but not without calling Jennifer. Unfortunately, she wasn't picking up.

"You've reached the office of Jennifer Hargrove. I'm either away from my desk or on another line. Please leave a short message and time that you called and I or my secretary will get back to you as soon as possible. Thank you." **BEEP**. Jake wanted to hang up but decided to go ahead.

"Jennifer. It's Jake. If you haven't seen it yet, the Herald article came out today and the store is now being bombarded with customers. Which is good, but, I'm going to have to be at the store most of the weekend, especially now with Jill out. I'll try to reach you later and you try to reach me too. Bye." Then he called George. George, on the other hand, picked up immediately.

"Jake! Congratulations! I'm so proud!!"

"George, I'm getting killed over here if you really want to know" replied Jake knowing this would set him off.

"Oh my dear! Reaping the benefits of phenomenal press and complaining!"

"Why don't you drive by and take a look at the line. Bear in mind that my manager is out sick or being kidnapped, I can't tell which."

"Uh-oh. That's not good."

"That's right, George, it isn't. I think I have to do an intervention tonight."

"Sounds fabulous, can I come?"

"No."

"Poo Jake. You really know how to hurt a girl."

"Listen, I'm going to be swamped for the next few days and I just wanted you to know, in case you need to get in touch with me."

"Why did you just sound like a passive aggressive diva?"

Jake laughed. He did kinda.

"You know I didn't mean that quite the way it came out. I'm actually being an incredibly thoughtful friend and letting you know that I'm going to be out of touch but not neglecting the people that I care about."

"Okay then, you're very sweet. Thank you Jake. By the way, you don't sound very hetero today. Don't mind my saying."

"Oh really? Well, don't be surprised if you get a call from jail. From me. Bye."

"Whaa?..." **CLICK**

Now Jake's phone was ringing. It was Jennifer.

"Hey! Jennifer! I'm glad you called me back so soon. I didn't want to miss you."

"Jake, I saw the Herald this morning. That's pretty incredible" she said. "So you are still available for the interview, right?"

"Well it's so crazy here and I can't leave the store."

"Are you kidding? She'll love it."

"I don't mean to be rude but I don't remember her name."

"Amanda. Miss Amanda Tisdale or *The* Amanda Tisdale. Either will do."

"Well bring Miss Amanda Tisdale on over. Friday right?"

"I'm pretty sure. I'll call you when I know definitely."

"Okay, just leave a message if I'm not here. Bye."

"Sure thi…" **CLICK**

At sundown, Jake was ready to just lay down on the kitchen floor and die. So was everyone else for that matter. But, he had a prior commitment with a few members of his staff. These evening plans, *no one* was going to be backing out of. So by the store's closing at 7pm, with the cleanup in full swing, Jake went over to all those who had volunteered, except for Nadia who was watching glumly, and reiterated the promise that they had made to him about coming tonight. He was emphatic that the day's work wouldn't be complete until they took a little trip. And paid a little visit. Jake tried to revive himself with another cup of coffee and by thinking angry, incensed thoughts. He practiced standing tall, looking solid as granite, and giving a steely-eyed stare.

"What's with Jake, yo?"

"Yeah, he looks like one of those little kids you catch making faces in the mirror."

Jake, of course, did not hear these comments while he was practicing. But to be fair, his ability of running things with Jill's absence was impressive. Nevertheless, it would take more than his face to convince any staff that he was going to bring down a rain of hurt on anyone. So, in the meantime Cupcake's most precious commodity would still require some additional protection.

It took about another hour to clean the place up in preparation for the morning. Jake liked everything done the night before so the next day staff could open with minimal prep time. When the last sponge was wrung out, all the staff, except for those looming around Jake, bolted out the door. Jake's baker's gang hung back, waiting for him to give them the address so that they could get this over with and go home, *finally*.

"Ok, everybody, we're gonna meet here," Jake gave everybody a piece of notebook paper with Jill's address on it and his cell phone number. "Let's all just take our own cars. If any of you guys get there before me, don't do anything. I'm serious. We'll meet in front of the apartment building."

So in single file: non-violence practicing Fred weighing in at 265; ready for anything Tony hitting the scales at 210; got no girlfriend and nothing to do tonight, since the last episode of Stranded aired last week Johnny slimming down to 200; and I don't much care who wins, I just like a good fight Raul weighing a completely average 195, left out the back door and got into their cars. Lastly, their boss, easily mistaken for a good-looking pedestrian, weighing in at an embarrassing 175 lbs., slipped into his car and drove off.

CHAPTER

THIRTY-NINE

Everybody: Fred, Johnny, Tony and Raul, all arrived before Jake despite the fact that he was the only one in the Porsche. It did not go unnoticed. Johnny was positive that a Toyota could out maneuver any car on the street, but he left that statement go for another time. All four waited in their cars, motors running and wasting gas, when they heard Jake drive up. He was glad that they hadn't blown off the front door of the apartment complex, but where were they? Driving around looking for a parking space, one by one he could make out each sitting in his car and while a. wondering what was up with that? b. he realized to his horror that after 6pm this became a hateful parking for residents only neighborhood. If the parasitic tow-truck driver can't see a plastic card hanging from your rear-view, your car was gone. You could be seeing your girlfriend to her door safe. You could be chasing or being chased by a mugger. You could be lying stabbed multiple times on a random front lawn. You could be on the verge of slipping into a diabetic coma. "Sorry. I don't make the rules," he'll shrug.

Pulling away from the curb, each waiting member of the furious five went back down the hill to go find metered parking, then walk back up the hill to Jill's building. By the time they found their way to the front door, everyone looked a little more wrecked than before. The work day had been no help at all.

"So what's the plan, boss?" asked Johnny.

"We, um, I, first ring the buzzer and see who answers" said Jake.

"Okay. Then what?" asked Johnny, clearly unsatisfied with the plan, thus far.

"Then, whether it's Jill at the intercom or not, we want to convince whomever it is that it's in their best interest to let us into the building" said Jake.

"OK, then we'll kick some ass!?" exulted Tony.

"No, then we'll go inside" said Jake calmly. So far, this plan was not very exciting.

"And?" said Fred who needed to get home and study.

"And then, once we're in the apartment, we'll see what's going on. But we need to get inside, first. If we have to take things a little further, we'll make that decision inside. Otherwise we're just here out of concern."

"I guess that's a plan" said Tony.

"You got any better ideas?" Jake was getting pissed.

"No, no boss. Sounds good. Let's do it."

"Oh and another thing, if and I stress if, we have to rough somebody up you wait for the signal from me."

"What's the signal?" asked Fred.

"'I'm sorry you feel that way'. 'I'm sorry you feel that way' is the signal. Okay?"

"Then what?"

"Then somebody should call the cops. Try and separate Jill from this guy whoever he is. Get her out of the apartment."

"Okay, okay, let's *go.*"

So following his plan to the letter, devised barely one minute prior, Jake pressed the intercom buzzer for Jill's apartment. The rest of the guys crowded around him to listen.

"Hello." It was a female voice. It sounded like Jill.

"It's Jill" said all the guys to each other.

"Jill, it's Jake and some of the guys from work. We wanted to make sure you were okay?" There was a long pause and then the door buzzer sounded.

"What was so hard about that, Jake?" asked Tony.

"Would you get in the door?" snapped Jake.

They waited for the elevator to come down and then piled in heading for the fifth floor.

"Which apartment is it?"

"#5G."

When the elevator opened they checked to make sure they saw fives on all the apartment doors, and once reassured, stepped out looking for Jill's. Jake tried to move up to the front to lead but it was difficult being the shrimp. He had to fight his way through and by then they were all standing in front of the door marked '5G'. Raul rang the door bell and an unfamiliar man came to the door. Everybody could hear Fred gulp. The rest of Jake's crew spread out in an attempt to appear more threatening and possibly dangerous. Jake established himself as the leader by stating:

"Good evening. May we speak with Jill? We wanted to make sure she's okay." Jill came to the door in her pajamas. Sure she looked tired but in keeping with the UN's guidelines for torture detailed in the Istanbul Protocol or the most recent Geneva Convention, Jake was a lame-ass. The apartment didn't smell of any questionable odors. There were no ligatures, ropes or cigarette butts lying strewn on the floor. There appeared to be plenty of fresh water and exposure to sunlight.

"Hey Jake, hey guys, what are you all doing here?" she asked. Her head had cleared and she only coughed occasionally.

"We were worried about you" said Fred.

"Oh that's really sweet, come on in." She and the strange man stepped back into the apartment and the liberation posse followed behind.

"Yeah, we wanted to make sure that you were on the mend. It's been a while since we've heard from you" said Jake. He wasn't going to come off looking less caring than anyone else.

"Yeah, how are you Jill? We miss you. Can we bring you anything?" offered Tony. Jill felt like she was going to tear up, but she pulled herself together and faced down the six men standing in her living room.

"Do you see what I mean Daddy?" Jake looked hard at this man. He wasn't aware of Jill having a boyfriend named Daddy.

"Yes, J., you work with some very fine fellas. Thanks guys for caring so much about my daughter." Daddy seemed sincere. Jake was trying to run quickly through his heterosexual relationship database to retrieve anything about men who refer to their girlfriends as "daughter." He was coming up with nothing. Maybe he was too stunned to run the program properly.

"It's a pleasure to meet you Mr. Ingram" said Fred.

"I'm sorry Daddy, where are my manners! This is Fred." Hello. "Tony." He nodded. "Johnny." Hello. "Daddy, this is Raul." Pleased to meet you. "And this is my wonderful boss who you've heard so much about, Jake. Jake Wellington. Jake, this is my Dad, Mr. Ingram." Mr. Ingram extended his hand to Jake and shook it. Or rather, crushed it. Jake burst out into a painful sweat, nearly letting loose a small squeak which he attempted to swallow, but choked upon instead.

"Are you alright son?"

"Yes, I'm fine. I'm pleased...I'm so pleased to finally meet you. You have a wonderful daughter, Mr. Ingram. I don't know what I'd do without her. She's a gem. Really." Jake continued having his hand crushed by Daddy, despite his best efforts to extricate it before tears of pain sprung from his eyes and he'd only have the one hand with which to wipe them away.

"Everybody, have a seat, can I get you guys something?" The now curious five sat down in Jill's living room in various sofas, loveseats and armchairs. Tony and Fred took the overstuffed loveseat and overstuffed it some more. Jake sat on the sofa with Mr. Ingram and Tony and Raul sat in the two chairs facing.

"No, I'm good, Jill, thanks" said Raul. Fred pulled himself out of the loveseat's death grip and followed her into the kitchen.

"Are you sure you don't want any help, Jill?"

"No, no, go back and sit down. I'll be right in." He turned around and Jill walked over to the refrigerator pretending to find something, but she was really starting to blubber.

"Jill are you all right, honey?" her Dad called out. She quickly grabbed a tissue and blew her nose.

"I'm fine Daddy. I'll be right out." Mr. Ingram turned back to his daughter's co-workers and asked again if they were comfortable. They all shook their heads 'yes'. "Are you sure I can't get you anything?" They all shook their heads 'no'.

"And you fellas drove all the way out here? Well I'm sorry that you feel that way."

CHAPTER FORTY

Neither Mr. Ingram nor Jill could understand why the whole living room exploded into such convulsive laughter. It was infectious enough that Jill was tempted to laugh too, but not knowing why, she remained quiet with very wide eyes. Her father, in turn, was just pleased that his daughter knew such a fine bunch of hard working fellas.

"Are you guys okay? Dad, did I miss something" Jill asked.

"Well whatever you missed J., I'm afraid I missed it as well" Mr. Ingram grinned confusedly.

Everyone sat around in the living room happily trading stories except for Fred who was getting jumpy. He had to get home and hit the books. They bragged about the Herald article and its resulting onslaught of customers.

"You seem like you're feeling better Jill. Are you sure you're doing okay?" asked Jake.

"I feel so much better, Jake, thanks. Dad came and stayed with me for the last few days to make sure I was alright." So Jill was a Daddy's girl. Jake would never have guessed it.

"I'm afraid I wouldn't let your daughter back into the shop even though she wanted to come" said Jake who was doing his best not to black out from exhaustion and nerves.

"You're a good man, Jake. Thanks for letting J. stay home. She needed to. And I apologize for being so curt with you on the phone. She looked so sick, I wasn't thinking properly." Wow, Jake didn't see that one coming.

"That's quite alright, sir, I understand completely." On that note, the 'fellas' were ready to leave. No violence? No reason to stay. One by one, they casually stood up to indicate that they were heading out. Jake took the cue.

"Well, it's getting late, at least it is for us, we're gonna have a long day tomorrow. But we're glad you're on the mend. Take you're time coming back, because you're going to put in some grueling hours when you're back and we need you to be strong. Okay?"

"Okay, Jake" smiled Jill.

"It was a pleasure meeting you fellas. I'd love to come by someday and see where J. works, but not this time out." Everybody moved en masse to the door which Tony, oddly, was able to unlock and open without anyone noticing.

"Bye Jill. We'll see you." They were in the hallway.

"Bye guys. Thanks for coming over to see me." She looked weepy again and knew that they could tell this time.

"Thanks fellas. Thanks a lot." Mr. Ingram shut the door behind them and they walked quickly to the elevator.

At the elevator bank Jake was half expecting to get smacked hard up side the back of his head. The floor doors eventually opened but no one said a thing. They walked in with Fred looking panic-struck and pressed 'L'.

"It was nice to see Jill" said Raul.

"Yeah, I didn't realize how much I missed her not being around" said Tony, a.k.a. 'Fingers'.

"Well, despite the fact that that guy turned out to be her father, thanks you guys for coming with me and checking out the situation" said Jake, waiting for the lampooning to begin.

"No problem Jake. Anytime you need me you just have to ask" said Johnny.

"I got nothing" said Fred.

"I'm sorry I messed up your study time Fred," said Jake.

"What's more important, Fred? Making sure Jill's okay or *homework?*" mocked Tony.

"Come on you guys, just because we didn't rough anybody up yet, don't start now. Everybody's going home. Got it?" A soft murmur of sheepish "yeahs" rolled out of the elevator as the doors opened.

"Alright, everybody, go home and I'll see you tomorrow first thing."

"Okay Jake, later."

"Fellas."

They practically ran down the hill praying there would be no tickets tucked under the wiper blades. Thankfully, there were none, well except for Fred, whose "SHIT!" bounced off the buildings and back at him. That's sucks, he could have used more change, thought Jake, knowing exactly what Fred had found sitting on his car. Jake sped back to his part of town, fast but legal, pretty much. He was dead tired and groaned at the thought that he would have to do this all over again tomorrow. Fuck, he remembered with a start, he had the Amanda Tisdale coming over with Jennifer. Well, there was no reason, he thought, to feel one way or the other, he'd never met this woman. However things turned out, it was out of his hands. He had more important things to think about. Like not falling asleep while driving.

Although he was tired, he wasn't too tired to spend more time than was necessary going over tonight rescue fiona.

Whether or not Jill ever found out the extent to which he was prepared to 'act', he would just have to wait and see. But he hoped that she would understand. He was wrong and overreacted. She was not victim of a death cult home invasion. She does not have a vicious boyfriend, who thinks little of tying up a poor flu-ridden woman, with the belt of her own chenille bathrobe. But he had shown how much he valued Jill, her safety, health and well being. Everybody did. So when she did find out, which she was going to eventually he was pretty sure, hopefully it would make her smile or give her a laugh and nobody, especially Jake, would have to be reminded of it again. Now whether or not he could expect the same from the guys was another story.

Chapter

Forty-One

Jennifer Hargrove spent the morning frantically trying to appease Amanda but to no avail. Judging from her endless complaints, *Extreme Leisure*'s West Coast offices weren't located in Century City but somewhere like, Little Rock. Jennifer thought, you could probably get anything you wanted even if you were in Little Rock. Well maybe not. But wherever she thought she was, Amanda was being impossible. She insisted on a *regular cup of coffee,* when no one in L.A. drinks that stuff. It's embarrassing to order it. It's embarrassing to see someone else order it. People out here wouldn't pour that hot filth into a planter because they have too much respect for the plant. It would be totally uncool, and worse, not at all 'green.' Jennifer had been living in LA long enough now to notice what New Yorkers can look like out of context and it wasn't always pretty. Amanda refused to order from any one of the local eateries; she wanted one of those greasy corn muffins in the plastic sealed wrapper. There are at least four noshes in Beverly Hills, but she only wanted a bagel from Zabar's and well have you ever had a bagel from Zabar's? And why did she have to be so loud? So vulgar in dismissing what she knew nothing about? And God bless her, but the Suit. Please. Okay, we'll give New York the evening wear, you really shouldn't wear thongs with a Galliano, but for day time, a Power Suit, even an 80s-inspired Power Dress, is just sad. It wears the stamp of 'loser' with a very large font size. Silk blouses with pencil skirts and black pumps as an alternative? Pitiful. They let the world know that you can 'Color Me Bland', or that you're a Macy's drone or, heaven forbid, 'I am a very pricey hooker and it's a secret!' What it comes down to is this: you never want your fashionable silhouette to tell the world that, first and foremost, you WORK FOR A LIVING. That you're a consumer, consuming. That is not style. That is not fashion. Never in a million years did Jennifer think New York chic could actually sicken a person. But there was definitely the taste of bile in her mouth. Jennifer had her epiphany.

So getting back to her harrowing morning, Amanda was feeling out of sorts, out of place and out of the loop. Not good for the fashion editor...very bad in fact. What to do? Why torture every one in sight, and that is exactly what she had been doing for the last two hours. She had no right. Absolutely no one had asked her to wear that disgusting wool bouclé suit. If she'd only brought the Armani, or any of her Lauren or Gucci, she would have been fine. Fabulous, in fact. Instead of awe, Amanda saw horror and disgust on their faces, as if she was suddenly missing an arm, or had an oozing bloody gash in her $500 haircut. She saw them look away. She saw them focus on their pedicures. She'd never known shame before. Not like this.

Jennifer, though not completely sympathetic, did her very best to maintain sympathetic composure. She catered to Amanda's every whim. She endured her snide remarks and tabulated on her computer's calculator the remaining hours, minutes and seconds before the bitch's departure. She also prayed to every known deity she could think of on such short notice. She knew she had to put in a call to Jake to warn him of their arrival but she thought it should wait a bit. In Amanda's presence she didn't like to be on the phone too much. She, the Amanda, was starting to show the early signs of paranoia. Not being fashion forward can do that to an aging fashionista. Jennifer assumed the French socialized mental health system had already discovered a syndrome for these women who suddenly lose their eye and slip into psychosis. 'Le Syndrome Carrie Bradshaw' perhaps. She typed in a brief outline while Amanda was off being a pain in the ass elsewhere. She could forward it to the French Embassy later.

LE SYNDROME CARRIE BRADSHAW

1. *Definition*: **SCB** is a psychological disorder effecting mostly affluent women predominantly from Post-Industrialized nations. The average age for those afflicted range from early to middle age and are often employed in professions dealing with media or culture. They do not, strictly speaking, have to be a member of the professional class. A small percentage, though less vulnerable, are members of the permanent leisure class. This sub-sect is sometimes referred to as suffering from the Syndrome Mondaine or **SM**.

2. *Causes*: The working hypothesis is that **SCB** carries the highest risk factor amongst women, and to a lesser degree men [no significant studies have been conducted as of the publication of this article] whose personal identity strongly holds that they are stylish and ahead of the rank and file in regards

to their self-representation. Tested, these women typically judge themselves as 98.5 - 102% superior to the rest of the known world in terms of their outward appearance, sartorially speaking. From within this distorted framework there is a sudden realization, whether based on fact or impression, that they are no longer in this top 3.5% and are now significantly lower. When tested, after diagnosis and/or hospitalization, they judged themselves as being in the range of 90-91.5%. The paradox of being in the top tier of a supremely judgmental society based on appearances and no longer possessing the appearances to belong there is a mentally crushing blow.

3. *Symptoms*: Symptoms include delusional thinking; difficulty forming and/or expressing ideas and concepts; spatial disorientation; disassociation; difficulty dressing and sorting through cosmetics cases and accessories; emotional upheaval, turmoil and in less than one dozen cases, fashion induced schizophrenia.

4. *Effects*: Effects can be long term if psychological counseling is not implemented quickly. Ultimately they are shunned from the very society they've come to dominate. They usually do not commit a preemptive strike by removing themselves from the above mentioned social cluster as the delusion becomes too powerful. Family and friends of those suffering from **SCB** must be gentle yet encouraging in allowing them to find safety in transitioning into a new form of self-representation. They should be encouraged to begin to rebuild a self-image based on current fashion trends and not hold on to nostalgic memories of former glory. In just one example, those still referring to the 80s must stop using hairspray, velvet headbands, bold colors and padded shoulders immediately. Under no circumstances should he/she be allowed

to wear oversized round black frames á la Carrie Donovan and her ilk. They should not be allowed to enter the Gap, H&M or Forever 21 without adequate supervision as this may induce a grand mal seizure.

5. *Reaction*: While **SCB** numbers are steadily growing, new treatments are being developed by mental health professionals both in academic and public health facilities.

> *5a. Shock Therapy*: Not limited to electroconvulsive charge-induced seizures, but also showing patients their wardrobe on other people, placing them in their closets for prolonged periods, supervised of course, and showing them recent photographs of themselves particularly in larger social assemblies.

> *5b. Reimmersion*: Taking patients, in a slower yet prolonged therapy program, back into au courant style houses with soft lighting, on long walks on liberal arts university campuses, art galleries on Tuesday mornings, also newsstands with extensive fashion magazines during weekday hours. Exposure to catwalks, overly tall adolescents, rows of white folding chairs and polyrhythmic dance music is strongly discouraged.

> *5c. Institutionalization*: In rare cases, patients do not respond to the realization that they are passé and assume a near catatonic state. The above mentioned therapies have proved to be useless in these cases and the current recommendation persists in placing them in a facility with little to no visual stimulation beyond providing a soft microfiber robe and slippers. Reading materials and/or mirrors are to be provided with a doctor's recommendation only.

References:

Vogue, issue 9, vol. 2, 2004; *Town and Country*, issue 4, vol.12, 2006; *Tatler Magazine*, issue 2, vol. 18, 2000.

Well that killed three-quarters of an hour. They would be leaving shortly, as soon as Amanda came back to her office, and she didn't want any trouble. As if on cue, Amanda stormed into the room looking suspicious as if she'd been mocked in her absence. With one arm Jennifer reached for her purse and with the other she reached over and hit 'delete'.

"Ready? The car's out front."

Chapter

Forty-Two

Jennifer and Amanda slipped into the limo and headed east through Century City. Jennifer called Jake on her cell phone to say that they were on their way.

"Hello? Jennifer?"

"This is Jennifer Hargrove. Hello. Ms. Tisdale and I are in the car and will be arriving in a few minutes. Just wanted to let you know." She hoped he could tell that she was in her professional voice and not a member of the Baader Meinhof.

"Ohhhhh. Boss right there? Okay, no problem. Listen, do you want me to have lunch prepared or do you want to go out or eat later on your own?"

"Hold on please, let me check with Ms. Tisdale." Jennifer put the phone on 'mute' and asked Amanda about lunch."

"Oh I don't know. Let's just do the interview and get lunch later" whined Amanda. Jennifer clicked mute off.

"Hello Mr. Wellington? Sorry to keep you waiting. Ms. Tisdale would like to eat at a later time if that's alright. We'll just conduct the interview. But thank you. That's fine. Yes. Goodbye." She snapped her phone shut and put it back into her purse.

Needless to say Jake was beyond thankful no time would be lost eating. The line was again snaking down the block and the cupcakes couldn't come out of the kitchen fast enough. Jill, thank god was ready to come back. She had called to say she'd try for Monday, but even her latest would be Wednesday. If business was still this intense, it would certainly save his ass to have Jill back to help him streamline this madness. They had to figure out a way to shorten the time to complete tasks, points of travel, avoid waste, and get the most out of what they had. They may have to hire another company for deliveries. In the midst of this chaos, profitable as it was, he had no time to make kissy face with a bitch lifestyle journalist. He didn't even see the point of tidying up; the Amanda Tisdale was just going to have to deal with the harsh reality of common labor.

Just as expected, someone in front spotted the black Lincoln Towncar is it drove passed the store looking for a parking space. I thought nobody drove those things anymore, Jake said to himself. Shouldn't it be a white Escalade or a Range Rover, at least? People on the street were starting to buzz; 2 lb. telephoto lenses started to peak out of doorways and other building crevices, as Jennifer and Amanda stepped onto the sidewalk. 'Are *they* anybody?,' telepathed one member of the line to another. Lips parted and whispered and heads nodded in agreement. They understood. No, they weren't. Dare I say it? Poor Amanda.

As she adjusted her fitted suit and smoothed her bob, she looked up only to catch a horrifying glimpse of the most fashionable hydra-centipede upon which she ever laid her eyes. It had already been looking at her, sizing her up. Each of its hundred heads, all different hair cuts, all different colors, all different over-sized designer eye frames. Each could move independently: flipping hair and shaking out an individual blow-dry; placing sunglasses atop a head or turning away to make a phone call, and turning back to stare some more. It was slowly inching its way into the mouth of what had to be the Cupcake. Jennifer didn't seem afraid at all. Amanda felt like she was experiencing something paranormal and felt herself start to hyperventilate. Jennifer noticed that her breathing was strange.

"Amanda, let's get into the store." She grabbed her by the elbow telling the driver to wait and pushed her quickly passed the monster and through the front door. Jake had just come through the kitchen partition and saw that the Amanda was looking peculiar. He brought them through to the back and sat them both down at his desk. He got Amanda a tall glass of water at once and opened the back door to let some air in.

"I am so sorry, Mr. Wellington, I don't know what came over me" explained Amanda as she took a sip and placed her glass back on the table. She shakily began to search for a handkerchief and her lipstick.

"It's the crowd, Ms. Tisdale. It can be overwhelming."

"My goodness." Her breathing was slowing down and she had brought out, much to Jennifer's regret, her YSL lipstick in Red Flame. Unless you're super pale, nobody, I mean nobody....oh forget it. Jake refilled her glass of iced water and took a brief look about his kitchen to make sure everything was in order, at least superficially. It looked impressive to him, so he went back to focusing on this swooning editor who was reapplying her lipstick. She was exactly as he had expected she would be. Brittle and plain, with bulging blue veins on her hands, she was in semi-desperate need of a couple weeks "rest" at the Peninsula Hotel. The rest that comes with a private nurse on call and soup through a straw.

"Shall we get started?" asked the Amanda, now that her clown mouth was back on.

"By all means. Let me just thank you again for taking the time out of what I know is a very busy schedule" said Jake. He looked her in the eye and maintained his gaze until she started to color.

Amanda cleared her throat slightly and pulled out a small notepad. Jennifer was privately amused at just how small it was. She had already taken her mini-recorder out of her purse and placed it where Amanda couldn't see it. She had extra batteries and another mini-cassette if the thing acted up on her.

"So Mr. Wellington…."

"Please, call me Jake. Everyone else does" he put his hand on the table and spread out his fingers. She was transfixed. And so it began. The Spider. The Fly. Or so he thought.

"Yes, of course, Jake. Tell me, how did you come to owning a cupcake bakery?"

He leaned back in this chair, Jake made sure to have a third one delivered and assembled before this interview took place, and ran his fingers through his hair. Maybe he wouldn't cut it. He went through the whole spiel all over again. She made a few little notes. No sentences from where he was sitting. He thought he saw her draw a smiley face. A crown. A heart. She worked the hell out of a five-pointed star.

"Now that there are several bakers doing cupcakes, what do you think of your competitors?" she was looking at her notebook drawing a circle and then a triangle.

"Truthfully, I think it's inspiring. It gives everyone an added boost to improve what they do. And the bakers out here doing this are very, very good." Good answer, she thought to herself. 'Bitch' was what came to his mind.

"What do you like most about your competitors, Jake?" She wouldn't drop it.

"Let me think, well the Adlers are extremely fun, they have a fresh, light-hearted approach. And the people behind

The Sweetness are just extremely professional. Their baking is superb." Damn, she thought, I can't get a straight answer. 'Twat' thought Jake.

"I know that there are others that have entered the cupcake business but those are the only other two who I can comment on. I've eaten their work on several occasions; the others I haven't tried to be honest." Does she know I'm banging Jennifer?, Jake wondered. "Anyway, everyone offers something different and I'm sure that most of those who can stay in the game are pretty good."

"What do you think sets *you* apart?" she asked looking up from her latest pretty pen doodle.

"Well, I'd like to think my baking is a little more sophisticated. I don't want to alienate anybody, to be sure, but I do try to push the boundaries just a little bit. I bake for *adults*, really." He placed special emphasis on the word 'adults', making it seem rather triple 'X' dirty as in *adult cinema*. Then he pushed his hair out of his eyes and looked at her. She reached for her glass of water.

"So Jake you see yourself as being ahead of the rest, then?" she asked, eyes starting to glow. Jennifer was getting uncomfortable.

"I would never claim that, no. I hope I didn't give you that impression. I meant in terms of my own sensibilities, nobody else's." He thought she was up to something.

"What are your plans for the future?" asked the Amanda Tisdale.

"Well, I'm presenting another line that should be out before the holidays."

"I hope their as good as what the Adlers just announced. Those organic cupcakes of theirs are to die for. Just brilliant."

"Pardon?"

CHAPTER
FORTY-THREE

The rest of the interview, for Jake, was a fuzzy erratic heartbeat blur. Jennifer watched aghast as Jake turned slightly pale, but thankfully, at least for his sake, he recovered nicely. Jake responded by saying that he hoped his own organic line would be just as good as any of his competitors, but each baker had a unique set of expectations. Amanda remained silent. Jake went on to say that he assumed everyone would present their own version before too long into the New Year. It was time for bakers to take that step. He asked that she not mention it in print since he had his own publicity schedule, but that he would send her all the pertinent information if she would like. She said that that wouldn't be necessary; he should just forward it to Jennifer. With that, she rose, doodle notebook in hand and made preparations to leave. Jennifer said her goodbyes with her furrowed brow inching its way up into her hairline and the helix of her ears matching Amanda's Red Flame-d lips. She guided Ms. Tisdale out past the hydra, now bigger and more curious, and walked her directly in hand to their waiting car. Jake said nothing but "Thank you very much for coming by" at the doorway and went back to work. No, it hadn't been a delight.

And then, Jake tried not to go into shock. There must have been some connection between the state that woman had been in when she arrived and how she later regained her equipoise. Regardless, he was blown the fuck away. But she couldn't possibly have known anything. Had *he* told anyone? He couldn't remember. He had to just forget it. But first, he called George.

"Jake! Where have you been?!" said George.

"I'm getting a beat down here at work and you know why, so why ask?"

"It's called being polite and enthusiastic?" said George calmly refusing to endure a man-tantrum, or mantrum, as he liked to call it.

"Sorry" said Jake.

"Okay Jake, what's going on?"

"There's this HORRENDOUS FIEND at *Extreme Leisure*."

"That could be anyone Jake, please be more specific" said George, encouraging Jake to express his feelings in a healthy manner.

"The Amanda Tisdale."

"Oh. Co-Manda. I'm sorry. She is quite the hob-goblin. Did she, in quotes, *interview* you today?"

"She did and for no fucking reason she tried to mess with my head. *I* was fine but now I'm really pissed." said Jake.

"She does that to everybody. Let it go. She likes to throw people off balance to get info. Is that all she did?"

"Think so."

"Don't worry about it Jake. Forget it. Let's go have a drink" said George. That's all he could come up with.

"George, it's the afternoon. I'm working; I have to make phone calls. Come over to my place later. Bring your trunks."
CLICK

"Whoa." George said to himself and put down his cell.

The first thing Jake did was call the Adler's bakery Sugar Peaks over in Brentwood.

"Hey is Jonas or Bette there? It's Jake Wellington calling."

"Hey man! How are you! This is Todd, man! Jonas is in back, hold on." He put him on hold. Who the hell was Todd?

"Jake!" Jonas came on the line after a minute or so. "Read that Herald article, man, you must be being attacked by the cupcake zombies, dude! Cup-Cake! Hehhhehhhehh. How the hell have you been?" Jonas tried his best not to sound like a rich Hollywood producer kid, but instead rather street. He thought it raised his credibility, despite being a cupcake baker. He could pull it off pretty well in Brentwood.

"Dude, you have no fucking idea. Listen, has *Extreme Leisure* contacted you guys yet?"

"No dude, why? Who are they anyway?" Fuck.

"They're this style magazine out of New York and one of the editor's was just here. She mentioned your new cupcakes."

"Dude, we don't have any new cupcakes. Who is this woman?"

"Amanda Tisdale."

"I don't think so dude, but I'll ask Bette. She wouldn't talk to someone without telling me though."

"Okay. Let me know. It's no big deal. Just thought it was out of line. Let's get together soon, alright?"

"Sure man. I'll call you later." He hung up. That bitch.

Now he had to figure out how to call Jennifer without losing his shit. She had warned him. He decided to just leave a message.

"You've reached the office of Jennifer Hargrove. I'm either away from my desk or on another line. Please leave a short message and time that you called and I or my secretary will....Hello Jake?" Jennifer came on the line.

"Hey."

"Hey, I'm sorry."

"Is it safe to talk?"

"Yeah, she's in the toilet, probably throwing up her lunch."

"Nice. I'm so glad to know her lunch can't stand to be around her either."

"Listen, I did warn you."

"Yeah, I know but I wasn't expecting to be manipulated."

"Come on, what about you with the Casanova routine?"

"No seriously, she lied to me to get information."

"Jake, what are you talking about?"

"Listen, come over tonight, George is…"

"Here she comes. Gotta go, bye Jake." **CLICK**

By three o'clock, the crowd outside was way too big for him to be on the phone obsessing about industrial espionage. He walked over to his spot by the kitchen partition to catch a brief glimpse at what was going on out there. Just as it had been since that damned article first appeared, insane. Jake realized that he had pretty much left his staff high and dry all day and although they had been cool about it, that was kind of shitty. He prayed that Jill could make it in on Monday but if she couldn't, they would just have to soldier on without her. Jake began the walkabout that he should have done around lunchtime. They would be open for four more hours, long enough time for him to check everything out and get on top of things, especially his own sanity. Thankfully, Nadia had done a run through twice already and stopped him before he started.

"Jake, I've gone through the kitchen and here's the list of what we need."

"Jeez, thanks Nadia." Jake was astonished. He loved his staff. "Do me a favor. See if you can verify that this stuff is going to be delivered, double what you have to and let me know okay? It's getting pretty late."

"Sure Jake."

Jake went back to inspecting the kitchen. He could see without looking very hard that there were a couple of infractions that he would be sited for if he didn't fix them immediately. With Nadia doing supplies, he spent the rest of the day looking the place over and fixing everything he could. He reprimanded more than a few for not keeping their workspaces cleaner and putting things back immediately. It was a little strange how for once they seemed to appreciate and respond positively to this kind of attention. He checked the temperatures of all the refrigerators and planned for a thorough scrub-down tonight after hours.

"Okay people, listen up. I know it's late but we've let this place get pretty messed up. I want everyone to clean up their area and then a little bit more when we close. I want it spotless. Floors too." You could hear the groan float around like very soft spoken, but unhappy phantom.

"That's right people. We're getting out of hand here. I'm staying late tonight too so...."

He went to the front again, and could see that the staff was not moving the line fast enough. For the first time in Janice's memory, which wasn't very long since she was a new hire, she saw Jake come into the store front prepared to serve customers. He switched his splattered apron for a clean one and a crowd gathered on the sidewalk to watch through the window. *And Lo He appeared Thus*, gorgeous and radiant, surrounded by *His Cupcakes* and *Their Bearers*. Janice thought she saw a putto barely miss crashing into the storefront window before flying off. Jake heard the gasp of recognition coming from the sidewalk and gritted his pearly white teeth into a smile, as he turned to the next customer.

"Who's next?" he asked.

CHAPTER FORTY-FOUR

The crowd was *thrilled* shitless because this never, *ever* happened. Jake knew to limit his public appearances. Unlike Her Sweetness, he didn't pretend to work the front. Jake feared that the line would actually start to slow down and he did have a point. The only solution, however, to the present crisis was to step in and reduce this line; just force these people to make their selections, pay and leave as quickly as humanly possible. He moved Margaret, the newest new hire, to the cash register and told her to stay there. He kept three staff behind the counter at all times, two taking orders only and one moving trays in and/or taking orders. He would be the barker in the center to make sure that no one dawdled. Order. Pay. MOVE IT!!!

"Yes may I help you?" he smiled again at the small bosomy blonde with dusky champagne highlights. She had a spaghetti strapped floor length dress on and had spent all this time staring at him instead deciding what flavors she wanted and how many. It seemed as though she may have some trouble speaking.

"Do you know what you would like?" Jake asked again soothingly. She nodded 'yes'.

"And how can I help you?" the crowd was focusing in on her catatonia.

"Clocklat?" She didn't appear foreign. And he couldn't see a retainer.

"Did you say *chocolate*? Yes, we have chocolate. What type of chocolate, dear?" She pointed her manicured index finger at the Mexican cocoa.

"How many would you like?" She slowly made a peace sign.

"That's two cocoa for the lady, ring her up." He barked. "Next, how can I help you?" The bosomy blonde stayed in place, not moving, not talking. The next woman, a bed head redhead found it necessary to sideswipe blondie over to the cashier area.

"Hi. Jake. It's Jake right? Oh God! Can I call my mother? It'll only take a sec! Oh my God! She's not going to believe this! She was supposed to come shopping with me today but she stayed home, she lives in Bixby Canyon. Oh my..."

"I'm sorry, no calls please, madame. Now what would you like?" Jake was going to crush this line.

"Oh, oh okay, sorry. Uh, I'll have three apple five spice and three mocha, and do you have lemon? Okay, well, the blood orange, three of those also, please." He wondered if he was enabling a bulimic. "Three apple, three orange, three mocha! Next!" Jake proceeded to holler orders until the line started to thin out. That took over an hour and it would be time to close pretty soon. He was restacking the boxes, stickers and wrapping paper when he heard:

"Hi, Jake." He turned around having stacked everything nicely only to see before his eyes, yep, Ellie. Shit. Super goddamn mother fucking shit fuck fuck.

"Ellie, what are you doing here?" He couldn't be cool with her anymore. She was freaking him out.

"Jake?"

"Come out of the line, please, I need to talk with you. NOW." Sweating, Jake came from around the counter and escorted Ellie out of the store and down the street. The line had been cut down considerably and he felt comfortable with leaving the four behind on their own for the time being. Ellie stopped allowing him to push her, and she turned around pissed.

"What is your problem Jake?" she spat.

"You're kidding right? What's my problem? You. Ellie, you're my problem." Ouch.

"How's that Jake? I just came by to say 'hi', I didn't realize that it was going to upset you so much."

"Ellie, listen." He knew that by softening the tone of his voice like he just did, he'd fucked up everything. Now she was going to play innocent and try to turn the tables. And she did.

"No *you* listen! All I did was walk through the door and you humiliate me in front of everyone!? I'm supposed to bring dessert to a dinner party and I thought 'Perfect. Cupcakes will be such a hit' and instead you….." she burst into tears. Oh for the love of Christ.

"Ellie." Now she had snot running down her face, streaking her spray foundation. Not a pretty sight for an innocent Beverly Hills passerby. It was like looking at the toothless homeless. She continued to sob, reaching into her gargantuan purse for a tiny packet of tissues. Jake couldn't help her. In fact, he wouldn't. She was full of it.

She found a tissue and proceeded to honk and blow and sniffle, waiting for him to say something comforting. But he didn't.

"Your mascara's smeared" he said calmly. Jake wasn't usually this mean. "You need to fix yourself up before you go to that 'dinner party'." The one in your head, he heard his head say. He hoped he was the only one that heard that. Well, fuck it if she did.

"Can I use your bathroom?"

"I don't think that that's a good idea, Ellie." She proceeded to start the waterworks again but this time it was different. This time she was mad. Both kinds of mad.

"I don't know why you have to be so mean to me Jake. I've never done anything to you. I came over here to help you but"

"But what?"

"Things have changed is all."

"Ellie I don't think you know what you're talking about."

"No I do actually. And soon, so will you." She gave him a funny look, funny in part because of the look in her the eye, but mostly because of seriously jacked up eyeliner and a snotty nose. She turned around and stormed off.

"Ellie." She raised her hand still clutching the tissue as if to say, 'save it.' She was gone. Relieved, Jake returned to the store where the last of the customers where placing their orders. He walked directly to the back of the kitchen. Everybody was cleaning up their areas fairly decently. Jake passed by each individual work station while the store got ready to close. He brought out the floor mops, a sight which upset everyone. As he passed the last storage shelves, situated a few feet from his phony office area, he saw what the Amanda Tisdale had spotted during the interview. Two one pound sacks of **organic** flour sat smiling down upon him, 'Hi Jake!'

CHAPTER

FORTY-FIVE

No sooner was Jake back home then he was in his trunks and swimming. He hadn't heated it and tough shit. It had been, in his estimation, a crap day. And frankly if this was success...... well at least they got the 'suck' part of it right. He hadn't spoken with either George or Jennifer and wondered if he would even see them tonight. That was okay. For a couple of minutes he entertained the insane idea of doing some light house work but realized he must be out of his mind. So Jake continued on with his laps until he could finally stop thinking about the Tisdale and the Ellie and work and the future of organic cupcakes. *Biologiques* they called it in France. Disgusting. How does one market *les petits gâteaux biologiques* anyway? He knew that he finally must be calming down because he was thinking about nonsense. Jake continued to do his laps and by the time his mind wandered over to the Irish Secession of radical Presbyterians, contemporary letterpresses and Australian wallpaper from the 1970s, the effects of the day were behind him.

It was nice not having that phone, no no no; his mind threatened to turn back to practical matters. Maybe he'd stay in a little longer. Jake flopped back onto his belly to swim again to the other side, when, of course, his cell went off somewhere. Although hesitant to answer it, he had invited people over and had to get out of the pool. He jumped out, grabbed a towel and checked who was on the line. It was George.

"George."

"Took you long enough. Am I calling at a bad time?"

"No, of course not, I was in the pool. Are you coming over?" asked Jake.

"I have a date tonight!" George squealed.

"But George, I cleaned up, and made dinner and"

"Shut up. You're swimming in your goddamn pool and just **barely** managed to get to the phone."

"Not true, my vacuum cleaner is really, really loud."

"How can you be in your pool vacuuming?"

"It's one of those automatic floor ones, a Bumble, but it makes such a racket."

"If only you *were* funny."

"So, who's tonight's victim?" asked Jake.

"No one you know" replied George.

"Okay, be vague and secretive. I don't want to hear about it. It will all end in tears, anyway."

"God, I hope so."

"Okay, George, I'm getting cold…hanging up now."

"Bye. Wish me luck!" **CLICK**

Should he call Jennifer? If he remembered correctly, she'd hung up on him. He decided to call Jill instead. He put on his robe and walked back into the house to make the call and start dinner. She picked up after three rings.

"Jake?"

"How are you feeling?"

"Oh my god, so much better Jake. You have *no* idea. It was either the burdock or the fermented soy bean, but man! Or maybe the forsythia?"

"Jill, you shouldn't really eat forsythia."

"No, Jesus, I'm talking about my Chinese herbals. Hello? I'm trying to remove excess heat." Jill explained with exasperation.

"Oh. Sorry. Are you still taking them?" Please say no.

"Right now, yeah. I don't want to get sick again."

"You can't get sick again Jill. We need you."

"Thanks Jake. That's sweet."

"So are you busy tonight? Do you want to come over? I'm making dinner."

"Uh." said Jill.

"Well if you're still feeling, you know, like you need your rest, I'll understand. I just thought it would be nice. We could catch up."

"What time?" asked Jill.

"Anytime. I'm swimming. You can swim if you want. You know it's good for circulation."

"I'll be there in twenty minutes."

Huh, he thought. He padded into the kitchen to see what there was to eat. Jake was considering grilling, then he examined his formerly fresh vegetables, now going a funky green and slightly hairy. He looked at the potatoes and the mushrooms, they were fine, but did not amount to much of a meal. It'll have to be delivered, which would be alright, he didn't feel much like standing around a kitchen again, truth be told. Jake placed an order at the deli of Canterbury Farmhouse. He got the baby greens salad with grilled hawai'ian onions, feta and crushed pineapple, the soft boiled eggs on top of assorted mixed wild mushrooms, thinly chopped ham with crème fraiche folded in, their fresh spinach stuffed chicken breasts and lastly the crispy gratin dauphinois. They could throw in some vanilla ice cream for dessert. He checked for his honey, got it, looked for his dried chili mangos, got those too. He put four bottles of pinot in the refrigerator and went back outside. Since the pool wasn't heated, he lit two of the fire pits and a fire in the den.

By the time he had got every fire going, having sadly lost his touch, the door bell rang. He opened the front door holding the burnt remnants of a rolled newspaper. What he saw holding a wine bottle in a paper bag and a big smile that indicates that nothing is on underneath, was Jennifer. Oh my god.

"Surprise!" she said, her perfect teeth ablaze.

"I should say so!" Jake's voice had gone up an octave. With his larynx frozen, he would soon have trouble with modulation and conveying emotion.

"Jake?"

"Jennifer!" he squeaked. "You're just in time." On this occasion, however, his mouth produced a strangled alto. "Jill's on her way over for dinner. George can't make it. Did you talk to him this afternoon? He's standing me up. He has a date." Oh god.

"Jill?" Jennifer was definitely was not wearing anything under the coat because she pushed her way in and slammed the door behind her. "Jake" she said pleadingly and opened her coat.

"Oh." He cleared his throat and went to put down the smoking roll of newspaper. "Come in and let me find you some clothes." Nice one Jake. Real smooth.

"No, I should leave." Jennifer felt a complete fool. But to be honest, arriving at anyone's house unannounced, naked but for your outer garments, is usually disastrous.

"Don't be silly. I'm glad you came. Just let me find you something to wear. Or do you want to skinny dip?" Jake grinned.

"I…"

"I have to warn you. I've lit some fires outside but the pool's not heated. You can put on a t-shirt and shorts? How's that?"

Before she could make up her mind, the door bell rang again.

"That must be Jill." Jennifer could no longer talk. Tears started to well up in her eyes. "Now go into my bedroom and find something you'd like to swim in while we wait for dinner to arrive and I see to Jill. You'll like her a lot. I promise." With that he kissed her on the mouth as one small tear rolled down her cheek. He wiped it away and gave her a big hug in her short and shiny Burberry trench. Sad face.

CHAPTER

FORTY-SIX

When Jake opened the door, Jill looked equally pleased to see him.

"Hi!" she said. "I told you twenty minutes!"

"Listen, while you were on your way, Jennifer came over."

"What?" Jill looked scary pissed.

"Yeah, she's putting on her swim stuff. Did you bring yours?"

"Wait. Jennifer. Jennifer is here? Why didn't you tell me?"

"It was a complete surprise. But it's fine. You're okay with it aren't you? I mean George was supposed to come too."

"George?"

"Jill, what's wrong with you? Aren't you swimming?"

Before she could say 'yes,' 'no' or 'fuck you I'm leaving,' Jennifer came out of the bedroom. She was barefoot, in one of Jake's t-shirts tied at her belly button and had a pair of his swim trunks tied tight and folded over.

"Hi," she extended her hand "I think we've met before. I'm Jennifer."

"Hi. I'm Jill. And I don't think we have actually." She put her hands on her hips in defiance.

"Jennifer, Jill has been incredibly sick and you shouldn't really touch her although I don't think she's contagious anymore. Right Jill?"

"I'm not really sure."

"Jennifer, would you like some wine? I think that we may need one more bottle. Would you do me a big favor and pour some glasses, please? Jill, where's your bathing suit?" He was going to pretend as if this was all completely normal, that he was just dealing with two brace faced seventh graders and hope for the best.

"I'm wearing it," she was still pretty fucking annoyed.

"Well, let me get some towels. Jennifer? Meet us by the pool, okay?"

"Uhm, okay." She was in the kitchen feeling lonely and idiotic. It's a little difficult to find a bottle opener and wine glasses when you're wading through your own tears. This was either going to be a momentary blip of feminine insecurity or the start of a very, very bad night. Only time would tell. 'Right,' she thought. The only thing for Jennifer to do was enter her sunny disposition zone and see what went down from within the bubble. Bubbles are good.

Outside Jennifer's bubble, Jill was having her own feminine insecurity blip, but it didn't look at all momentary from where Jake was standing.

"I thought it was just gonna be the two of us catching up Jake?" she accused.

"Would you relax? Do five laps and then we'll have a drink." He left again to look around for Jennifer. She must be in the bedroom, he thought, so he went back outside. He found Jill still standing by the pool looking petulant.

"Listen, let's do the laps together. Get in the pool, Jill."
She stood with a lower lip threatening to poke out further
than her nose. "I mean it. Come ON!" Jake took off his robe
and dove into the pool. Still freezing.

"AHFFKADEFKEHEH!" he shrieked as his balls shriv-
eled. "Go tell Jennifer to get out here and leave the chilled
wine inside." He choked on some pool water while Jill turned
on her heels and stomped back into the den.

"Jake says leave the wine and come into the freezing water!" she barked, turned around and left. Jennifer was in the
bathroom wiping her eyes when she heard someone bellow
something.

"Hello?" she asked. No answer. She went back into
the kitchen and between sniffles got the bottle opened, and
walked outside with it and three juice glasses.

"I couldn't find the wine glasses, Jake."

"Hold on, I'll go get them. You too get in the pool. Be
warned it's very cold. Five laps each or no dinner." He got
out and grabbed a towel on his way inside. He got three
glasses and brought towels out from the linen cabinet. He
thought he heard splashing and laughter but it must be those
horrible kids from next door.

Sure enough it was the neighbors next door because Jill
and Jennifer were facing off, waiting for something to happen. Jake could tell that each was waiting for the other to
leave.

"Okay, I don't know about you two, but I'm getting in the
pool. Then I'm making dinner. I'm having my wine. And
I'm having a good time. *You two* can stand there all night for
all I care." He dove back into the pool and proceeded to do
his laps. Each time he raised his head for air he tried to catch
a glimpse of what they were doing but it was pretty difficult.

They would have to come to some kind of understanding. Jake was sick of doing nothing wrong and being in the doghouse. Fuck 'em.

After his fourth lap he started to warm up. It wasn't his intention to seem like a freakish host but he couldn't stop; he needed to stay warm and safe. So on he went, stroke after stroke, from one end of the pool to the other. By the time he had finished, the girls' heads were wet and bobbing.

"Would you get out of the way so we can swim?" yelled Jill.

"Yeah, move it!" yelled Jennifer. They both cracked up. Sisterhood *is* powerful.

Jake got out of the pool, dried off and grabbed a glass of wine. On the way into the den the doorbell rang for the third time; it was the delivery guy. Perfect. He could pull dinner together while they bonded at his expense. You couldn't say that Jake didn't know women. By the time he'd finished setting the table, they'd be fast friends and ready to bully him all night. Well at least George couldn't make it. Otherwise it would have been three against one.

He brought the food into the kitchen and set it all on the counter. He could hear the girls splashing around and chatting. Jennifer had Jill laughing. Jill was pouring Jennifer another glass of wine. God, I hope they don't get sloppy drunk and start braiding each other's hair. He placed every dish in a server bowl, created more flames by placing candles on the table and left them unattended. Jake went back outside for the hundredth time to find his robe.

"Come in!" they called out in unison. God, not that again.

"Dinner's ready. You guys should come out."

They both started to whine, showing the first signs of menstrual synchronicity.

"Maybe after we eat, but it'll probably be too cold. Come on. Get out of the pool." Jake clapped his hand. He'd never been a woman wrangler before. Never needed to be and wasn't going to start now. Nonetheless, he knew that he had to keep a firm grip on them otherwise this gathering would go rogue and turn into a shitty slumber party.

The two came out of the pool and took the towel that he offered each.

"Okay, the food's on the table. You two come inside and get warm. And bring the wine."

CHAPTER
FORTY-SEVEN

The table flickered and steamed; Jennifer thought that it looked divine, as usual. She and Jill salivated while they huddled over the spread, while Jake went and got more blankets and throws for them. Holding a pile of wool, microfiber and cashmere, he heard the door bell ring again.

"Can one of you get that?" he yelled over the contents in his arms.

"Jake, we're half naked. No." replied Jill.

"Jill! I think you're cured!"

"Fuck you Jake!"

Jennifer laughed and Jake had to stop himself from shooting her an evil glance.

He dropped everything in his arms on to the floor. At the front door, through the peep hole, stood George.

"George? I thought you had a date?" Jake opened the door wide.

"Yes, well it was a quick one." George stepped into the foyer dressed in black corduroy slacks, a bright blue polo under a black merino v-neck sweater and no hat. Jake couldn't remember ever having seen the actual shape of George's head before. Kind of round.

"Where's your hat, George? And where are your trunks?"

"My hat is gone and I'm afraid that I can't swim tonight Jake. Got a little something going on down there. Might have some trouble sitting down too, come to think of it."

"Just a thought but that date may have been just a little too quick, George."

"Don't be silly." He waved him off. Where's Jennifer?"

"Getting some dinner in the living room. Are you hungry?"

"Starved," he said, patting his belly.

"Well, help yourself. Jill's over too."

George turned to show Jake his look of co-conspiratorial intrigue and then turned to follow the aroma wafting from the other room. Jake, confused and/or disgusted went back into his bedroom. He yelled out to the other guests his latest and final arrival.

"George's here. He's date's over."

"Over where?" mumbled Jennifer. She and Jill were putting the food on plates and she was focusing.

"Oh Jennifer, come here. I love you." George gave Jennifer as big a hug as he could manage without allowing her to get any of his clothing wet. He merely leaned forward from the waist offering Jennifer his shoulders to pat. Sweet. By this time, Jake was in his shower, getting his back blasted by a perfectly modulated staccato of warm water. It was probably rude to do this with a room full of people, especially when some of them were most likely freezing, but it was his house and he felt like it. If, for what ever reason, the evening took a turn and it became a really trying night, he was going to get the name of that shrink. He did a quick sudsing and turned off the water. He wiped the condensation off his mirror and leaned in closely. How are you holding up Jake? Are *you* okay?, he asked himself. His hair line didn't look to be receding. He pulled at his cheeks: facial elasticity holding steady. He couldn't see his possible bald spot as usual and besides, there was way too much steam. He could have George take a look, but not tonight, not with the ladies present. He toweled off quickly so his guests wouldn't start to wonder what was taking him so long, being a host and all. As he tried to slip past the living room to get to his closets, he caught a glimpse of George with his pants pulled slightly off his ass and Jill and Jennifer peering over closely. Jill was wearing her reading glasses and saw his pink flesh streak by.

"Hey Jake come take a look" said Jill taking off her 1.75 drugstore spectacles.

"Huh?"

"George got a tattoo tonight" garbled Jennifer, her mouth full of potatoes.

"You what?" Dressing fast, Jake came over and grabbed a dinner plate and silverware.

"I got a tattoo. That's why I can't swim and I don't have my hat. Can I please eat now? I'm not a science project." He was still standing there with his ass out while three individuals helped themselves to food and wine. It didn't seem fair or dignified.

"Okay, let him go. George here's your plate." Jake waited for him to finish zipping up his trousers and adjust his belt before handing over the china.

"Thank you. I was starting to feel a little vulnerable."

"I can assure you that *that* is not possible" said Jennifer poking her fork at him with her mouth full. She put her plate down. "I'm going to take a shower and find some clothes." *Find* some clothes?, wondered Jill.

"The tattoo, George. What is it? I can't make it out." she asked while pondering Jennifer's exact words.

"It's a swallow, darling. It's so I remember to eat."

"I would have thought it was so you don't get lost," said Jennifer in the hallway leading to the bathroom.

"But you have to remember to look at your *ass*, George, before it can remind you to do anything else."

"True, I suppose. Now move aside, I'm weak with hunger."

"George, how could you have been raked over with a needle and still be such a princess?"

"That's a very good question." The topic was now closed. George loaded up his plate and ignored him. He wanted to hear no more mention of his ass, his date, or his hat which he easily accomplished with a happy food stuffed smile on his face.

Jennifer found some more towels and walked into Jake's messed up bathroom. She turned on the shower and kicked away his clothes as daintily as possible. The water was perfect. She could stay in here forever, she thought. But there was a knock on the door. Jake no doubt.

"Jake?" she asked.

"Yeah, what are you going to wear?" he'd popped his head into the steam just a crack.

"I don't know. Give me some pajama bottoms and a sweat shirt."

"Are you staying over?"

"Dumb question."

"Right. Sorry. I'll leave some things out for you. They'll be on the bed." Jake went back to Jill and George.

"Jill, are you going to take a shower? I need to give you some towels."

"When I'm done eating I'll take one. Thanks." She and George were talking about something that he couldn't quite make out. He got another glass of wine and came over. They, in turn, shut up as he approached. He sat in ignorance by the fire. Ho hum, thought the host. And in my own house.

Out came Jennifer who switched places with Jill. Jake followed her to show her where there were more towels. When he finally got back to the dining table....not a scrap of food remained.   That makes things easy; he thought and cleared away the plates and flatware. Jake sat down again, this time Jennifer cozying up next to him. She placed a big sloppy kiss on his cheek and smiled. George was sitting with some difficulty, so he gave up eating his off his lap. He was finished anyway. Instead, he occupied himself by admiring Jennifer and Jake, taking credit for it all. Jake wondered if it would be too rude to wipe that oily spot off his face. He left it alone.

CHAPTER
FORTY-EIGHT

Everything seemed to be going smoothly after all. The dinner was devoured, the swimming swum, the dessert a sly success. Jake had scooped four bowls with the vanilla ice cream, topped them with thinly sliced dried chili mango, drizzled honey and just a bit of crushed chewy peppermint candy for color and cool heat. His friends lazed by the fire, bowls and spoons in hand, and shoveled the icy contents down. NOTE: It's safe to say that Jake liked mints with dessert; it was better than an Altoid and just as effective.

George smacked his lips just a few times too many, got up slowly, preparing to leave. He had a faraway look which meant either he was overfull or had a sore bum from a bird tattoo. Jake saw him to the door and told him not to worry about the hat. Jake was exhausted himself, having been the boss for too many hours. But not Jennifer. And not Jill. They were wide awake and chattering away about work and living in L.A. and shoes. Mostly shoes. The three of them lay about the living room, with the fire sparking into embers, and Jake slowly passing into coma.

"Jake?" said Jill softly.

"Mmmhmmm." Jake wriggled his nose with his eyes still closed.

"Jake, you're not sleeping are you?" she spoke again.

Jake slowly opened his eyes and looked at her.

"No, I'm awake." He sat up. "Hunh?"

"I'm gonna get going. I need my rest too."

"I'm up." Jake bounced off the sofa forcing himself into semi-consciousness but nearly falling over in the process.

"Thanks for dinner and the pool and everything" said Jill.

"We didn't get to catch up" said Jake rubbing his eyes.

"We can catch up later" she said, putting on her coat. She kissed him on the cheek and gave him a long, hopefully not contagious, hug. "Goodnight. Tell Jennifer 'goodnight' for me."

"'Night. See you soon. Drive safely." He closed the door behind her and stumbled into the kitchen. Jennifer had already placed all the plates in soapy water. The dining table had been completely cleared and the place almost looked like it did before anyone had come over.

"You didn't have to do that" he said.

"I know but you're tired. Let me get my things and I'll call you tomorrow."

"You're leaving?" he was awake now.

"Yeah. I'll call you. Thanks for dinner and sorry about surprising you like that."

"You sure?"

"I'm sure. I'll return these clothes, but I need something to get home in." she laughed. They embraced for a long time and kissed but she pulled away and left him to his empty house.

Jake couldn't really complain. He was good for nothing but sleep. So after making sure that all his fires were out, he locked up, turned off the lights and crawled into bed.

He didn't remember the water being this perfect. He had never turned the heat on, that much he knew, yet it was a perfect 82 degrees. He was down at the bottom of the deep end examining the tile work but then, he was on the shallow end with his eyes open underwater. He could see perfectly two female figures, except for the water rippling, kneeling towards him at the other end where he'd just been a second ago. He paused to consider those urban tales of the chlorinated pool nymphs and whether or not they could roam from one backyard to another. Water nymphs can't be trusted, so he stayed where he was and popped his head out of the water. There weren't even nymphs, it was Jill and Jennifer.

"Hey! What are you doing here?" he asked, wiping his eyes. They turned, synchronized, to look at him, but didn't say anything. What is with women and this shit? I am *so* sick of it, he thought.

"Um, didn't I lock the door? God, that sounded rude, I'm sorry. So, uh, what's going on?" Jake was getting nervous. In actual fact, he'd just kicked off the top cover of his bed linen.

Jennifer, he noticed, had irises that were a little too big, and though she kept looking at him, when she opened her mouth to speak, nothing came out. Her mouth was moving alright, but he couldn't hear anything.

"Jennifer, what? I can't hear you." He shook his head but this was no swimmer's ear. He looked around for his sunglasses or spf cream or a towel or a bat, anything. He couldn't move towards her. Jennifer kept on mouthing something that he still couldn't make out and then Jill started to as well. Jill looked smaller than usual, once he focused his gaze upon her. Her body was a bit too small and her head was a bit too large.

"Come on you guys. This isn't funny." Both of them were wearing clothes that he had never seen them in before. Ugly, unkempt clothes. And now that he was really looking, they both looked kind of beat up and dirty. He was holding on to the side of the pool trying to tread water, when the doors leading to the living room opened up and out walked Ellie. She was completely naked except for this weird streak of something muddy which spread across her stomach and on up to her face. She walked out slowly and touched Jennifer and Jill. Jennifer started to dribble out of the side of her mouth and then she vomited into his pool. He watched horrified as it swirled around his perfect turquoise water and he tried to get out. He couldn't; he was frozen. Then she slipped under the water and disappeared. Jill also started to hemorrhage the same sticky ooze, falling over onto the tiles, laying there while this gushing mess gathered by her knees. It formed a narrow line and drizzled into the water.

"Stop it!" he cried out. Jennifer was gone. Jill laid there, her eyes staring into nothing. Ellie, naked, slowly rose up onto her feet and turned towards him, her left arm reaching. Again he tried to move, to jump out of the pool, but he couldn't. As she approached, her hand getting closer and closer, he opened his mouth to scream but nothing came out.

He woke up. His bed clothes were all over the floor and he was in a sweat.

CHAPTER
FORTY-NINE

George got a frantic call at 6 in the morning, Sunday.

"What?" For the first time, George wasn't his usual over-enthusiastic self when Jake called.

"George?"

"Do you have any idea what time it is, Jake?"

"I'm sorry. I had a horrible, horrible Ellie dream. The second one."

"Eeeew. That is disturbing and everything but um, so what? It's just a," George didn't bother to stifle his yawn.

"Dream. I know. But tell me what *you* do after waking up in a cold sweat? Tell me how'd *you* feel?" yelled Jake.

"Alright, alright. That *is* horrible. Are you sure you didn't fall asleep with MTV on?" He yawned again. Silence. "OK, what can I do so that I can go back to sleep?"

"I want the names of those shrinks!"

"Oh, Jake! At last! It's a breakthrough!" George was awake. He sat straight up in his reproduction silver-leafed cherub bed, stretching his arms in one of his favorite cheerleader poses. "It's not like you're fucked up or anything, Jake, but I still think you're turning a wonderful corner. I'm so proud of you! Now listen, I'm going to text them to you as soon as I wake up again. It's Sunday, Jake. Big hug!" He hung up.

Finishing one task prompted Jake to finish another. He looked around his bedclothes and decided his next project would be to straighten out the tangled mess. Better yet, he switched the linen out and threw the sweaty ones in the corner to wash later. Once the last blanket was spread out, he crawled back in. Afraid of dreaming of Ellie again, but too tired to put up much of a fight, Jake was asleep before he had enough time to think about the dream vomit in his beautiful pool.

Jill, on the other hand, enjoyed pure uninterrupted sleep. She didn't have to pee, or blow her nose, or slosh down a glass of water to stop choking. She didn't have nightmares or phones waking her up. She was a lucky girl. By the time she finally accepted the fact that she had to get out of bed, it was 10am. Briefly, Jill entertained the idea of calling Jake and spending the afternoon in his pool but maybe he wouldn't be too thrilled at seeing so much of her so soon. If she didn't relapse she'd be back into work tomorrow, so she decided to spend the day close to home. Again.

A moment passed and Jill decided that that was just not possible. I have to get out of here, she thought. She walked into her bathroom and pulled out a bottle of astralagus from her medicine cabinet, out of which she took two capsules and swallowed them with tap water. She took another shower, poured herself some green tea and sat staring bored shitless, in her robe, in the living room. Jill could not watch another movie or cable or sleep or read. She wasn't going to stare into the refrigerator or out the window. She decided to narrow down her myriad of choices of just two. Either she could call Jake, risk being a phone call unwelcome and unanswered; just in hopes of getting back into his freezing pool and get sick again. Or she could go to the Korean Spa cross town and be detoxified and pummeled to supple baby softness. One second of deliberation and detoxified baby softness it would be.

She had no trouble getting an appointment, which seemed a bit odd. I guess it's because it's a Sunday, she thought. Jill left her car and keys with the valet and walked in. At the counter, she was greeted, eventually, with gross reluctance. Ah, sweet emotional and physical abuse, beauty is thine end! She walked into the crowded changing area and grabbed a towel, pinning up her hair. She stripped down, wrapped the towel around her middle and made her first stop, the whirlpool. Actually she won't be going there, it's way too crowded. Some of the larger women, waved her on. Fine. Next stop the mugwort pool. It was hot as hell. She ignored the stares and the endless variations in body types that were adding up in her head. She stayed as long as she could take it before making her way to the cold pool. This time she didn't play nice, she just shoved her way in. Jill had two steam rooms left. After she had been in the cold pool long enough to be annoying to others, she got out and moved on. One was constructed out of stone and jade, and the other one, just stone. Both were extremely hot, but a toxin can be very stubborn.

As she came out of the last room, an attendant dressed in the official uniform of a black bra and panty set, called out the name of the next client for treatment. She barked a mangled, palsied squawk but being that 'Jill' is just one syllable, it was still recognizable. Her time had come at last. She lay on the table naked, except for that same old towel and worried that she hadn't shaved. Not that she could do anything about it now, except perhaps to close her eyes. She gritted her teeth and prepared to be exfoliated down to the bone. Standing over her, the masseuse smelled of the delicious lemony scrub which she proceeded to slather all over her. Jill lay on her stomach while the silent woman swirled it round her shoulders, back, butt, down her legs and on to her feet. She was really very generous and thorough. She didn't skimp on the product at all, which is quite nice and a refreshing change of pace.

And so it began. What had been a swirling, became an industrial scrub, an exterior house paint scraping, a macrodermabrasion. Could a sugar scrub land one in the emergency room? Jill thought that if she flailed a little she could alert them to her distress, but she was being pushed around so much on the table, it wasn't at all noticeable. She tried to turn her head to meet her attendant eye to eye but she feared she'd break her neck or have it broken for her. She moaned loudly but that didn't work either. So she discarded her dignity and just started to yell.

"You! Are! Hurting! Me!"

The attendant stopped immediately and barked:

"Too rough?" Was that mockery she heard somewhere in those two syllables? Jill leapt to a sitting position and stared at her. She saw no name plate on the black acrylic bra. Jill appraised her arms looking for blood and jumped off the table.

"We're done."

"Don't you want the shower. You're very greasy."

"Yes I want the shower! Where is it?" Jill was still so mad that she didn't think of what was to come. By my watch, it read Lamb To Slaughter Time. Like an indignant Dorothy in the shitty backwoods part of Oz, she followed the women's pointing finger; didn't give her a gratuity and stormed off towards of the sound of running water.

Well, forget the Wizard, poor Jill's final stage of spa detox was much more like the shower scene in 'Carrie'. There were locker rooms, showers, cruel females and water. Maybe even a little blood. Did I mention the water? So much water. The force of which was strong enough to peel off her already tender epidermis. She looked around in terror. No one was crying. No naked white women were running for the door or slumped in the shower's corner mumbling nonsensically to themselves. So she withstood it, she manned up and she didn't cry either. When the shower nozzle was finally turned off, she stumbled away with her blessèd survival. Strangely, Jill saw a tunnel of white light and decided to make her way towards it. Maybe it was her time after all. She'd had a good run; she had no complaints. Maybe her little dog Skip, who got run over when she was six, would be waiting for her. She stumbled for another ten paces or so until she made it to the other side. Walking into that ethereal veil of light, which was fluorescent, she found herself standing in the noisy dressing room area.

She put her clothes back on a fast as she could, rushed the valet and peeled. She wouldn't look back and she couldn't calm down for at least five lights. This was when Jill reached out and stroked her arm. Sinfully smooth. Softer than the ass of a ewe. She'd make an appointment for next month at the very latest.

CHAPTER FIFTY

Jennifer, on the other hand, did stay in her apartment for the rest of the weekend. She had to write the entire article that Amanda was going to carry under her own by-line, as usual. She sat in her bathrobe facing her laptop, but stared at the blank screen for what seemed an age. Amanda hadn't done as much research or interviews as she should have; she had poo-poo'd the whole endeavor, but she would not be seen missing the boat on this one. Jennifer thought that she had been angered by the indifference she'd been shown. But, Amanda still wanted all of the credit and intended on doing none of the work. So no change there. Jennifer knew the boundaries of her own position, so here she sat with a tankard of water by her side, staring at her screen saver and then back out the window. The birds looked happy, she thought. Why couldn't she be a bird?

The notes that Amanda had taken were mostly comprised of 0's and *'s and her initials worked over so hard that their impression went through to the sheets underneath. They had visited The Sweetness, Sugar Peaks and Cupcake but by then she was tired and wanted to go back to the hotel. Never mind that there were several worthy cupcake bakeries in town; Amanda was done. Jennifer had decided long ago that she was not going to fill in Amanda's research gaps; she would only work with what she was given. However, in this case, she had a butt load of doodling. But that was okay. Obviously, Jennifer had a lot of experience replicating Amanda's style. It was easy and bone-head breezy, Sylvia Plath-era *Mademoiselle*. This was *Extreme Leisure*, mind you, and there would be no gravitas. She looked back out the window and put it together in her head in moments.

DRAFT
EXTREME LEISURE
December Issue
What People Do When They Can't Live in New York
By Amanda Tisdale, East Coast Editor

Saluti! Baci a tutti i miei cari! As you know from my last column I mentioned that I would be journeying to the left coast to see what those wild colonials are up to! As you can well imagine skin exposure passes for fashion and although the restaurant scene is intense, nobody eats! I can assure you that I felt absolutely overdressed wearing lipstick, but alas, such is the life of style columnist from NYC! I might as well have been in Guam! Needless to say, miei dolci, I cannot be kept away, whether it be the cloistered bedchambers of *l'ancienne noblesse* or a starlet's walk-in closet, if there is utter fabulousness to be discovered I will have at it!

This past month, I was sent out on assignment to investigate the West Coast's take on that racing locomotive of a trend: cupcakes. Yes, you read that correctly, cupcakes! People are passionate about cupcakes out here and that ought to have told me something from the start, don't you think? It's taken quite seriously, chéries. For Los Angelenos it's as important as the opera; as teeth gnashing, as the daily health report on Manhattan's oldest living heiress. I kid you not! But work is work and I do as I am told, so I was off to research this rather unusual phenomenon.

I left the Best Coast for the West Coast and immediately set about for discovery. The cupcake, as you know of course, is a small children's pastry. A bit of cake in paper, with a dollop of sweet frosting atop. Sometimes, it has sprinkles, sometimes it has a gaudy plastic ring. Strictly for the kiddies! I know that it is somewhat of a trend here too, in lower Manhattan of course, but really, we're all adults are we not? Would the Prince of Wales eat a cupcake? I should say not! It's a ridiculous question.

But I must accept this, whether I understand it or not, like Yohji Yamamoto's couture in 1979. I told myself that I would go to no more than three. The alleged (as they insist on saying on the telly) top three, of course. That being The Sweetness, tucked away in a cozy mews in West Hollywood; Sugar Peaks, a mid century modern meets French chandeliered frénésie in Santa Monica; and the sleek and industrial Cupcake in Beverly Hills. My tasters and I first hit West Hollywood, were we sat and chatted with the utterly charming proprietress Miss Deborah Sanchez. She is the grand dame of the baking world in this so-called city. Her cupcakes are only a small portion of her total menu, which is divine and terribly fattening! A must for those coming to the City of Angels. We next stopped by the brother-sister enterprise run by the Adlers. Ah to be young and gorgeous! I can't say the same for the menu. It was so-so. But those kids are a delight and the store is gorgeous! I suggested that they sell shoes! Last on our whirlwind tour was Jake Wellington's Cupcake in, oh so chic, Beverly Hills. We tasted a wide variety and he was delighted to mention that an organic menu was forthcoming. Can you imagine! The treats were yum-yums but frankly a tad too sweet for my taste. Darlings, you know that Amanda prefers something a little more sophisticated.

All in all, I must admit it was very interesting, but I am so glad to be home. Los Angeles can keep its trends and its movie stars, yours truly is a New York City girl.

À la prochaine fois!

AT

Jake was going to kill her. She would prepare him before the issue hit the stands and hopefully he would be forgiving. But this was her job, and she did it well. Amanda would make her usual obnoxious criticisms and maybe, if she was lucky, stay away for a good long while. This last trip, seemed to have been a little too much for her.

CHAPTER
FIFTY-ONE

Jake got to the gym early Monday morning, hoping it would put him in the right frame of mind for the week. His trainer, Mike, worked him over good and he felt good. The previous week had been somewhat difficult and challenging. He'd pigged out over the weekend, so he was going to hit the ground running this week, of that he was certain. Mike was impressed.

"I like this new dedication, Jake."

"I've got a lot on my plate right now."

"I hear you. Keep up the good work." Typical man talk. That entire conversation would have taken at least two and a half hours had it been between two women. Jake did the last of his reps and hit the showers. He was out of there by 8:30am.

The minute he hit the bakery it hit him back. Janice was the first to get to him. She was holding the phone and wanted her cash.

"Heyah's yah pho-uhn. Heyah's the note-boo-uk. I suspect thayut you'allreadeh know that you'all have a bituvaproblem."

"What do you mean?" as if he didn't know.

"You gawt a crayank callah, or suhm obb-sayist luvah. I don't know wee-ich." What she was really saying was "pay me." Jake reached into his back pocket with one hand, grabbed the phone and set it down with the other. He paid her and she walked away counting her bills.

"Do I need to look through this?" he asked raising the notebook.

"Nawt reallay. Ah suggest you chaange yowah numbah."

Jake had a better idea. He wasn't going to have a land line any more. He threw the notebook into the nearest trashcan.

Next up was Jill. He gave her a big germicide fortified hug.

"Jill, I'm so glad you're back."

"Me too. Listen, don't mean to be curt, but I just got off the phone with Jaime Thornton's people."

"Who's that?"

"Jesus, Jake."

"I'm sorry! Who is he?"

"It's a she, Jake. The biggest scandal-grubbing pop star of the moment, that's who."

"Oh."

"Anyway, she's turning seventeen and her people have placed a massive order for pick-up Saturday afternoon. Oh and by the way, we're really, really busy. I've never seen it like this before." Jake gave her his 'are you fucking for real?' look.

"You said 'yes' I'm assuming?"

"Of course."

"Good." He walked over to the coffee machine. There was nothing in it. He could have said something, but he kept his mouth shut and made the morning's first brew.

"Can you define "massive" more precisely Jill?" Jake said while the coffee machine began to spit and sizzle.

"They want twenty dozen. Don't do the math, that's 240."

"Since that last article we've had to double up, you might want to order just for that party separately."

"Sounds good. Thanks for dinner, by the way. That was great. Jennifer is really nice, I like her." Jill stood next to Jake and they both stared impatiently at the coffee maker.

"Thanks. I like her too."

"So are you two serious?" she asked not really wanting to know.

"I don't know. Too soon to say." Jill's shoulders relaxed. "Uhp, there's goes my phone, hold on."

"George."

"I'm sorry Jake. I'm in a *huge* rush but listen, here are the numbers for those shrinks. Gotta pen?"

"Go ahead." Jake grabbed a pad and pen off the work table under Jill's curious gaze.

"Now call this one first. Her name is Dr. Gillian Thomkinson-Price. 310-578-0907. She's fabulous. I think you'll really like her. If she's booked, call Dr. Anne Mendelson. She's also very good. And a hoot. 310-899-6107. Let me know what you think. I'm swamped this morning, can't talk." **CLICK**

Jake snapped his phone shut while Jill continued to stare at him.

"Check up" he said. "Nothing serious. Just a physical."

"What happened to your other doctor?"

"I thinking I might switch." He'd never lied to Jill before. At least he didn't remember doing so.

The coffee began to drip when his cell went off again.

"Goddammit. Oh it's George again. 'Yes?'"

"You didn't tell me that you were doing the Thornton party?"

"I just found out five minutes ago. Why?"

"She's a brunette now."

"Meaning?"

"And she just got out of jail."

"George you're not making any sense."

"God Jake! When Jaime's gone brunette or when Mädchen Browne is blonde....it means big TROUBLE!!!!!!"

"What does that have to do with me exactly?"

"Nothing. I just thought you knew that's all. I told you she's out of jail, right?"

"Yes George. She's turning seventeen."

"44 minutes."

"She got out 44 minutes ago?"

"No, she was locked up for 44 minutes. Total. Caged heat can't *get warm* that fast Jake!"

"Bye George." **CLICK**

Eventually, the coffee maker finished sputtering and Jill poured herself the first cup. Jake grabbed for the second and held the warm mug in his hands and considered today's brush with lunacy.

"Is there something I should now about regarding this Jaime party?"

"I wouldn't think so. Why?"

"When are we delivering?"

"Saturday at 1."

"Okay. Let's go over some stuff." They went to the back room, Jill being welcomed back every five seconds or so. The staff's relief was palpable but Jake tried to assume it was because of him.

"Glad to see you, Jill." Thanks.

"Welcome back, Jill." Thanks.

"Looking really good, Jill." Thanks.

"Take it easy Jill. We can't lose you." Thanks.

This went on until they reached the 'office' area and sat down. They put down their coffee cups and Jake set about bringing her up to speed. He reviewed all the press visits, the customer increase totals. He left out the business with Ellie.

CHAPTER
FIFTY-TWO

Another week passed with no organic menu. For Jake, it was taking too long. He would do it now before this super successful business bullshit began to really fuck him up. Whether by accepting or by ignoring, he didn't know which, the thick crowds and kitchen chaos, he'd have to move forward. He was just waiting for certain staff members to come forward, asking for a quiet moment to talk, then asking for a raise. Was he going to say no? Probably.

Jill got a late afternoon call from the local show "Hail California!" saying that "they" (meaning the host and his camera man) wanted to "swing on bah." He told her to go ahead and set it up, but to make sure that Janice was in on that one.

"Why?"

"Trust me."

"They're coming early next week."

"Fine."

Continuous local coverage like this was going to insure that his customer numbers remained high. Jake was going to have to consider opening another store, sooner rather than later. Maybe I'll start looking for spaces in the New Year, he thought. That meant a new site to prepare, new staff to train. But it also meant more money; which meant arithmetic.

"I hate to come down on you so hard this week, Jill, but I'm going to be asking a lot out of you for awhile."

"I know Jake."

"First off, we have to get the organic line in order. Like yesterday."

"But."

"No buts. It has to be done. Get someone to cover the party for Saturday so you and I can do this."

"Okay, Jake. Whatever you say."

"In fact I want those people from that TV show to be the first to publicize it."

Jill couldn't come up with a retort because it was actually a great idea. And besides, she had insisted on being here, and now that she was, she knew she'd better keep her mouth shut. Well, at least she would try really hard. "I'll have to take more American Ginseng," she thought, "and I should be fine."

"Now let's go over what I was thinking of doing. Most of the ingredients are already here" said Jake. She noticed that he'd become kind of bossy while she had been out sick. He reviewed some of his ideas with her: a Meyer lemon zest cake with a nutty maple frosting; a pear chutney cake with vanilla buttercream; a fig cake with rose petal infused cherry frosting; an almond cake with infused earl grey frosting, and a sarsaparilla bundt with a tangerine frosting. He wanted to try out a chocolate cake with cassis, topped with a white nougat frosting; a chocolate curry cake with a vanilla frosting, dusted with chili powder and finished off with a tiny drizzle of Thai tea syrup. He liked the idea of adding black sesame seeds on top of *something*. She was pretty impressed but once again, it had to be *severely* edited. And who does organic Thai tea syrup? Jill also had some serious doubts about the fig. She began by suggesting that he drop the rose petals

"Well then let's just put rose petals on top" he said.

"Rose petal. One rose petal. Singular."

"Okay. One. Or a marigold petal or two." Jill ignored him.

"You have everything here, now?"

"Well I'm not sure if I have all the ingredients for white nougat and I know that I don't have any petals. We can send someone out for that. It has to be organic, though."

"Organic petals?"

"Well, my balls are the ones crushed if even the orange flower water isn't organic. Even the paper cups. We can't just call it organic and have it not be, you know. It's the Law."

"You're right. You're absolutely right. We can get it all down the street at the health food store. And since you're going crazy on this one how about a matcha latte cake with a coconut cream frosting to go under those black sesame seeds?"

"I love it!" Jake put down his coffee mug and hugged her. "God your skin is so soft. Did your fever do this to you?" Jill was so taken aback that all that she could manage was some incoherent mumbling about fresh lemons. Making no sense, Jake stopped listening.

"Let's get Fred. FRED!" Jake hollered.

"Fred's not here, he's taking some exam" said Tony. Seconds later, Fred came walking out of the toilet.

"Excuse me, Fred is here, Fred was in the loo" Fred said.

"Sorry, man" said Tony, "I thought you said you weren't coming in today." Fred gave him a funny look and turned to Jake.

"Yes, Jake, you called for me?" He bent over slightly, not in a gracious bow, but to make sure his fly was zipped.

"Fred, yes, here's a list and some cash to cover it. I want you to go find this stuff and make *sure* that it is all organic. It is *imperative* that it is *all* organic. Go to Complete and Total Foods. I want everything in the bag to have an organic sticker on it. If you can't find something, then go to Ecalpemos. If they don't have Meyer lemons, don't worry about it. There's a hundred in it for you if you can do it in less than 2 hours." Considering his weight, Fred was out the back door pretty damn fast.

"Make sure it's organic!" Jake yelled once last time. But there was so much noise in the kitchen, had Fred heard him? Did he bring his cell phone? Did he have Jake's number?

"Now, what can we start working on in the mean time?" Jake pulled out all his purchases that he placed on that shelf in the back. "Let's do the sarsaparilla and the earl grey."

"Okay, Jake" Jill was cautiously skeptical.

Ignoring the din around them, Jake cleared off enough space to start making cakes. If anyone had a question, they had to take it to Nadia or Janice first. They had about eight or so recipes to work out and keep only the very best. In other words, this was going to be a long night.

CHAPTER FIFTY-THREE

Fred got back in 1 hour and 25 minutes. He carried two jam-packed bags with a third in the car and the sweat was rolling down the sides of his face and coating his back. As a result, all the shopping bags were wet on top, so Jill insisted that he unpack them all and go wash up. She even went so far as to make him sort the ingredients according to recipe. Then he would get a crisp bill.

Jake and Jill had started work on the first two when Jake's cell phone went off. It was Jennifer.

"Hey!"

"You're in a good mood! What's up?"

"That horrible woman is gone and I am so relieved you have no idea! Are you busy?"

"Actually I'm swamped. I have to get something ready for early next week but what's your weekend look like? I know it's only Monday."

"Well as of today it's free. Do you want to try to schedule something?" Jennifer asked. She felt like she was arranging a playdate. And in a way she was.

"Yeah, let's take that drive up the coast."

"Sounds great. We'll go even if it rains."

"I'll call you back later and we can figure everything out. Right now I have to go. Okay?"

"That's fine. Bye Jake." **CLICK**

Of course, Jill was eavesdropping the entire time, as usual. Something about the conversation between them seemed lifeless to her, but she couldn't figure out what exactly or why. Jennifer seemed nice enough. Beautiful. Charming. Well-Spoken. But it's true, she no longer made Jill feel jealous or possessive. And none of them ever did. Without her realizing it, she'd just met another girl that would arrive on the scene and sooner rather than later, depart. She didn't need a clock. I wonder if Jake knows, she thought. Maybe that's what he likes about them, was the next thought.

She and Jake baked for the rest of the day and the day after. And the day after that. And the day after that. By the end of Thursday they had narrowed it down to five. Pear chutney (adding a tiny dash of chili powder to the batter): you haf maid eet. You arr safe. Fig cake with white nougat: you have maid eet past the judjes. Rainier cherry with almond cake and earl grey frosting: you are safe. Sarsaparilla with tangerine: concrachulations, urine. Und finally Sweet matcha latte with coconut and black sesame: you maid eet. Congratulations, all auf you. Meyer und Cassis und Curry, please step forwart. I'm sorry. U ahl suck. Yourout. Auf Wiedersehen. Kisses. If those winning cupcakes could hug each other and wipe tears away from their little cupcake eyes, they would have done.

Jake set out the final selection of organics so that staff could have a taste and give their opinions. He had never done this before. Usually they're so sick after a few months at the bakery that they have no interest in touching another cupcake for the rest of their lives. But this time they were intrigued enough by what had absorbed Jake and Jill's attention so completely, that they had to check it out for themselves. It was also the first time that Jake did not compromise in appealing to customers who strictly wanted comfort food. For the first time Jake would be making his client base work a little bit harder. He would either fail utterly or get the validation that said that he could maintain his popularity and be more adventurous at the same time.

Jennifer called while staff was milling around tasting.

"Jake?"

"Hey there!"

"You sound so excited!"

"I survived the week! How are you?" he asked watching Nadia and Janice seriously contemplating the fig and then the sarsparilla.

"I'm doing well, Jake, thanks. I don't want to take you away from work but I called to find out what time you wanted to start out on Saturday?" Jake thought she sounded a wee bit cold.

"Um, let me think. If I pick you up around 10 in the morning, we can drive up to Santa Barbara and come back Sunday afternoon. Is that okay? If I can't get reservations, you'll just have to be surprised. How's that?"

"Sounds really wonderful. I can't wait" said Jennifer, warming up just a smidge.

"Well I've got to get back to work, I'll see you on Saturday. Bye."

"Bye." Jill was standing there staring right at him.

"What?" he asked.

"Uh" said Jill, realizing she'd been caught.

"You say something?" asked Jake.

"Nope." said Jill. She turned her back to him "So guys which ones do you like? Should we drop any?"

Jake noticed that the staff had pretty much forgotten about the line out front, so he kindly suggested that they reserve their comments until after the work day. They took the hint and went back to their responsibilities while still managing to grab at the cupcakes on the table. For some, this was lunch and possibly dinner. He walked to the back of the kitchen and put a call in to George.

"Jake!"

"Hey George. Help me out man."

"I'd love to. What can I do?"

"I need a house. I'm taking Jennifer up the coast for Saturday and Sunday. Do you know anybody who's not using their's? I know it's a long shot but why not ask?"

"Actually, if you give me a little time I'm sure I can come up with something. Aren't you still doing the Thornton party?"

"Yeah, why?"

"Don't you want to be around for that? What if something goes wrong?"

"Do me a favor George. *Call* me if something goes wrong. And if you find me a house, you'll know *exactly* where I am."

"Oooh I love it when you talk tough. Seriously, I love it. But no, seriously Jake, I wouldn't want anything to go wrong with the Thornton people. They are very high profile."

"What's could possibly go wrong?"

"I'm just saying."

"Everything will be fine. I'll certainly hear about it if there's trouble. I'm only supplying cupcakes George."

"Okay. If you say so. I'll call you later."

Why was George being so paranoid? Jake's contribution to this birthday party was pretty minimal. I can't be the only provider of dessert. I'm sure they'll have a birthday cake too, he thought.

When he came back into the kitchen all the cupcakes had been eaten. He hadn't tasted any. Not one.

"Jill did you taste any of them?"

"No, because I never had the OPPORTUNITY" she turned and yelled at the remaining staff wiping frosting off their mouths.

CHAPTER
FIFTY-FOUR

George called back Friday night at 10:30.

"George you're a little late getting back to me."

"Listen Jake, you've been asking a lot out of me lately. I would show a little more gratitude and a little less attitude."

"Bad date?"

"Stuff it."

"Okay, I'm sorry. I'll take you out for a spa treatment in the next two weeks. Promise. I'll even get you drunk."

"That's better. Now here's the info. You lucked out. The house is in Santa Barbara, the keys and address are here with me. You'll have to stop by my place Saturday morning to pick them up by 8am. Sharp."

"What?"

"By 8am. No kvetching. I'm doing you a huge favor, Jake."

"Alright. Thank you George."

"That's better. Now you have to be out of there by 12pm on Sunday. Absolutely. Do you understand?"

"Of course."

"If anything goes wrong. I will come and kill you. This is a super *huge* client's house. Neither they nor their staff knows that you're going to be there. They're in London until Tuesday, but the servants will be arriving early. There had better be no trace of either of you two. Otherwise it's murder. Mine *and* yours."

"Got it. I'll see you at 8am. Thanks a lot. Really, George, thank you."

"Murder. Jake. MUR-*der*." **CLICK**

Jake had to call Jennifer and tell her that their day would be starting out a lot earlier than planned. The phone rang but she did not pick up. It was kind of late, and she could be out so, he left a message.

"Call me if you can't make the time, otherwise meet me at my place at 8am. I'll see you then. Bye."

Jennifer was sound asleep and didn't get Jake's message until she was finding her way to the bathroom at 5:30 the next morning to pee. Once back in bed and under the sheets, she clumsily set her alarm clock for seven and let her head hit the pillow for a second time. Her thoughts about packing and daytime temperatures evaporated without her noticing them morph into an office scene with Amanda. Jennifer was now fast asleep. In her dream Amanda was reading Jennifer's ghostwritten cupcake article. She had a queer look on her face; a grin or a grimace, you never could quite tell with her. Amanda let out an occasional snort, which was a good sign and then she put down the proofs and looked over at Jennifer.

"I know you're fucking him" she pronounced.

"Excuse me?"

"This article," she said tapping, her finger with noticeably chipped red polish. "This article reeks of your sex. I can smell it. Don't you have the dignity to at least bathe?!"

"Amanda! Please!"

"I didn't let you come out to Los Angeles to become a common *whore!*" she sniffed. Jennifer got up to leave the office.

"I don't know what's come over you Amanda, but I won't allow you to stand there and..."

"And what?" she charged at her and grabbed hold of her arm. Jennifer tried to shake her loose and got scratched in doing so.

"Get a hold of yourself!" She finally shook Amanda free and went off to the ladies room.

It wasn't where it was supposed to be. Jennifer found herself walking in circles with the blood starting to run down her arm. She had no tissue so she held her arm out and away from her body. Approaching another editor's desk, she came up to some low level assistants who were obviously gossiping. They turned and look at her questioningly but were soon disinterested. She looked down to see that she was now bleeding on the carpet.

"Is there a box of Kleenex over here?"

"No." They returned to their conversation.

She walked away in frustration, at last finding the bathroom, which she must have passed several times. When she got inside Amanda was already in there, waiting for her.

"What are you doing here? You need to stay away from me!"

"Stay away from you? My dear! You *work* for me!"

Jennifer was trembling by this point, trying to get the light activated faucet to start working and keep the dripping blood in the sink basin from splashing. Finally after the third or fourth swipe of her elbow it turned on, freezing cold, and she started to wash away the blood. It wasn't that much.

"Amanda, you need to leave."

Amanda had already walked out of the bathroom and was in the common office area talking very, very loudly. Jennifer couldn't quite make out what she was saying but she did hear the following words distinctly: fucking, Jennifer, whore. Same stuff. No, there were some new ones too: opportunist, user, cocksucker, liar and maybe even tramp. She couldn't tell, she may have said cramp.

The bathroom had gone "paper towel" free but Jennifer chose not to blow dry her arm. Instead she went into a stall for toilet paper. Toilets hadn't yet replaced their rolls with a crotch and ass hot air blower, thank god. A lady's got panties to deal with. Well I suppose with a thong.... She pulled off a long stretch of paper and started dabbing at her scratch, or rather, arm when one of the west coast head honchos (male) came into the bathroom.

"I'm alright, Frank, thanks, but this *is* the ladies room?" Frank approached looking nonplussed.

"I just want you to know...." he began, while Jennifer continued to dab at her arm. "...that you have brought *unspeakable* shame upon this company with your *disgusting* behavior."

"What? Frank! I'm bleeding! Amanda attacked me!"

"You leave Amanda out of this. What that poor woman has had to put up with! I can't believe it. I want you to go back to your office and get your things together. We'll forward you your severance." With that he was gone.

Jennifer looked at her reflection in the mirror and started to cry. But no tears would flow, her eyes weren't even red. She swished her hand back and forth under the faucet until the water flowed and she could splash her face. She didn't know how she was going to pull herself together. She may even need a tetanus shot. Once out of the bathroom, she saw that a crowd of office workers, none of whom she recognized had gathered in the hallway to watch her every move. She made her way back to her office when the alarm went off. It was seven a.m.

CHAPTER

FIFTY-FIVE

When Jennifer got to Jake's house, she looked a wreck. That's what happens when the last of a good night's sleep includes a nightmare. She had dark circles and a frown and looked liked she spent the night puking.

"Are you okay? You want to cancel? It's okay if you're not up to it."

"I had a bad night's sleep. I'll be fine."

He leaned over and kissed her gently and threw her very light overnight bag in the back. I forgot to tell her that this car has no room for luggage, he thought.

They drove over to George's and Jake left the car running while he got out and rang the doorbell. Jennifer watched from her seat as George answered the door in his bathrobe and slippers, handed Jake an envelope, a piece of paper and wagged his finger at him. He pointed at the sleep mask on his head and closed the door.

"That was easy" said Jake as he got back into the car.

"Hmmmm."

"I'm not going to ask again if you are you're up for this but how about some breakfast?"

"Let's eat later, okay? She kissed his cheek, and settled back in her seat. I would like some coffee though."

Jake swung by one of the local coffee bars and while waiting on his order looked over George's map. The directions to the house looked simple enough. They would be there by 10, 10:30 at the absolute latest. Jake brought the coffee back to the car, handing Jennifer her's through the passenger's side window and got back in, the papers in his teeth.

They drove east to the 101. The nice thing about driving to Santa Barbara was that it was so easy. They would stay on the 101 N until they got into town. Jennifer had finished her coffee by the time they were on Highland and he could see out the corner of his eye that she was going back to sleep. He reached back and pulled an afghan out from behind and handed it to her.

"Try to get some sleep and I'll wake you up when we get there."

What's he doing with a trading blanket in the car, she thought, and fell off to sleep again.

The freeway was open the whole way up. Since, it was 9am on a Saturday morning; most people weren't out of the house yet. It would get pretty damn full, but by that time, they would already be at their destination. If they came back at this same time tomorrow, he thought, it would be even emptier. Jake was going to sit on the idea of leaving early tomorrow morning for a while. We'll see how things go. He'd never spent the weekend with someone so soon. Did this make them a couple? If so, wondering about the state of a relationship with a person who, while sitting next to you, would rather be asleep, may not be an encouraging sign. A very bad sign in fact. Jennifer was nice but well, maybe it's too soon, he told himself, again. As far as Jake could tell they may both be curious, but they were also equally detached. The weekend would probably determine whether or not they continued on or broke it off, but he wanted that to happen nicely. He hoped she was the sort with whom you could remain friends. Who wouldn't burn down your house or kill your kitty.

Jennifer was out cold until they got off the freeway and turned onto Ysidro Road. Jake now realized why George was being such a control freak. He hadn't really looked closely at the directions but now he knew that they weren't really in Santa Barbara, they were in Montecito. Jake's jaw dropped open and a "holy fucking shit" popped out before he could stop it. Jennifer now was sitting up and alert, sensitized to the smell of copious amounts of money.

"Did you sleep okay?" Jake asked. Jennifer was trying to demurely dot the drool off the right side of her face. She looked down briefly to make sure she hadn't made a spot.

"Yes. I'm sorry. I really needed that extra hour" she said.

He handed her the paper with the directions and asked her to tell him where to go from Ysidro Road. There were an awful lot of traditional mansions. She liked. He hated. She told him where to turn as they passed one multi-million dollar spread after another. It made Beverly Hills look kind of rough. Visitors must feel great shame over their hardscrabble origins like Malibu or the Holmby Hills when they come out here. He looked back over at Jennifer, bemused to see how wide awake she was now. She was dazzled and dazed, like a sleepy panther in a parakeet aviary; no more so than when she saw the house where they would be spending the night.

It sat atop a perch overlooking the coastline surrounded by an overabundance of lush plantings, all alien to the region. The house bore a sign which read "The Wooden Beam." This must belong to a porn producer, Jake thought. Oddly there were no mounted cameras or security gates, which is why Jake and Jennifer would be breaking in so easily.

"They really should do something about their security system" he said. Jennifer just laughed. The Wooden Beam was, from what they could see so far, a *huge* modernist inspired estate. There were no other homes anywhere nearby, so no one would know that they were there. He pulled into the long circular drive and parked. The paper that George gave him had the lock code, as well as the directions. These people were rather stupid, he thought. And George is just awful. Jill grabbed her nearly empty overnight bag out from the back and followed Jake to the front door. He let her punch in the code and key the door. A very happy click resounded and they walked in.

Now he understood why George had said 'murder' so many times. The foyer was ridiculous, more of a Great Hall that eventually spilled into an even larger and more grandiose sitting room. What seemed a football field away, were the floor to ceiling windows which looked out over the Pacific. Jennifer squealed. She threw down her bag and started running. She ran to her left and disappeared. He heard her scream out.

"Jennifer are you okay?...(no response)...Take off your shoes!"

"Oh my god! Come here! I'm in the bathroom!"

He followed the sound of shrieks and yips until he found her, barefoot, in what must have been the sickest bathroom he had ever seen. The digital interface controlled shower could be entered from the left or right side leaving the sliding glass enclosure panes open or closed. The walls were decorated with brightly colored Turkish iznik tiles interspersed with smaller groupings of translucent colored glass. The flooring was made of the same glass tile as the walls, but cut in a larger variety of sizes. Water could come from at least eight stainless steel showerhead tiles. There was a fireplace, flatscreen TV with DVD player, ceiling stereo speakers and Jennifer was taking off her clothes.

CHAPTER

FIFTY-SIX

"Jennifer what are you doing?

"I'm getting into the shower silly! What does it look like I'm doing?"

Jake couldn't figure out how to say quickly enough, much less at all, that a. the owner's don't know that we're here; b. they must never know; c. you can't use the towels, therefore d. you can't take a shower. He figured if he had to use the laundry room and dry everything, it would turn the night away from work, into another night of, well, work. Jennifer had by now thrown her clothes all over the floor which Jake immediately put in a neat pile. He stared at her for a while and then he left the bathroom. Not knowing how she would react to the rest of the house he decided to view the property for his and her own personal safety. Some people just can't handle mega money.

He popped into the kitchen. It was pretty standard for sick rich. It had everything that everybody else with a load of cash had. There was a central food prep table with a black marble top, ebonized mahogany panels and matching Italian stools. The cabinets were ebonized as well, the appliances, sub-zero, the wall color, an antique white. With so much black, it was a necessity. The floors were bleached Egyptian travertine. There would be no spillage of the grape juice or slopping of the cranberry sauce. These people obviously didn't cook. This was a kitchen for people, who while entertaining, stopped by to show it to their guests. He opened the fridge and it was very clean. Not a single food item. What made the kitchen beautiful was what one could see from within it. Floor to ceiling windows on the two adjoining walls looked out onto gorgeous views of the ocean and an overgrown English garden.

He walked out of the kitchen and into the living room. It was spacious in tones of cream and birch, sparsely furnished with more Italian furniture and more of those same immense windows. The area rug must have cost a cool 100 grand, he thought. It was Turkish also, bleached by the sun into an array of gorgeous apricots, corals and soft golden tones. It went pinky peach even. It was lovely. He wished that he was enjoying it more but he was getting the George-induced shakes. 'Mur-*der*' kept repeating and repeating in his head. His libido was shriveling to nothing. He might not even be able to sleep. They would most definitely leave first thing in the morning.

Jennifer was now out of the shower with a glazed look on her face. Thankfully she hadn't washed her hair; and hopefully there would be no soap suds to clean up.

"How was your shower?" he asked.

"I didn't shower. I was just checking out the water pressure." she said.

"And?"

"Fucking amazing."

"It's a nice house."

"Uh-huh."

"Well I was going to check out the rest of the house and go outside. Care to join me?"

"Let's go!" She put down a little too roughly, a porcelain urn with a little too much ormolu for his blood pressure.

They peeked into the bedroom which, for some strange reason, was all Anglo-Bahamian. Pineapple finials and white gauze and draped canopies.

"They must have had a house in the Caribbean and shipped the stuff here."

"I guess. I hate it."

"Me too." He was surprised. He assumed that she would have wrapped herself up in the bedclothes, losing a precious earring by now.

On their way outside, there were more bedrooms and bathrooms and hallways and guest rooms but after awhile, it gets a bit dull and repetitive. The lawns were perfectly manicured for polo by the ocean except that fast ponies would likely fall off the edge and die. There was a pool, of course, and a veritable haven of overgrown foliage for the vermin. Like everything else, just a bit too much of everything.

"They must be English."

"What?" asked Jake.

"The owners. They must be English."

"I thought they were Turkish."

"Don't you know them?"

"No. It's the summer house of friends of friends." Kind of true. Two degrees of separation from a complete lie isn't so bad.

"Oh, well I think they're globe trotting colonialist, imperialists who like big, Italian furniture and sub-zero refrigerators."

"Or Egyptians who were educated in England and had a summer place in Mustique and somehow lost a load of cash and washed up in Montecito."

"Hmmm. That's entirely possible" said Jennifer. "I like that. But there's no telling with the jet-set."

"No telling indeed." Jake was getting tired of talking like a git. He took her by the hand and they walked down a narrow pathway to the beach. The water would be too cold to swim in, but it was still beautiful to look at. They walked about holding hands, both lost in their own private thoughts about the filthy, filthy rich. Jennifer liked them. Jake, not so sure. Maybe if he wasn't a trespasser he would have felt differently.

"Let's have lunch?" offered Jennifer.

"We should drive into town" replied Jake, who really meant, let's make a mess from a safe distance.

She agreed and they climbed back up the sandy pathway and locked the house up. Jake made sure they had the paper with the combination on it. They drove back into the village and bought sandwiches, fruit, wine, cheese and chocolate. Jake bought paper plates and napkins, and plastic silverware and cups. Jennifer thought that that was a bit strange.

"Let's have a picnic. And we need a bigger blanket. The one in the car's too small" said Jake.

"Um, sure." The general store manager told them where they could buy picnic blankets and throws and where the drug store was.

"Did you bring your toothbrush?" Jake asked.

"Yes?" What was he talking about?

Jake decided he better not propose buying bath towels or bed sheets. But he did purchase another two bottles of wine.

"Are you trying to get me drunk, Jake?"

"Yes."

Back they drove and parked the car in the circular lane. Jake prepared to go into the back garden and lay everything out on the grass but Jennifer was having none of it.

"Let's eat inside, okay?"

"But we got all this stuff."

"I know we did. But I really want to eat inside. I like it in there."

Jake didn't know how he could refuse without seeming stranger than he did already, so he relented. Thankfully, the fireplaces were electric. They could lay out the picnic blankets on the rug. While she stood beside him wondering what he was doing, he prepared lunch. He opened the pre-chilled white wine; he doubted red was ever allowed in this household, and poured.

"Why aren't we sitting at the table?"

"Cheers" said Jake. She got on the floor beside him and they tapped their plastic cups. Jennifer stared at comfortable chairs, while she sipped her wine. Jake's cell phone went off. It was George.

"Yes George?"

"Jake, sorry to bother you but I thought that you should know that the birthday party is off. Have you heard from the store?"

"No. All I know is that they've paid for their cupcakes and they've been delivered so we're cool."

"Well, I'm glad *someone* got paid. Anyway, the birthday girl got pulled over again by the police this morning at 4am. DUI. Naked as a lima bean on the 405!"

"Can this wait?"

"Sure. Call me when you get back into town and don't spill anything." **CLICK**

CHAPTER FIFTY-SEVEN

Jake did his best to pen Jennifer in the living room. They had lunch on the blanket and then sat together on the big couch watching the flatscreen. He had fed her just enough wine that the fatigue resulting from a bad night's sleep came back with a vengeance. She was out cold by 5pm. He figured when she woke up they could leave. He kept the fire lit and lay there with her snoozing under his arm. This had been a hell of a weird day, he thought. And night. He turned the volume down and fell asleep himself.

Jennifer woke up at 4 for her wee hours of the morning pee. When she looked for all empty wine bottles, she was astonished to see only one. That would explain why she had no hangover and finally felt completely rested. Once out of the bathroom, she looked around the kitchen for something to eat. Nothing. Back in the living room, she drank water from her sports bottle and nibbled on some leftover cheese. She snuggled back under Jake's arm and lay there waiting for him to wake up. It didn't look like there was going to be any sex. Maybe that was just as well because yesterday's dream was still so unsettling. She wasn't a whore no matter what Amanda said.

When Jake woke up it was 7am and Jill was already packed up to go. That was easy enough since they were wearing the same clothes. Both had fallen asleep in this comfort cradle and woke up again with ease. It must have dual drug classifications, extreme luxury, acting both as a stimulant and as a depressant. I wonder for whom it was psychosis inducing, Jake wondered, slightly appalled. He was a little grossed out by Jennifer to be honest. He'd never seen anybody wake up out of a dead stupor and fly into mania in a big house like that before. Had the house made her bi-polar? Or narcoleptic-maniacal?

The car was packed up and humming by 7:30. While Jennifer waited in the passenger seat, Jake went over all the places they had been throughout the house to make sure nothing had been left behind. Or moved. Or touched. Once confident that there were no fingerprints, he was ready to make the drive back. That store clerk couldn't say anything because that store clerk didn't know anything.

When they pulled up to his place Jennifer immediately hopped into her own car.

"Don't you want to come in for a sec?"

"No, I gotta get back home. I still have work. That was pretty amazing, though Jake. Thanks."

"Sorry we couldn't stay longer."

"It was perfect, really. Sorry I slept the whole time. I was more exhausted than I realized. I'll have to make it up to you." She sounded a tad insincere to Jake's ear.

"Maybe you're working yourself too hard. You should ease up a bit. By the way how did that article go?" There was a longer pause than expected.

"It's finished. I haven't heard word back yet." Jennifer turned over her engine.

"Great. Good for you. When's it coming out?"

"Not sure." Jennifer blew him a kiss. "Bye, Jake. Thanks again."

Jake had the rest of the afternoon to think about their excursion. He was certain that he would never do that again. Wherever he thought they be might be going, they definitely weren't. He knew now that he had no real feelings for her; what he had liked about her was her composure and polish. But Jake would have had a better time up there by himself, or with George. Or Fred. Or Jill. He knew that he had to find a nice way of breaking it off. She kind of gave him the creeps but why he couldn't say. She may be polished and composed but still felt that he needed to take a shower.

Since it was Sunday afternoon, Jake was certain that it would be safe to put in a call to George.

"Jake."

"George what more did you hear about the party? Nobody's called me but you."

"Jake, I thought this was a social call. But you're all business."

"That's not true. I figured that you were the most important person to talk to."

"Well, that is true but no, I haven't heard a thing. As far as I know, the party went on without her. It was a huge hit from what I hear. I think I will get paid after all. So how was the weekend?"

"It sucked. I don't think I want to see Jennifer any more, George."

"But why?" he whined. "She's such a nice girl. What happened?"

"Nothing, George. That's the whole point. I may as well have taken a corpse."

"Jake, that's not nice."

"But it's true. She's nice and everything but I'm done. When you're done you don't need any more time to figure things out, you know what I mean."

"All too well, Jake, all too well. Have you told her?"

"Not yet, soon. So keep you're mouth shut, George."

"I beg your pardon Jake?"

"Just what I said."

"When do I get my spa treatment and alcohol?"

"How about some time next week? You pick the place. By the way, where are the people who own 'The Wooden Beam' from?"

"What?"

"The house? In Montecito? The owners? Where are they from?"

"They named it 'The Wooden Beam'? That's cute. Uh, Japan. They're Japanese."

木 製 の 梁

CHAPTER

FIFTY-EIGHT

Jill spent all of Tuesday morning on the phone with the producers of "Hail California!" She had expected that they would show up with video around ten and now their arrival time was up in the air. Jill had already given them the speech about not being disruptive during business hours. Ten in the morning was still pushing it as far as she was concerned, even for a weekday, but now they wanted to show up later in the afternoon and she refused the request.

"I wish that you had called with these schedule changes earlier. We can't have a crew here during our busiest time."

"Can we come at the end of the day?"

"The place will be a mess and there won't be product. How about tomorrow, early morning?"

"Matt is going out of town. It has to be today. How about 4:30?"

"Make it 2pm." So much for her tough talk.

"Deal. See you then."

Jill didn't even know who this person was but she went back and told everyone to be ready for a crew after the lunch crowd.

"They're going to be here at 2pm guys." Her statement was met with less than an enthusiastic reaction.

"Every time those people come, the store gets busier" complained Raul.

"That's good. We want that."

"Why?"

"Raul." He raised his hands in defeat and went back to his cake batter.

Jake was late. It was 9:45 and just now Jill could hear his car revving into the space and the engine turning off.

"Matt Partmenter is coming late."

"Matt who?"

"The host and crew of "Hail California!" changed their arrival time. They're coming at 2 o'clock."

"Okay."

"They were originally scheduled to come in this morning."

"Oh. Sorry. Why didn't you call me?"

"Because they called and cancelled."

"Oh. Well that's good isn't it?"

"Yeah, it's fine."

Jill was getting irritated. Why was he being so *odd*?

"Jake are you alright?" Jill couldn't remember whether or not she'd already asked him that question.

"Yeah, I got a lot on my mind."

"Care to talk" she poured him his cup of coffee.

"Not really. But thanks."

Hmmm. While Jill hung on a pre-menstrual precipice of losing her temper, being offended, crying, thinking about new shoes or just forgetting about it, Jake interrupted her and started talking again.

"Well everything's ready for them, right?" he asked.

"Yep." Very casual. Nicely done.

"So, they're gonna be here 3-1/2 hours later than expected? Well, let's just get on with it and try to keep things tidy. In fact. *I'll* tidy." Jake went off to find his cleaning products. He busied himself with counter tops and windows. He spot cleaned and swept. He re-stocked the plastic gloves and surface counter cleaner. He looked over the food storage areas for debris and the scourge of any baker, crumbs. Staff understood this to mean that Jake didn't get laid.

"How was your weekend?" Jill asked.

"It sucked." Jake replied.

"What do you mean? Didn't you..."

"I don't want to talk about it right now."

Jill felt as if the sun had burst open through her stomach, spreading warmth and joy from deep, deep down. Lit up like a Christmas tree, she went around doing this and that, staying out of Jake's cleaning frenzy. She noticed that the threat of the Health Inspector brought out a little bit of OCD with him. And why was she horny?

"Can someone get the dust out of these air vents, please!" Jake hollered.

After three hours of this behavior, Jill began assembling gift packages for the "Hail California!" host and crew, a copy of the press release for the producer, assuming she could read, and the shopping bags laid out and ready for packing. No sooner had she folded the extra tissue and put aside the logo stickers, a commotion began to rumble from up front. Jake came from out the kitchen, saying

"I got this. Go get Janice."

Jill was busy pinching her cheeks for color.

"What?" she said between squeezes.

"Go get Janice. Meet me up at the front."

Jake passed her by and went out to meet and great.

Standing in the store front was an immensely tall gentleman who dwarfed his crew by at least a foot.

"Whah helloo theyah." Matt outstretched his big hand towards Jake. Jake didn't seem to have to move far to meet up with it.

"Hello. I'm Jake." They shook hands briskly while Jill and Janice came up and stood in the partition. The crew, rather, the cameraman had set up and Matt had his mike in hand in unbelievably fast timing.

"Are we all ready? Wah don't you two ladies step bayack just a biyit. Let's gow people!" Jake looked over at Jill and Janice to make sure they were moving back into the kitchen. They had taken two tiny steps and weren't budging.

"Welcome to 'Haiyal Caleeforhnya'! Weah heyah at the ECLUSIVE baakeree CUP CAYKE. Heeyah on my raaat is the onah, Jayake Wellingtun! I'm SO pleayused to MEET you!" Jake tried not to look pained as he smiled and nodded his head.

"Mah gawd! These are just thee most beeYOUtiful cupcayakes! Get a shot of these Joey." Jake stepped back so Joey could get a good closeup.

"Theyah lahk little pieces of AART! I beyt they tayaste GOOD too!" Jake didn't miss the cue and presented him with an array of the regular cupcakes. They were cut into small pieces.

"Uuuum! Mah GAWD. These are de-LI-CIOUS!" Not to be out done, the 'li' and 'cious' had come out with a vengeance to meet the 'de.' "So TELL me, how many CUPCAYKES do you all BAYKE in a DAY?"

"At our busiest, we range anywhere from 2-1/2 to 3 thousand."

"That's AMAZING! AH cayan't BELIEVE it! Did you say up to THREE THOUSAND a DAIY?!"

"That's correct Matt."

"These AHR wuhnerfuhl! I cuhn SEE WHAH! Well let's all have a LOOK at the BAHCK if you don't MAHND!" Jake stepped back with his arms opening into a wide second. For some reason he was acting like a member of the corps de ballet. Then he brought his arms forward and down. Jill didn't know what to think at this point.

"Hah! Ahm Matt! Plu-leeyuhsed to meet yuu!" He outstretched his hand in greeting Jill and Janice.

"Hello, I'm Jill, store manager" said Jill.

"Hayh!!" said Janice without explaining who she was. Matt looked thunderstruck. Their molecular genetic codes were synching and beginning to hum.

"Wah are you a southan gayl?

"Thaht's raht."

"Do you LAHKE working heyah?"

"Ah luv it!"

"Ah can SEE whah! And y'all have to be carefuhl not to EAT TOO MUHCH! Don'tcha?"

Before his staff was felled by an explosive group aneurysm, Jake tried to move everyone out of the store front with intense eyeball work. But it was useless. Matt looked down upon him, holding his ground steady.

"Now what ah y'all workin' ohn?" asked Matt trying to push his way further into the back kitchen area.

"We've just developed a line of organic cupcakes." Jake beamed.

"AH LAHN OF ORGANIC CUPCAYKES?" he repeated as he was prone to do.

"Yes, we're really happy with them. They're made only with ingredients in accordance with the State of California's strict organic food code. Would you care to try some?" Jake was finally able to lure him back to the cake displays.

Jake presented him again with a selection of cupcakes, this time the new ones.

"OH. MA. GAWD. Did you say these are COMPLETELY ORGANIC?"

"Completely."

"Whah they are inCREdiBUL. Taste this Joey." Joey stepped forward with the camera on his shoulder and grabbed a small piece, a part of which broke off and fell to the floor.

"Well ah want to thank you'all for having us heah in your WUHNERFUL establishment."

"Thanks for coming."

"That's CUPCAYK, located heyah in EXCLUSIVE bevuhly HILLS. Another example of what makes CALIFORNIA...."

Somewhere way out in the street came a high decibal shrieking. It just went on and on. It didn't even sound human, more like a something from the LA Zoo that had become really, really irritated.

CHAPTER
FIFTY-NINE

"Whaht on EARTH? Get a shot of this Joey."

It was Ellie. She was screaming and thrashing about on the sidewalk with pedestrians and store customers standing back in horror. Jake and Jill and Janice and everybody else on staff came running into the store front and watched while she was in the throes of a Beverly Hills meltdown. People were taking out their cell phones to snap pictures. Drivers were honking and waving their arms in support. Chauffeurs leaned against their limos looking bored. Some re-crossed their legs. Some continued to read the paper.

"How could you Jake! HOW COULD YOU! You can't treat me like this! I WON'T LET YOU!!!!!" She started screaming again. Somehow she had managed to get a selection of cupcakes strapped onto her body like some granny terrorist wrapped in plastic explosives. But whatever point she was trying to make with them, she couldn't quite as they didn't explode. They fell in clumps off her body every time she moved or yelled out. Joey could have told her that, what with leaving his broken off cupcake clump inside on the floor to absolutely no response. It just didn't strike anyone as political.

"This is *just like* Robertson" said someone to the right. A family of tourists across the street posed together making sure that Ellie was in all their shots.

"Call for help" said Jake. Jill went back into the kitchen and quickly dialed 911.

Ellie continued to smash cupcakes on herself. She rubbed her face in frosting and mumbled incoherently between barks. Thankfully she was making no sense and beyond screaming his name (and a lot of women do), Jake couldn't really be implicated. This being Beverly Hills, the police showed up in less than two minutes. Ellie swung her arms about threateningly, covered in sticky frosting.

"It's alright lady. Everything's going to be *okay*." The lady cop hitched up her pants by her belt. Despite being a perfectly respectable size 8, all her bulk was added paraphernalia packed around her hips. Jill wondered about the center of gravity on female police officers.

"YOU GET AWAY FROM ME! IS HE FUCKING YOU TOO!? GOD! BLESSED! JESUS!" Jake looked at his shoes and Jill's mouth fell open. Joey had been filming the whole thing up until now.

"Turn that camera off please, sir" said the second officer. Matt came out from behind the camera.

"Well hellooo theyah officer. Ahm Matt Parmenter. Weyah from "Haiyal California!" and weyall ah doing a peeeus…"

"Please step aside sir." The officers restrained Ellie despite a fair deal of frosting getting onto their uniforms and placed her in the back of the squad car. They perfomed the bending of the head forward procedure which is always on TV, but this time they got cake and frosting all over their hands and the door frame. It made her head slip around and she could have easily hurt herself and sued for excessive use of force and abuse of power under the color of authority. She might be crazy, but she was a crazy lawyer.

"Should have brought our latex gloves, Captain."

"That's alright. Let's just get her in the vehicle."

The "Hail California!" crew went back into the store when they saw a second squad car approach. Jill was already in the kitchen packing up their goodie bags. She brought them over, handed the bags out and showed them the way to the back door.

"Won't that police officah requiyah a stayatmeyent?" Matt asked.

"I'll give them all your information. Not to worry. But you guys should really leave. We'll take care of everything and thanks for dropping by."

"Thayank youu. It's beeen a REEYAL PLEAYASURAH" said Matt. He mentioned that one of his producers would call when the piece was edited and send a copy of the episode with its screening date. Jill thanked them, opened the back door and let them out. As far as "Hail California!" was concerned, this *was* golden.

Going back out front, Jill saw that the crowd, besides actual customers, had been dispersed. It wasn't a crime scene so Jake could go ahead and clean up the sidewalk after he finished giving a statement. He said that he had known the woman in college but had no idea that she was unstable. No, they had no relationship. No, she had never shown signs of odd behavior before. Jake said he didn't even know how she got the cupcakes, much less how they got on her body without causing a commotion earlier. The lady officer thought he was lying. She jotted down a little note in her booklet. Jake said, he didn't have her phone number, did not know where she lived and had not been in touch with her beyond her coming to the bakery to say hello once, a long time ago.

"You're welcome to talk with anyone on my staff. If that's all, I would like to clean up the front." The officer nodded her head in agreement and slid her pen into her back pocket. She turned to look at Ellie in the back seat trying to break out with her dirty feet. She had made a smeary mess all over the back seat and windows.

"Who's gonna clean that up?" said the second officer in disgust.

They thanked Jake, gave him a police precinct card and drove away. The second squad car soon followed. What Jake didn't know was that he was gonna be in the tabloids from now on. He'd finally arrived.

While Jake was busy cleaning and wondering if he had handled the skirmish correctly, Jennifer was working. She had called New York to find out where the editorial copy revisions were. She asked to speak to Sammy, the Assistant to the Assistant Editor.

"This is Sammy."

"Sammy this is Jennifer Hargrove. I'm calling from L.A."

"Holy shit, Jennifer! How the hell are ya? When ya comin' back?"

"Um, you never know Sammy. Listen can you do me a favor?"

"That all depends. What do you need?"

"I need a copy of the revisions for the Tisdale piece for the December issue."

"Hold on." Sammy took so long; Jennifer had filed both hands and was getting ready to pluck her brows.

"I got the copy here. Sorry it took so long."

"Can you fax them to me?"

"Why?

"I want to see the changes."

"There aren't any. It's running just as it is."

This is the part where Jennifer made the mistake by calling Jake. She was gloating. She had lost that feeling of guilt about misrepresenting her article because she was too busy fantasizing about a career coup, that was hardly going to happen. Amanda had just figured out how to keep Jennifer out of New York and take credit for her work in Los Angeles at the same time. He didn't pick up so she just left a message.

"Hello Jake! Great news! Amanda loves the article! Call me! Bye."

Jake wasn't picking up his phone. When he heard the message later he realized that he would have to call her back and break up. He felt kind of sick. Maybe they could play phone tag and then break up.

He went back outside with a bucket of soapy water. He had to be very careful and not get anyone wet. No shoes. No lambskin anything. How does one remove frosting from designer lambskin? Ellie had made quite a little mess out here, he thought. There was cake and frosting globs on the window and door. Some globs flew on to parking meters, some on to nearby cars and a little on the side of the building. He saw one of those limo drivers licking his fingers. This was going take a while to get rid of. He wiped down the front window for the second time today and was drenched in sweat by the time he walked back into the store with all of his cleaning equipment. He didn't want to risk any inspector seeing this at all. And why hadn't anybody asked for his photo?

CHAPTER SIXTY

Jill was pretty adamant that the staff pull themselves together. She corralled everyone back into the kitchen and demanded order.

"Okay everybody THAT'S ENOUGH!" Jill, if they remembered correctly, had no problem with yelling when the situation required it. Staff that had been bent over cackling, knocking each other shoulder to shoulder, or comparing Ellie impressions were stopped dead.

"Do you think Jake is going to want to see this? Pull your shit together and GET BACK TO WORK! NOW!" Jill clapped her hands together several times and her nostrils flared. She was back. The Enforcer. In times like these there's nothing an employee can do but turn around and count sticks of sweet creamery butter.

It took some 20 minutes for staff to finally focus on what they had been doing before the afternoon's outburst, but it required fear. Being terrorized into silence so effectively by such a petite manager, had reactivated the latent but all too lively PTSD from various catholic school upbringings. Memories of Sister Mary Evangeline made Ellie vanish and order was re-stored. Jake came back in after finally cleaning up, to a quiet, efficient work place. It was like a church in there. He looked over at Jill. Jill's face was a blank sheet of calm.

"Is everything cleaned up in front, Jake?" she asked in soothing tones.

"Yeah, I think I got it all. The customers are coming back back in" he said heavily.

"Are there any photographers out there?"

"None that I could see."

"Well hopefully we won't be on the news."

NO SUCH LUCK

Thanks to the efficiency of local websites scooping the latest scandal-plagued starlets, and the fact that unbe-knownst to Jake or Jill, one such starlet was walking with her entourage towards the store, (but still two blocks away) when Ellie went ka-boom, the entire video feed and tele-photo zoom lens stills had been sent to every news and gos-sip source. If thanks can be given, it was due to the fact that many of the stories that ran focused on said scandal-plagued starlet, a certain pencil thin Tracey Minturn, who may have wanted some cupcakes that day, but never got any. Some of the tabloid titles read:

- **TURNED AROUND!**
- **NO CAKES FOR THIS CUPCAKE!**
- **STARLET AVOIDS ARTILLERY FIRE FROM CUPCAKE COMMANDO CUTIE!**
- **LOVED MY CUPCAKE MORE THAN YOU!**

Neither Jake nor Tracey knew what the stories were more about; 'Jake's lunacy inducing cupcakes, they're that good' as one late night talk show host quipped; Ellie's being enlisted in the war to "fight Terrorism" or Tracey, who could create a scene from two blocks away, she was that charismatic. As Ellie was currently undergoing a psychological evaluation, *she* didn't know what to think. During her "absence" however, software designers created downloadable Ellies who you could watch go through her moves backwards, forwards, slow-mo or fast forward. She could replace the cursor on your computer. She became the dancing animation figure for insurance quotes, mortgages, and diets that work. You could 'send' her through any number of social networking platforms. Graphic t's and caps emblazoned with **I'm Having A Cupcake Crack-Up!** were selling out on Robertson and Melrose, Hollywood Blvd. and at Venice Beach. The line at Jake's store became impossible, this time for good.

Sadly, the whole organics launch was completely lost by this other news coverage, never gaining more than a bit of obligatory copy in specialty food magazines. The line was extremely popular without additional press, but if Jake was going to have this type of media coverage by the mainstream, serious food journalists would sniff and walk away. Which is what they did. Well Jake had sold out, hadn't he? Jill told him that maybe he was just too good looking.

Jake tried not to focus on it but instead tried to appease the line that now wrapped around the block. He would not grant interviews but that didn't stop the press from trying to crawl up his ass. Now he understood how truly horrible it was to be followed incessantly while doing absolutely nothing interesting. Being photogenic got him little sidebars every week, linking him to people he had never met, questioning his sexual orientation, watching him eat a sandwich, discreetly picking his nose.

Jennifer was thrilled and although she hadn't talked to him she loved the fact that she was dating someone in the weeklies. She had neither seen him nor talked with him since that glorious weekend in Montecito, so she decided she better check in again. She'd already told everybody that they were a couple.

"Jake!" He'd picked up at last.

"Sorry, I haven't talked to you in awhile. As you probably know…"

"How could I not!" she sounded a little hysterical.

"Jennifer, I'm glad you called" he started out, trying to sound solemn.

"Jake?" Jennifer's armpits started schpitzing.

"I don't think we should see each other anymore." There, he said it. Done.

"WHAT? ARE YOU BREAKING UP WITH ME?" Jennifer shrieked.

"I'm too busy to be in a relationship right now. I don't even have time to sleep." What was she going to say to that? It was the truth. True, he left out the "there's something unnamable yet phony about you that sickens me" or "don't worry, you'll find someone with more money" or "I'm the first step on a long food chain, I wish you well" adages. They weren't necessary. He did add this, though:

"You're too new to Los Angeles to get involved with someone who's not even around."

Good one. She needs more time and experiences to realize that, in this town, being involved with a phantom isn't really settling. It could be interpreted as trading up.

"Jennifer, are you there?"

"Do you mean to tell me that you are breaking up with me on the telephone?" She tried to remain calm. Jake didn't know what to say to that one with any politesse, and 'yes' seemed rather callous. So he settled for the tried and true:

"I hope that we can be friends in the future. When you're ready."

He didn't mean to sound like a cad. Besides, he hadn't seen her article yet.

"Well I don't know what to say, Jake. I'm frankly astonished." She wasn't going to go quietly. This was going to drag on for a little bit longer.

"Don't be. It's just not going to work out. It's not right for you."

"How do you know what is right for me?" she was crying now. He looked at his watch.

"Okay, it isn't right for me, then. It's unfair to me." That made no sense but he stopped hearing her sniffles. He felt confident that he could wrap it up now.

"Listen, Jennifer. You're a great girl. You're beautiful. You're smart. You need the right guy. I want you to find him. It isn't me."

"Fine. Good bye Jake."

"Bye. Take care." **CLICK**

Jake wiped the sweat from his brow and went back to work. Every eavesdropping employee exhaled deeply. Jake did it again.

CHAPTER
SIXTY-ONE

George could barely contain himself. You just cannot pay an image consultant to create the coup that Jake had just pulled off. And all by himself, for the love of Christ. George wanted to know every fundamental detail, to understand all the petty nuances and greater complexities and yet, and yet that little bitch Jake didn't want to talk about it.

"It was horrible, George" he'd say.

"Oh, I can only imagine, Jake." George would say in comforting tones when inside his head, he was whining and flaying about. Tell me you! Tell ME!!!!!! But Jake wouldn't. All George had was the leftover consumer detritus: the video feed, the magazines, the jokes. George knew that there was more, there had to be, a camera can only capture one angle at a time and he wanted to know every single one of them. Neither was Tracey Minturn talking. Her publicist advised her stringently that if she opened her mouth about an event that she didn't even witness, she would sound even more the idiot, something she didn't need to be doing at this point in her career. She needed to go to Africa or Sri Lanka. Adopt something. She issued a brief release stating "how she hoped that that poor unfortunate woman (Ellie) was getting all the help she needed and that admitting you had a problem was the first step in a long and challenging journey. She wished her the best of luck." Tracey, herself, had been in and out of rehab a few times, even at her young age and it was nice to finally have the opportunity to say that shit about someone else. She felt the incident had been poorly timed since she didn't have anything of her own coming out to promote, so that was gonna do it for the Minturn camp for awhile. Or so she thought. The recent onslaught of publicity gave an old producer 'acquaintance' the bright idea to release her shelved and underage porno *Beth: Bad and Beyond* on DVD. Tracey immediately went back into rehab to wait for this to all die down.

Poor George was left so grossly unsatisfied. What he didn't know was that there was an extensive amount of footage shot by Joey filed away somewhere in the "Hail California!" production offices. The segment had been aired immediately following the kerfuffle, but with the kerfuffle bit cut out; instead replaced with an abrupt cutaway shot and the final sentences by Matt redubbed. Maybe one day, if the Fates allow, George will see this footage and die a happy man.

The only scoop he did get, however, was an advance copy of the *Extreme Leisure* issue in which Jake appeared. Given that the by-line was Amanda's it was completely acceptable. But he knew that she hadn't written it. And so did Jake. So he called him.

"George."

"Jake, I'm sitting here with a copy of the latest *Extreme Leisure*. By any chance did Jennifer send you a copy?"

"No. We broke up remember?"

"Of course I know that, so she didn't send you an issue?"

"No?"

"Shall I read it to you over the phone?"

"George, I'm super busy. Fax it okay?"

"Will do. Bye." **CLICK**

George faxed over the one page 'editorial spread' and Jake picked it up a minute later. He called George back.

"What a fucking bitch!"

"That's not fair, she wrote it as Amanda. Not as herself. That's exactly how Amanda writes" said George hastily.

"Are you defending her?"

"Well no, not exactly but she was just doing her job. It will have no effect, believe me. The best thing you can do is to forget it. That's just how important it is."

"You're the one who wanted me in that fucking piece of shit magazine in the first place George."

"But that was before you entered Valhalla. Now you're untouchable. My work is done. And you're welcome." With that Jake actually laughed which was good because it had been awhile.

"And besides you broke up with her so what difference does it make, really? It's not even much of a put down. If you can read between the lines, she did okay."

"What are you talking about, George?"

"God, why do I have to spell *everything* out? If she's going to sing the praises of Her Sweetness, how seriously can one take it? The Adlers should open a shoe store? It's a joke. You should send her a thank you note!"

"You know what, I think I will. Jill and I are having a drink tonight. Care to join us?" Jake asked.

"You owe me alcohol so that's perfect. Where?"

"Casa Ocho Nueve Diez. Around 7:30. It's gonna be an early night for me, though. See you there." **CLICK**

What Jake didn't tell him, is that he was indeed being swamped with phone calls and letters from investment companies, the very thing Ellie arrived on the scene promoting. Too ironic, really. He was only talking about it with Jill, but he was pretty sure that another store would have to be opened as soon as they were able. They would move forward because with these crowds they had no other choice. This was always the way he had wanted to do it, so he was comfortable. He could set his own terms; being that he was at this moment a very hot property. He had to finally get a real business manager. And a traditional banking arrangement would be the only involvement he would consider for the time being. Jake promised himself he would have a second store by the New Year

Jill had become, through this trying period, an ever closer confidante. She had been there for so long and he had always known that she had his best interests at heart when offering an opinion. He also knew that such loyalty had to be a two-way street. She had become a talent in her own right, and could easily, although he knew she wouldn't, start her own bakery and be a very able rival. He was considering offering her a full partnership but he would discuss that with the business manager that he was yet to hire. He would also talk to George about it.

As far as Jennifer was concerned, George was right. He had no right to be angry. In comparison to his current situation the article was irrelevant. What she *had* owed him was leveling with him about the tactic she was taking in covering her own ass. He hadn't known her well enough yet; something to bear in mind the next time he dropped his pants.

CHAPTER
SIXTY-TWO

Jill and Jake and George were all gathered at the bar at Casa Ocho Nueve Diez by 8pm. It was a tiny little place, barely room to place your order. If you were lucky enough to get a chair and got nestled in real cozy, the evil eye lurked from all about you, coming from the late arrivals. Lucky for them a three seat alcove opened up and they dashed in disgracefully and took it.

"You beeches" sneered some foreign person with a fucked-up accent.

George looked amused. And amusing in a black pin-stripe suit, black dress shirt, black mother-of-pearl cufflinks, a wide, white silk tie and white patent leather loafers. Completed by his latest small black pork pie. Again with the pork pies. He saw they're confusion.

"It's Kray Twins. 1966."

"Okay George, but you're still cute" said Jill.

"True but that's beside the point." George replied. "I need another drink" he remarked with an ennui as if to say "shut it." Jill could see that he was having difficulty choosing between being an east London hoodlum or *Le Grand Dauphin*.

George, after a time, went back to admiring the flocked damask wall paper and the chandeliers, a bit low, he thought. He matched the mahogany bar quite nicely and could see that the proprietors too were fond of a touch of mother-of-pearl. If you used it with restraint, it was rather nice. As he was admiring himself next to the décor, he happened to look over at Jake and Jill. They were talking about something work-related, of course, and for the first time it occurred to him that they made a cute... Oh my god, he thought, how could I have been so incredibly blind? They were adorable. Why hadn't he seen it before? They listened closely to each other and laughed at each other's remarks. They were sincere and respectful and what's more, fun to be with, which is more important anyway. Jake caught him looking at him and then Jill.

"George?"

"Yes?"

"What's going on under the hat?"

"Should I take it off? We *are* inside."

"No leave it on. I like it." said Jill.

"So Jake when do I get my mani-cure?"

"Well, you know I'm really busy right now."

"Jake you promised."

"I know, I'm sorry. Give me a break. I'm feeding you drinks aren't I?"

"True. True." George pondered his martini, confident that he had thrown Jake off the scent. "I'll have another one, please Jake."

"Me too" said Jill. The looks from the standing customers were rank as Jake waved over the bartender. He ordered one more round and said that he was cutting them off.

While waiting for their drinks to arrive, two long limbed blondes approached the banquette next to them.

"Excuse me" said the one in a sheer white on white empire waisted shift dress.

"Yes?" replied Jill. The blonde ignored her.

"Excuse me. Aren't you that guy that owns that *fabulous* bakery near by? Jake? I'm sorry. I don't remember you're name." Well I'll be damned, thought George.

"Wellington. Jake Wellington. And yes." Jill was disgusted.

"I hate to ask, but can I have your autograph?"

"Me too!"

"My what?"

"They want your autograph" replied George, taking a long pull from his martini and fondling his plastic monkey.

"Um, sure I guess. Do you have a pen?" They both anxiously looked through their gojiro sized purses only to come up with one gnawed ball point pen. And some gum.

"Will this do?" Blonde No. 1 handed him two drinks napkins.

Jake was not about to ask them their names or make ridiculous small talk. He would learn to do this bit later. He signed his name quickly and handed their napkins back.

"Here you go."

"Thanks!" Blonde No. 2 flipped her mane as they walked away. "Isn't he *gorgeous*?"

"Oh my fucking god" said George watching them leave.

"Shut up" replied Jake.

"How long before he dumps us?" asked Jill.

"I've got an egg timer, girl."

"Set it."

"Alright you guys, finish you're drinks and let's go."

As it turned out, George kept his opinions to himself and did no more matchmaking. Let them figure it out on their own, he told himself. Jake saw Jennifer very seldom, running into her at the occasional event, always on the arm of some bejowled business tycoon looking for a well educated east coast trophy wife. He wanted to whisper into their hairy ears "she's from Michigan!" but he let it pass.

He and Jill found another site, this time in West Hollywood, which they hoped to open in another six months. He did find a business manager and he did make Jill a full partner. Of the second store. They would be looking for a third and fourth and fifth in Santa Monica, San Francisco and New York, respectively. Despite her unfortunate tactics, Ellie had been right telling Jake exactly what he needed to do. He really had her to thank in the end. And as soon as she got out of the UCLA Neuropsychiatric Hospital, he would do just that. He wasn't going to send a card though. In the meantime, he would learn to enjoy his new found minor celebrity and bake a hell of a lot more cupcakes. Maybe he would lead a Cupcake Nation after all.